LIGHTNING
Dragon
THE BRIDE HUNT BOOK 4

CHARLENE HARTNADY

Copyright and Disclaimer
Copyright © February 2017, Charlene Hartnady
Cover Art by Melody Simmons
Copy Edited by KR
Proofread by Brigitte Billings (brigittebillings@gmail.com)
Formatted by Integrity-Formatting
Produced in South Africa

Published by Charlene Hartnady
PO BOX 456, Melrose Arch,
Johannesburg, South Africa, 2176
charlene.hartnady@gmail.com

Lightning Dragon is a work of fiction and characters, events and dialogue found within are of the author's imagination and are not to be construed as real. Any resemblance to actual events or persons, either living or deceased, is purely coincidental.
With the exception of quotes used in reviews no part of this book may be reproduced or shared in any form or by any means, electronic or mechanical, including but not limited to digital copying, file sharing, audio recording, email and printing without prior consent in writing from the author

First Paperback Edition 2017

CHAPTER 1

She'd nailed it.
Nailed it!
Excitement coursed through her. This was the break she needed. Jessica Woodruff was amazing. She was talented and would make a fantastic mentor. They'd gotten along like a house on fire, it was like they had known each other for years. The older woman was definitely someone she could see herself working for. The interview was a piece of cake. Tammy had sailed through it. If she didn't get the job, she would be really shocked. Then again . . . she sighed and grabbed the leather strap on her bag tighter. Her stomach gave a little clench. She tried to pick up the pace, to put her energy into something worthwhile. Any faster though, and she'd be jogging.

Try as she might, she couldn't help but think about the position. Graphic design was something Tammy loved. Something she was good at. The only problem was that the industry was small. Too damned small. Her past still haunted her. The skeletons in her closet were still very much alive and still very pissed. One skeleton in particular . . .

Bastard.

She walked faster and glanced at the watch on her wrist. Damn, she was going to be late – and for the second time this week. Carlos was going to give her grief and quite rightly so. Two interviews in one week.

Two.

She was on a roll. The thought of working for Jessica filled her with excitement. Squashed Orange was a small agency but they were on the up and up. Tammy wanted to be a part of that. The thought of the other interview she did this week had her hands turning clammy and her heart racing. There was a part of her that wanted nothing to do with that one. Mating a vampire. *Really?* Is that what her life had come to? All of her studies, her hard work? All meaningless. None of it mattered. If given the chance, would she really go to the vampire castle and beg some guy to take her on? Beg a guy to take care of her? What choice did she have? Then again, there was the payout. It didn't feel right to go down that road though.

The last two years had been long and hard. Living from hand to mouth. Begging for extra shifts to make rent. Some days the only meals she ate were the ones that came free at work. One meal per shift. It couldn't go on.

Tammy picked up the pace, she approached the door with a sign that said 'Staff Entrance' above it in peeling red paint. Just as she reached for the door handle, her phone rang. She took the device out of her purse.

Shit!

It was a landline number she didn't recognize offhand. For a quick second she thought about ignoring it. Carlos was going to have her ass. Without giving herself a chance to think about it any longer, she answered the phone.

"Good day, is this Tamara Schiffer?" It was a woman's voice. Formally delivered and not one she recognized.

"Yes, I'm Tamara."

"Hi . . ." A deep breath. "I'm Allison, I'm calling about your interview earlier this week."

Double shit!

Tammy swallowed hard, her heart rate picked up. "Oh . . . okay." She pinched her lips together, closed her eyes and waited to hear what Allison had to say.

"We think that you would be a good fit for our program . . ." the woman paused.

Tammy nodded once feeling like an idiot since the other woman couldn't see her. "That's great," she stammered.

"We need you to come in for a briefing on the third of next month. That's next Thursday," Allison added. "You will be required to sign a non-disclosure agreement which will be emailed to you before the close of business today. Make sure that you have your lawyer look at it between now and the time you come in."

Her lawyer. Yeah right. "Okay. No problem," her voice sounded squeaky. She couldn't believe this was happening.

"Oh and, Miss Schiffer . . ."

"Yes?" Her mind raced. *Shit!* A vampire. Could she go through with it? Hopefully she wouldn't have to. Maybe the graphic design position would come through as well. *Oh please let that one come through.* Miracles happened! They did, didn't they?

"Congratulations! We've had tens of thousands of applicants from all over the country. Less than half a percent made it. You are one of the lucky few."

Maybe Allison could hear the hesitancy in her voice. "Thank you. I appreciate it." She worked hard to inject some enthusiasm into her voice.

"I'll send all the information together with the agreement. Be ready to leave within a day of the briefing." That wasn't an issue, Tammy had casual employment. There weren't enough shifts to go around at the moment as it was. Besides, Carlos had always been good to her. Hard but fair. They said their goodbyes and she disconnected the call, shoving her phone back into her purse.

Her mind was still reeling. Being accepted into the program meant getting paid. They received an enormous daily allowance. One week in the program would pay two months' rent. It would take the pressure off of her in a big way. Maybe she'd find love in the process. Tammy had to stop herself from laughing out loud. *Yeah right.*

One thing was for sure, her luck seemed to be changing. Which gave her hope that the position at Squashed Orange would still come through. A real job. One that would allow her to stand on her own two feet. She would take the spot in the vampire program if she needed to, but she would still feel guilty about entering it only for the money when so many women were looking for love. When these vampires were seeking mates. It sounded like they were desperate. Hopefully she wouldn't have to go down that road.

If it came to it though, she'd make the most of the opportunity. She wasn't so crazy that she would jump in and tie herself to another person just for the sake of a secure future. She also wasn't so naïve as to believe in 'the one.' On the other hand, she hadn't had much luck with human men so maybe a vampire was just what she needed. Maybe she could start over on a clean slate and build a future. Worst case scenario, she'd get a break from the rigors of real life for a couple of days. Three square meals a day sounded like music to her ears.

Tammy took a deep breath and pushed the door open. Carlos was waiting for her. He looked at his watch and then pointedly at her.

"I know, I know . . ." Tammy held up a hand. "I'm so sorry."

"Save it. Not only are you late but you missed the weekly meeting."

Tamara felt her eyes widen. She blew out a breath. "Shit!" She rubbed her forehead. "I'm really sorry. I don't know how I forgot about it. The interview went on for forever. Jessica asked me to help out with an ad she's working on. She wanted to see how we worked together and to see if . . ." Tamara licked her lips, feeling excitement course through her as she relived the last hour and a half. "If I could deliver the goods."

Carlos didn't look impressed. He pushed off from the counter and dropped his hands to his sides. He finally gave a quick nod. "Get your ass in there." He pointed to the double door with his thumb. "Natalie is covering for you." They were working skeleton staff which meant that the server from the previous shift had to work overtime – for free. They'd all filled in for one another on occasion so it wasn't a big deal. It wasn't like she made a habit of it. Not normally. It still made her feel really guilty though.

Tammy pulled a neatly folded apron from her bag and tied it around her waist.

Carlos sighed. "How did it go?" Her boss stared at her pointedly. Although his voice was still gruff, his eyes glinted.

Tamara tried to hold back a grin and failed.

"That good, huh?" Carlos smiled back. "I'm still angry about you being late. In fact, you're closing up tonight."

"It's James' turn to . . . never mind," she quickly added when his eyes narrowed. "It went really well. I loved every minute of it . . . okay, maybe not the first five minutes and waiting for the interview was horrible, but once I got in there and we got to talking . . ."

"This Jessica lady sounds nice."

"Oh she is! Really nice in a 'kick ass and take no prisoners' kind of way. She's dynamic and so damned good at what she does. It's little wonder the company is doing so well."

"I take it she's open-minded?" He raised his brows.

"We'll soon find out since I nailed the interview."

"One day someone will see through the bullshit. They'll see you and know that you aren't capable of those things you were accused of."

"Lying, cheating and stealing, you mean?"

"It's crazy that anyone would think that of you. I believed in you . . . gave you a chance."

"Yeah, but you knew me from before. Still, I can't thank you enough for giving me a chance when no one else would." She felt her eyes sting.

Carlos smiled, the skin around his eyes crinkling. He shrugged. "There's no way you did those things. Did you put me down as a reference?"

Tammy nodded. "Not that it will help much . . . no offence. Agencies generally want references from other agencies."

"You never know. Now," he pointed towards the swinging doors, "get in there before you miss your whole shift. Oh . . ." His eyes darted to his shoes for a second or two before he made eye contact with her again. "The roster for next week is up. We're still on a skeleton staff for the next couple of weeks. Business is bound to pick up soon though."

Tamara didn't like the tension in the air or the way Carlos kept dropping eye contact. He rocked his weight from one foot to the other. She walked over to the cork board and glanced at the roster. "Oh my word!" she muttered under her breath. "Three shifts? Are you serious?"

Carlos shook his head. "I'm sorry. It doesn't make

sense to have more than one of you per shift, for the majority of the time we're just not busy enough."

"I get that, but three . . . I need at least four just to make ends meet." Just to pay the rent. Any other bills and food would come out of tips. This was a small diner; they didn't make much in tips.

"There is nothing I can do. There was a shift going earlier, if you'd been at the meeting you—"

"I was at an interview," she tried to keep the anger and frustration from her voice. "You know this."

"I told you to swap shifts."

"Thursday evenings are the best money."

Carlos pinched the bridge of his nose and closed his eyes. "I'm sorry, Tam," he finally said. "There's nothing I can do. I need to be fair to all my staff."

Tammy nodded, feeling like an ass. "I know. I'm sorry I complained. I'm just nervous, if I don't make rent . . ." she let the sentence die. "I'll be fine," she quickly added, seeing the look of concern on Carlos' face. It wasn't fair of her to put the blame and responsibility on his shoulders. She was an adult and responsible for her own past, as well as her future.

"Do you need a loan? I could help out with a small—"

Tamara put up a hand. "No . . . no, I'll be fine. Thanks though." Times were just as tough on Carlos. He had a family to take care of. Three kids, the youngest of whom was still in diapers. No, she'd get by.

"Are you sure, I—" Her phone rang, silencing her boss. He looked down at her purse and frowned.

"Shit! Sorry." Tammy pulled the phone out of her bag, intent on silencing the device, and saw that it was the agency. "Oh god! It's them!" she blurted. "It's Squashed Orange." Her heart-rate accelerated. She could barely breathe. She locked eyes with Carlos.

He must've seen the panic reflected there because he gave a nod. "Take it. I'll meet you out front in a few minutes." He gave her arm a squeeze as he walked past.

It was too soon. A call this quick had to be bad news. Then again, maybe it was a good thing. Jessica seemed like the type of person to make snap decisions.

Tammy sucked in a deep breath, her hand shook as she pressed down on the green button. "Hello?" Thankfully her voice sounded normal.

"Good day, is this Tamara Schiffer?"

Oh no! The woman sounded formal. Too rigid. "Speaking." There was just the hint of a squeak in Tammy's voice. She couldn't be blamed.

"I'm calling to inform you that you were unsuccessful in your bid. Thank you for applying."

Shit!

"Why?" It just slipped out. Stupid thing to ask when she knew why. There was only one reason she didn't get this job. One slimy, asshole of a reason.

The woman on the other end of the line hesitated for a few moments. "We called the previous company you were with and . . ." A long, drawn-out pause. This was followed by a heavy sigh. "You shouldn't waste people's time like that."

What the . . . ?

"Jessica is a busy person. She was excited about working with you," the woman said in a clipped tone.

"I was excited about joining your company as well, and for the record, Chris Collins is a liar."

Another sigh. "Thank you for your time, Miss Schiffer."

"Christopher is my jilted ex-boyfriend but I'm sure he didn't mention that."

"Please stop . . . you're only making things worse. We can add sleeping with the boss to your long list of reasons why *not* to hire you."

Tammy felt her mouth gape open but quickly pulled herself together. "We were partners," she half yelled. Only Chris had never officially given her shares like he'd promised.

"We both know that's not true." Of course it was true . . . well, not exactly, since a person's word counted for shit.

"He made all of those things up," she practically whispered, talking more to herself than the other woman.

The lady on the other end of the line must have heard her. "You were arrested, put inside a jail cell . . . correct me if I'm wrong."

Fuck!

"If it wasn't for Mr. Collins dropping the charges, you'd be in jail now. As far as I'm concerned the man is a saint."

She couldn't help the snort that was pulled from her. If he was a saint, then she was an angel in heaven.

The woman paused. Tammy could almost hear her irritation through the phone line. "You can thank your—"

"I was framed." Tamara knew how she sounded. She sounded as guilty as sin, as guilty as the freaking devil himself and there was nothing she could do about it. "He was angry when I left him. He framed me. I didn't do any of it."

"You left him?" The lady sounded incredulous. Tammy couldn't blame her. Chris was a smooth-talking charmer. It was the reason she'd fallen for him in the first place. That and his good looks. "Hmmmm. It doesn't matter, the decision has been made." There was a soft click as she put the phone down on the other end.

Tammy's throat felt clogged. Her eyes stung and her nose threatened to run. Tamara sniffed a few times and sucked in a deep breath. *Shit! Double freaking shit.* Why did it still hurt so bad? Two years and, at times like this, it was like it had happened yesterday. Christopher *fucking* Collins had ruined her life and there wasn't a damn thing she could do about it. Crying wouldn't help. She'd done plenty of that.

The Program.

It wasn't something she ever saw herself getting involved in. Not that she had anything against vampires. She just didn't like the idea of relying on another person again, especially a man. Then again, these guys weren't men. A shiver ran through her. Like someone was walking over her grave.

She'd take part. It wasn't like she had much of a choice. It would mean going against what she knew was right. Her father would be so disappointed in her if he knew what she was planning. She'd get in, earn the money she needed to start over and then get out.

One week. Not so long. There was no chance of her falling for anyone, so she wasn't worried about that. Tammy didn't like the idea of stringing someone along, so she'd make sure that no one fell for her either. One week and then she was out of there. She only wished it had never come to this.

CHAPTER 2

Ten days later . . .

How had she ever thought that this would be better? That being out here in the middle of nowhere was better than her two-bit, rat-infested apartment. Tamara looked around her. Tall mountains spanned in all directions. The valleys were made up of thick forests and open plains of tall grass. The peaks were snowcapped. The sky was dark blue and cloudless. In short, it was breathtakingly beautiful. She'd passed a small herd of deer earlier and a waterfall . . . an honest-to-god waterfall! Okay, so maybe this was better than her apartment. Way better.

Despite her sweater and jeans, she was freezing her ass off though. She had always enjoyed winter but this was ridiculous. Her toes felt like ice blocks. It wasn't her fault she didn't have hiking boots and thermal gear. Tammy didn't have much, period. Her teeth chattered. At this rate she was going to die of hypothermia before one of those shifters caught up with her.

Dragon shifters.

Lord up above . . . she couldn't believe that she was here, in the middle of the mountains, being hunted by huge men who could turn into savage beasts. There was a small part of her that found the whole thing exciting. It was a tiny part. The rest of her questioned her own sanity. To add to her predicament, she had to stay for two weeks. Two whole weeks! Guilt churned in her gut. She was here for the money. Although she wasn't about to admit that to them, she was going to be clear about not being interested in long-term. She had to at least try to be honest.

She needed to be careful how she worded things since she'd told her interviewer that she was keen on dating and mating a non-human. Tammy didn't want to get booted and lose the cash but she didn't want to string someone along either. So far, everyone had been really nice. They'd got to see the men last night at dinner. It seemed like a lifetime ago. The big shifter guys had eyeballed the five of them like there was no tomorrow. One or two had smiled almost shyly while others had winked and grinned. They seemed sweet enough, considering. There was no interaction permitted so she had only learned what the Fire King's mate, Roxy had told them.

"How are you holding up?" Claire asked from behind her, pulling her from her thoughts.

"Fine." Puffs of white plumed as she spoke. Her breath came in hard pants. Tammy picked up the pace, the brisk movement helped keep her warm.

"Here." She could hear a rustle from behind her. "Please stop being so darned heroic and take the gloves."

"I'm fine."

"Your lips are blue."

Tammy had to laugh. "You can't even see my lips."

"Don't have to. I can hear your teeth chattering, and I can hear how cold you are by the sound of your voice," Claire sounded concerned.

Tammy stopped. She smiled as Claire came up next to her. The other woman's big, blue eyes widened. She reminded Tammy of a porcelain doll. Tiny, delicate, she had wisps of blond hair which fell in ringlets around her face. Most of her shoulder-length hair was neatly tucked into a woolen hat. "I knew it, your lips *are* halfway to being blue. I can't believe they dropped you off wearing so little clothing. Crazy."

"It won't be long before we're nabbed by a couple of those big brutes and then it's off to their castle, and to a really big fireplace, and steaming plates of food." Tammy's mouth filled with saliva while the rest of her hurt from the numbing cold.

Claire frowned. "It could be a while yet. I'm sure most of them would've followed the bigger group." She and Claire had chosen to break away from the others. They had been advised that it was the best course of action. That, and that they get as far away as possible.

The stronger, higher-ranking shifters were faster and had the most stamina. Not that Tammy cared who she ended up with. The dragon shifter community ran differently though. It wasn't a money-based society.

She'd use the time she had wisely. She needed to reflect

and decide what to do about her future. "I hope they make it quick." Tammy rubbed her hands together.

Claire smiled. She pulled off the other glove and held them out to Tamara. "Stop being so stubborn. Warm extremities make a big difference."

Tammy smiled. "Thanks." She took the gloves and pulled them on. She had to stop herself from groaning at how good they felt. Claire was right, just having her hands warmed made her feel instantly better. "I still can't believe I'm here," she blurted.

Claire gave her head a shake. "Me neither. My dad almost had a heart attack when I put my leave in."

"You work for your dad?" Tammy stepped forward and Claire followed. They began walking again, only not quite as fast as before. Her thigh muscles felt stiff, her whole body was tired. Claire was much smaller than her, she must be feeling it as well.

The other woman nodded. "Yeah!" She rolled her eyes. "I should feel lucky; instead, on most days, I feel trapped."

"Is your dad a control freak?"

"More like my mom is one. My dad goes along with everything she says. As my parents' only child, I'm being groomed to take over the family business . . . or should I say, empire. I'm expected to marry within my circle – that's how mom puts it." Claire rolled her eyes again. "I'm done with working day in and day out in a job I don't enjoy. Sales, logistics, marketing, merchandising . . . it's all coming out of my ears. I'm done with the functions and the not so subtle set-ups with 'respectable,'" she made quote signs with her fingers, "men. Nope! Not for me. I've tried to tell them . . . to tell *her* but they won't listen. So," she gave a mischievous smile. "Here I am. Maybe it is me just being rebellious. Maybe it won't amount to anything, but I don't care." She spun in a circle. "I'm here," she grinned. "For once in my life I feel young and carefree, I feel like anything is possible."

Claire's enthusiasm was catching, Tammy found herself smiling.

"What about you?" Claire glanced at Tammy. She had shoved her hands deep into her jacket pockets.

Tammy shrugged. "I needed a change."

After a couple of seconds Tammy said. "Cryptic. Why the sudden urge?"

"I just felt like I'd hit a dead-end. I saw the newspaper article advertising dates with vampires and here I am." Tammy looked around her, once again feeling awe and wonder and nervousness. There was also excitement. Maybe something would come of this after all.

"Yeah, here we are. I love the vampires but there is something about these dragon shifters that gets me all . . ." Claire made a groaning noise, "fired up." She laughed at her own joke.

"They're definitely easy on the eye." *Extremely easy on the eye.* She'd found herself blushing a few times at dinner. Good thing she had sworn off men who were too hot for their own good.

The other woman gave another groan. "And hard on the panties. Good thing I brought enough pairs for regular changes," Claire giggled and Tammy couldn't help but do the same.

"I haven't had sex in so long, I don't remember how it goes anymore." Tammy gave a shake of the head.

"You poor—" Claire was cut short when someone roared behind them. It was deep and scary. The noise punctured through from somewhere down the valley. They both turned in time to see the clash.

It was a group of five or six guys against two. It looked like the shifters had caught up to them. They were fighting over them. Even though this had been expected, her heart still sped up.

"Is this happening?" she whispered.

"Yes, it is!" Claire was smiling, her eyes bright with excitement.

Another roar drew her back to the fight. All of the men were shirtless. Even though the clash took place a couple of hundred feet away, they all still looked huge. Muscles bulged and rippled. There were loud grunts and growls and several even harsher roars.

"Oh, my god!" Claire wrapped a hand around her mouth. Her eyes were wide. "That's so damned hot." It was clearly the two guys with their backs to them against the other . . . she did a quick count . . . five of them.

"We should get going." Tammy suddenly felt queasy. She couldn't take her eyes off the fighting men. There was a loud cracking noise and one of the guys flew backwards. He didn't get back up. The others carried on undeterred.

Claire made a noise for 'no.' "It wouldn't do us any

good." Another guy went flying, Tammy could see blood pouring down his face. They were so barbaric. So base. Although Tammy felt a bit ill, she struggled to tear her eyes off the fighting mass of men. There was another cracking noise as one of the guys kneed another guy in the face.

She winced at the horrible sound. "Flip . . . sheesh. Um . . ." Tammy licked her lips. "They're aggressive. They're . . ." She didn't know what else to say. Her hands shook so she folded her arms across her chest. Maybe this was a bad idea. Two weeks. All she had to do was get through two weeks.

"They're magnificent," Claire sighed. "Perfect."

Some women liked this type of testosterone fest. Tammy wasn't one of them. Having said that, she couldn't seem to make herself stop watching. Within a half a minute, it was just the two guys left. They both turned at the same time. They both had dark features and were both equally big and broad . . . terrifying was a better description.

"Oh, my lord!" Claire whispered, barely loud enough for her to hear. "Look at their chests."

Both of the men had golden markings. Bright and strangely beautiful. Their chests were broad, muscled with pecs that could have a grown woman on her knees in a second. Good thing she didn't fall for stuff like that. They moved damn quickly. The one said something to the other one and he nodded as they approached.

They may have looked alike from afar, but up close they

were night and day. The one guy had purple-colored eyes. It was a weird hue, unlike anything she'd seen before coming to dragon shifter territory. Those purple-colored irises seemed fairly normal with the shifter dragons. Only this guy's eyes were bright and so vivid that they almost looked like jewels. He was beautiful. Plain and simple. Drop dead gorgeous as the saying went. She felt a little light-headed looking at him, so she looked away.

The other guy had eyes that seemed as black as the night itself. He was a little more muscled, although not quite as tall as Hunkboy, next to him. He wasn't nearly as good-looking but seriously attractive, nonetheless, in a dark, brooding kind of a way.

She noticed that Hunkboy was focused on her while the brooding one was eyeballing the hell out of Claire who gave another one of her sighs.

Tammy glanced at the other woman and sure enough, her eyes were focused on the brooding one.

Shit!

That meant that the good-looking one was hers . . . her eyes shot to Hunkboy. He winked at her. The son of a bitch actually winked. There were smears of blood on his arms and drops of blood all over his chest.

She felt a zing of . . . *arousal.* Arousal? Really? At a time like this? No damned way. No! She didn't do over-the-top good-looking men. She'd only made that mistake once—with Christopher *fucking* Collins – and look where it had landed her. *Right here* is where. *With no other choices* is where.

There was a moaning sound from next to her. Tammy

glanced towards Claire who had her tongue down Brooding's throat. One leg was around the back of his thigh.

Great!

The smell of musk hit her. Not the kind you find in a bottle. Not the kind with a fancy name like white musk or vanilla musk. This was the real kind. The kind that smelled like a wild animal. It had a clean edge to it though. Soap and musk. Another zing hit her square in the clit as she realized that not only did she like the way the guy smelled, she loved it.

What the hell was wrong with her?

His purple eyes narrowed in on hers and he gave a half smile. "Hey." The smile widened and dimples appeared on either side of his mouth. A full mouth. Lips like that didn't belong on a man. Such kissable, soft looking lips.

"I'm not going to hurt you." He raised both hands, which ironically, were bloody. Not a lot considering the carnage these two had left behind them, but, there was still blood on them.

Tammy's brain raced at a million miles a minute. She didn't do hunky guys. She didn't do charmers. For just a second, she was tempted to tell him to take a hike. Then it dawned on her that maybe this wasn't such a bad thing. He was ridiculously good-looking which meant that she wasn't going to fall for him. *Forget it.* An average Joe would be more of a threat to her. Also, he was a royal which meant that he got privileges. He wouldn't be as desperate for a woman, so there was less of a chance that he would fall for her. Roxy had mentioned last night that the non-royals, the guys with the silver chests, only got to be with a woman twice a year. They hardly ever won a woman during the hunts, so if they managed to snag one, they would hold on with both hands. She didn't want to string someone like that along, it wouldn't be fair. Hunkboy over here was way better looking than Chris even. He more than likely had women fall over their feet to be near him. Tammy had to bite her lip to stop herself from laughing. Of course a guy like him wouldn't fall for a girl like her. That made him perfect.

None of the jocks had ever looked at her, let alone given her the time of day. Not that there was anything wrong with her mind, you. She refused to live on lettuce leaves and, as a result, she had an ass on her and a good set of thighs. Although she had lost a bit of weight lately but not by choice.

She didn't dye her hair or pluck her brows or tint her lashes. Her nails were short and she didn't paint them because she hated regular touch ups, so they would end up with chipped polish. In short, she couldn't be bothered. Having said that, her hair was really glossy and thick. She liked her eyes, they were big and almond shaped like her mother's. Her boobs were a generous handful and still firm. Beauty queen, no, but beautiful in her own way . . . you bet.

Back to the pretty boy dilemma at hand. Should she run for the hills or allow him to kiss her and take her home? Like she'd said earlier, an average Joe would be more inclined to fall for her. Especially one who was starved for companionship. Hunkboy was a safe bet.

"I'm not going to hurt you," he repeated, then caught her staring at his hands. "Um . . ." He frowned and looked down. "Oh fuck," he muttered, clasping his hands behind his back. His Adam's apple bobbed as he swallowed hard. "I swear you're safe. Hand-to-hand combat is normal amongst my kind."

"I know," Tammy finally managed to choke out. "We were briefed."

CHAPTER 3

*B*y Scale.
By Claw.
And by all that was winged.

This female was exquisite. Utter perfection. Her hair was dark and silky. It hung down her back to between her shoulder blades. Her eyes were large and expressive. They were the color of melted chocolate. Thunder loved chocolate. The taste. The way it melted in his mouth. He couldn't get enough of the stuff and he had a feeling she would be no different.

Her lips were raspberry-kissed. He couldn't help but to wonder if her nipples would be painted with the same brush. He caught another snoutful of her delicious scent. It made his mouth water for a taste. Made his dick twitch. Thunder had to suppress a growl, especially when her words from earlier ran through his memory.

I haven't had sex in so long, I don't remember how it goes anymore.

He was thankful that Granite hadn't put up a fight when he'd said that he wanted this one. The taller of the two females. The darker of the two. He knew from the moment he saw her that he had to have her. It had made him fight harder. The poor fucks hadn't known what hit them when they dared to try and claim what was his. The group of lessers had tried hard and had failed just as hard. The idiots were worn down from the chase and stupid for trying to keep up in the first place.

The female spoke. He had to concentrate to catch what she was saying. "I know," she paused. "We were briefed."

"Good. Then you understand that fighting is normal for us. Bleeding and fighting tend to go hand-in-hand as well, and I wanted to make sure they stayed down," he added the last and gave her a smile. One that always worked on the human females in the bars they frequented during the stag runs.

She nodded but there was no return smile forthcoming. There was no blushing or sneaky looks from under her lashes. What he did get was the lingering scent of her fear. Thunder was concerned that she might shun him for dealing so harshly with the lessers. She didn't look sure of him. The only time he'd ever had a problem with human females was during the hunt. There was a female on the previous hunt who had turned him down flat. It looked like this one might follow suit, which felt unacceptable to him. This type of wariness was not something he was used to, so he was not sure how to deal with it. Ignoring the situation had not worked well for him last time, so this time he planned on treading carefully.

There were no males within hearing range, so they had

a little bit of time. The gorgeous female before him was skittish, liable to bolt at any second. She was also, despite being nervous, aroused by him. It was a strange combination. The scent of her arousal was intoxicating, Thunder had to work to keep himself from sniffing her. However, the low growl that left his throat could not be helped.

Her eyes widened and she clasped and unclasped her hands. On a base level, she would understand what his growls meant. On a conscious level though, she might take them as a threat.

"Like I said," Thunder gently touched her arm. Thank fuck she didn't flinch or pull away. "You are safe with me . . ."

"Where are you going?" the light-haired human shouted. Both he and the dark beauty turned towards the commotion.

Granite strode away, the human female had a puzzled expression on her face and her hands were on her hips. "You can't just leave!" she shouted after him. "Hey!" she added when he didn't respond.

Granite paused, he glanced back. "One of the others will be here to claim you soon." He kept on walking.

"What about you?" her voice was a high-pitched.

Granite didn't answer, he shifted into his dragon form. Both females gasped.

"Wait!" the light-haired one called after him as he took to the sky. The female finally turned towards them. Granite was a speck in the sky. "Was it something I said?

Something I did?"

Thunder shook his head. "Do not let Granite concern you. He is a base male with the manners of a chimpanzee." He lifted his eyes in thought. "Then again, chimpanzees are friendly, chipper creatures. He has all the manners of a bear with a sore tooth and a bad case of tick infestation. What he said is correct. There are hundreds of males willing to fight for an opportunity to be with you."

"Do I take a seat here and wait. I really can't believe that just happened. I've never been so humiliated in all my life."

Thunder smiled at the female. "Do not let an asshole like him worry you. You should keep going, the males love the chase . . . they will fight harder. I'm sure you want the best possible candidate," he winked at her to put her at ease.

"I thought I had that already." She gave a shiver. "I fully expected him to throw me over his shoulder so that he could take me somewhere a little more private and claim the hell out of me." She shrugged. "Oh well." She looked at the dark-haired beauty at his side. "Good luck! It looks like you found yourself a keeper." Then she proceeded to eyeball the hell out of him before sighing and walking away.

"You too," the human at his side replied.

The light-haired woman walked away.

He hated being so unsure of how to proceed. Females in the bars they frequented would come to him. They would invite him to have sex with them. He never had to do much of anything except show up and deliver.

"I don't get it. I thought a guy claimed a girl by kissing her," the female frowned. "What did Claire mean when she said she wanted him to put her over his shoulder and claim her fully . . . in private. I also don't get why the guy just left."

"Granite is hard to read and even harder to understand. He knows what he wants and how he wants it. Your friend obviously wasn't it. I'm not sure that any female will meet up with his expectations. This isn't the first time he's walked away from one . . ." he paused. "As to your other question," he continued, "a male will claim a female when he kisses her but if he wants to claim her properly, he will need to really get his scent onto her. It will tell others to stay away. It is the best way to ensure that no other males will try and fight him for her."

"Get his scent on her?" she seemed to be speaking to herself.

"He will come inside her. His seed will mark her."

"Oh!" The word came out sounding shrill, she averted her gaze. Her cheeks turned pink and the scent of her arousal surrounded them. Melted chocolate. He wanted a taste.

A rumble left him. His dick woke up. As in all the way up. Thunder tried to breathe through his mouth. Human females were easily scared by erections. Especially dragon shifter erections. Human males were not nearly as well endowed. "That will . . ." he cleared his throat, "keep the others away for sure."

"Um . . . I'm not having sex with you." Her eyes were wide and that scent of fear was back.

"We don't need to have sex . . . just yet. It's better if a couple does have sex as soon as possible, but it's not necessary. I would never force you, so do not be concerned. That's not my thing. I'm into mutual pleasure. My partner should definitely scream and cry out but only because she is enjoying herself."

The female smiled. "TMI, buddy."

"TM . . . what?"

"Too much information," her smile widened. By all that was scaly, she was even more beautiful when she smiled. Thunder couldn't help but take a step towards her. Just a small one. "I disagree. You need to know what you might be getting into."

She folded her arms. "I'm listening."

"I know how to fuck, so at least I can give you great pleasure, even if we are not compatible as mates. It's also important that you know I enjoy sucking clit."

The human choked out a strangled laugh. "You didn't just say that," she shook her head. "I've never heard of such a thing."

"Wait a minute," Thunder put his hand up, snagging her attention. "Are you telling me you've never had your clit sucked?" *The fuck!*

Her mouth fell open for a half a second. "That's none of your business." She blushed harder. The smell of chocolate only grew more intense. His mouth watered for a lick, a suck, a good old taste.

"What I'm trying to say is that it may not work out between us but I could show you a really good time." He shrugged trying to look indifferent. He wasn't though. Not by a long fucking shot.

Interest flared in her chocolate stare. "Really now?" That delicious scent of her arousal was intoxicating. She smiled. "I like the sound of that because I'm here for a good time as well." She looked shocked at her admission. "I must be honest, I'm not sure about the whole mating thing."

Hearing her say that put his scales up. "Why are you here then?" His voice came out sounding gruff. "It was my understanding that females interested in mating with non-humans were selected for the hunt. If you do not wish to mate, then you should not be here. Did you lie when they questioned you?" Thunder was done with bullshit. If her answer didn't appease him she was out of here. As in going back to Walton Springs. It didn't matter how much his dick wanted her. He needed a mate not a plaything.

"Easy, big boy! I would love to fall in love and live happily ever after with the man of my dreams, but let's just say I'm a touch jaded. I'm one of those clichéd cases where a girl got her heart broken and is struggling to trust again. I doubt that you or any other man is capable of winning my heart again."

Thunder couldn't help but smile. It wasn't a humorous or flirty grin, it was downright feral. The human sucked in a breath and took a step back. Her pupils dilated a fraction and her heart picked up speed. "Firstly, I'm no boy." He took a step towards her. "And for your information, I'm not a man either, I'm a red-blooded dragon male in his prime," his voice had deepened. He took another step towards her and she swallowed thickly. "I am Thunder," he beat a fist on his chest. "King of the Air dragons. Ruler and defender of my people. I am gold. A royal, and I fucking love a challenge. I will win your heart even if it is the last thing I do."

Her breathing sped up along with her heart-rate. Her pupils continued to dilate. Her arousal had his cock lengthening and thickening a whole lot more. Thunder growled loudly as he circled his arms around her middle and pulled her flush against him.

"Please don't kick me in the balls," he muttered as he crushed his lips against hers. He couldn't be gentle or careful. He was done taking his time. Done treading carefully.

Thankfully, the female melted against him with a whimper. Her soft lips parted and he pillaged her mouth.

Fucking perfection.

So damned soft. Thunder took ahold of her ass. His erection pressed firmly against her belly. It couldn't be helped. He threaded his fingers into her hair and deepened the kiss. Her soft breasts crushed against him. She tasted decadent. Like chocolate, only better. *Much fucking better.* She whimpered again. Music to his ears. A good start, but he wanted more. He wanted a whole damned symphony.

Thunder cupped her chin and deepened the kiss further. He lifted her from her feet, fitting her more snuggly against him. Her little hands were on him, sliding up his chest, over his shoulders and onto his back. Her nails dug into him.

Then the human started to pull away from him and wriggled from his grasp. She was breathing fast. Her eyes were wide in . . . shock. It was more than that, it was panic. She touched a finger to her lips. They were swollen and wet from his kiss. If his mouth was anything to go by, they would be tingling as well. His whole body was on fire. By the way she rubbed her thighs together and by the flush on her cheeks he could gather that she was right there with him.

As his mind began to clear, he had to question why the fuck he had said that. He hadn't planned on boasting about his position so early on. Not after what happened in the last hunt. He wanted a female who wasn't concerned with all of that. The titles, the prestige, the lifestyle.

He knew why though; he'd told her because he had to. This was his female. He was as sure of it as he was about his next breath. She was his or would be soon if he had anything to say about it.

Instead of a sweet smile or soft giggle, her eyes narrowed like she was angry with him. "If you think you can break out those sexy dimples and use this . . ." she waved her hand up and down in front of him. "hunky body to charm your way into my panties, you are very mistaken."

It seemed the little human was upset that she was

attracted to him. *Oh yes!* This female was his alright. It was up to him to convince her of that.

Thunder couldn't help but smile, noticing how her frown deepened. "Mmmmm . . . so you think I have a hunky b—"

Talons wrapped around her body and jerked her upwards. The human screamed. Before he could act, a forked tail lashed out, knocking him from his feet. Thunder went flying backwards, the back of his head hit the ground hard. His teeth cracked together on landing and he instantly tasted blood.

He heard the loud flap of wings beating. Thunder struggled to open his eyes. Pain flared from the back of his skull, radiating down his spine.

The light stung his eyes. His head throbbed but Thunder clawed his way to his feet anyway. The dragon was a mere speck on the horizon. It had a silver chest. He recognized the beast's scent. One of its talons on its left hind leg.

It was Cloud. One of his own Pinnacle males. A feeling of dread grabbed ahold of him. *Dammit all to hell!* He had suspected that the male wasn't stable and this proved it.

No!

Maybe there was another explanation. *What though?* Thunder racked his brain but came up with nothing.

Hell and damnation. There was no other explanation. He had known it deep down. Should never have let him take part in the hunt. Cloud had clearly gone over the deep end. Who could blame him?

Thunder grabbed the back of his neck and squeezed. What the hell was he going to do? Doing nothing wasn't an option. Following on foot? Nope, wouldn't work either. It would take too long to get to them and to talk some sense into the male before it was too late. Before he did something he would regret. The hunt rules were clear though, if he shifted into his dragon form it was an immediate disqualification from the hunt. No exceptions! If he was disqualified, he wouldn't be able to have the human. *Unacceptable!* Thunder roared in anger and frustration. Was the human in immediate danger? Cloud would never hurt an innocent, or would he?

Fuck! Thunder roared again as indecision warred inside of him. It seemed that today was the day for experiencing abnormal emotions. Indecision being one of them. *What the hell was he going to do?*

CHAPTER 4

Her stomach lurched so hard she gagged. Her head felt heavy. Her skin numb from the cold. Her hair whipped about her face, flicking so hard that it stung.

The dragon was moving fast. Its great wings flapping in a quick rhythm. Way faster than the one that had dropped her off at the start of the hunt earlier today. Her stomach clenched again and it was all she could do not to throw up. She tasted bile and tried to swallow. Tammy opened her eyes but they watered so badly that she was forced to close them again. Besides, they were so high it made her head spin just to look down.

Her mind raced. Panic threatened to overtake her. Was this allowed? Was it normal hunt behavior? She remembered Roxy saying something about the dragons not being allowed to shift into their animal forms during the hunt. Not even to get back home. Had she misunderstood?

No! Roxy had been clear about that. The woman was the Fire King's mate, pregnant with his child. She was really helpful and friendly and she had been very clear about the guys having to stay in human form during the entire hunt. They could fight one another. Even dispute a claim, unless a couple had actually done the deed, but they couldn't do what this guy had just done. It was illegal. Unfair. Wrong. She forced herself to calm down. That hunky shifter had seen the whole thing. Thunder had seen it all go down.

Well sort of. No, not really. He'd been knocked out for the count. Thunder had flown at least ten, if not fifteen feet. She hadn't seen him get up either. Maybe he hadn't seen much after all. She was too busy trying to stop herself from screaming and from being sick to take serious notice. Did that mean that she was alone in this? That no one was coming to her rescue?

It was hard to think while blood rushed through her body. With a head this heavy and stomach wound so tightly. It was hard to breathe even though air rushed past her. She clutched at the scaly talons that were wrapped around her waist. She squeezed her eyes shut and tried to stay calm. It wouldn't do to lose it. What if this dragon dropped her?

The beast in question slowed. His wings beat in a rhythmic fashion and they seemed to hover. Then he dropped, plummeting towards the earth. Tammy tried to scream but she couldn't. Her stomach lurched and she gagged all over again. It was worse this time. She felt saliva run up her cheeks and top lip. Just when she thought her head might explode, he slowed down again.

Tammy gulped in air. She could feel that she was

shaking. Her feet touched something hard and he let go. Tammy's legs crumpled and she fell, using her hands to keep herself from hitting the ground.

The earth was rocky and littered with stones. Pain hit her palms as the little sharp points abraded her skin. She'd lost the gloves Claire had given her. It was a stupid thing to think of now.

She stayed in a crumpled heap, trying hard to catch her breath. Then she wiped her face on her sweater sleeves to remove the saliva, sweat, snot and tears.

The sweat was the crazy part. She was shivering from the cold and sweating from the fear. It was a strange combination that left her feeling chilled to the bone.

Tammy heard footfalls and the crunch of gravel. She tried to stand. It took a couple of tries before her jelly legs finally obeyed her. Her hair was a mess. It hung over her eyes. Tammy swiped her hand over her face. The guy was big, like all the shifters. He was built as well but he had a strange look in his eyes. She couldn't quite put her finger on it. All she knew was that she didn't like it. She didn't much like him. A feeling of dread rushed through her and she took a step back. Her whole body shook with fatigue and fear.

Tammy forced herself to stop and stand her ground. She squared her shoulders. "Who are you?" Her voice was croaky and shook.

The guy walked right up to her and picked her up. "Hey!" she shrieked, sounding a tad hysterical. Which was good considering she was all the way there. "Put me down!" She tried to jerk free but his grip on her tightened.

"Do not fight me," the guy said, sounding altogether too calm for her liking. He had dark hair which had been cut close to his scalp and was clean-shaven.

"What are you doing?" She tried hard to break free but it was clear that it wasn't going to happen. Not unless he allowed it. Her mouth dropped open as they entered a cave. It was spacious without being ridiculously big. It was dirty and rocky and by all intents and purposes, it was what you'd expect from a cave. Except, there was a bed smack dab in the middle of the space. It was a four-poster bed complete with lacy drapes and satin sheets. Several candles burned on the jagged bits that jutted out on the rocky walls. A small fire burned in a hollowed out section of rock. Her eyes stayed focused on the bed.

Shit!

This couldn't be good. "Don't you dare even think about . . ." she managed to get out between ragged breaths. She changed the line of conversation, not wanting to give him any ideas. Also, if she continued to panic like this she might end up hyperventilating. "You're not allowed to do this. It's against your laws, against my laws," she cried out in fear as he threw her on the soft mattress. After bouncing once, she scrambled backwards putting as much space between her and the shifter as she could.

"I don't care about shifter lores," he spat, his eyes were haunted and filled with more anger than she had ever seen before. His whole body was tense. She kept her eyes on his since he was naked. "I care even less about human laws."

Oh god! This wasn't good.

"Please," she licked her lips. "Don't do this."

The guy frowned. "I'm not some kind of monster, so you can relax," he added.

Yeah right. Excuse me if I don't believe you.

He sucked in a deep breath. "I am owed. My kingdom, my people . . ." he clenched his teeth, "they all owe me. Above all, I am owed by my king, Thunder. How does the saying go?" He looked up to the ceiling. Not that you could actually see the ceiling, it was swallowed up by the dark. "Ah yes! An eye for an eye . . . or in this case, a female for a female." His voice broke and he swallowed hard but seemed to shake it off quickly.

"Look . . ." Tammy had to try to get through to this nut job. "I don't know what kind of beef you have with your . . . people and your king, but it has nothing to do with me."

The guy smiled and the glint was back. "It has everything to do with you."

She shook her head. "No way. This isn't right. Thunder already claimed me, you—"

"It doesn't matter what Thunder did or didn't do. I could care less. You are mine now."

"What?" She shook her head. "No! Forget it."

He narrowed his icy blue eyes. "Oh yes, female, and the sooner you start to realize it the better." He took a step towards her.

"No!" she yelled. "Don't come near me!" This lunatic

had decided she was his. She just hoped that he didn't plan on proving it.

He grit his teeth for a moment. "I won't force myself on you, so you can calm down. My name is Cloud. I wish to talk to you. I am your mate so it is in your best interest to get to know me since we will be spending a lot of time together. Forever, to be exact."

"Your mate? Don't I have a say in this?"

He shook his head. "No. Get used to it and we'll get along just fine."

Tammy relaxed just a little despite his whole 'you are my mate' attitude. She didn't trust this guy but she felt safe, at least, for the moment. That crazy look in his eyes had eased up. Maybe she could rationalize with him. "Let me get this straight, you took me because you think I belong to Thunder?"

He nodded. "You do belong to him."

"I don't though. Just because he claimed me does not mean I am his or that I agreed to mating him. The original agreement was two weeks, not a lifetime." Maybe she needed to talk to him in a way that he understood.

Cloud made a growling noise. "I heard him promise to win your heart before he claimed you." He pulled a face. "You would've ended up mating him so therefore—"

"Bullshit!" Tammy said. "That's ridiculous. I hadn't agreed to anything. In fact, if you'd listened to what I had to say you'd—"

"You were as good as mated to the male. The rest would've simply been a formality, going through the motions as they say. No!" He shook his head. "This is not up for discussion."

Tammy made a noise that showed her frustration. "Why won't you listen? You don't even know me. How do you know you and I are well suited? You might end up finding me the most irritating person on earth. You might struggle to live with me. You might even hate me. What then?"

He shrugged. "Mates should be accepting and forgiving of each other." He looked like he meant it. "I could never hate you. I will cherish you. What is your name, mate?"

Tammy shook her head. "You sound like a crazy person. Do you know that?"

"I'm not crazy!" he yelled, looking every bit the looney tune. "Why does everyone keep questioning my mental capacity?"

Maybe because you're nuts! Tammy bit down on her lower lip to keep herself from saying it. She held up her hands. "Take it easy. My name is Tamara."

Cloud smiled. "There, that wasn't so hard, was it?"

Tammy didn't answer him.

"We don't have much time. It won't take Thunder more than a couple of hours to make it back to the lair and to send a search party. They will have a good idea of where to search since there aren't many places in Air territory that are suitable for a human."

Thank god! That meant that Thunder had seen them. It sounded like the Air king would have a good idea who had taken her and where they were. Something about what he had said nagged at her. "Time for what?" As soon as the words left her mouth, Tammy wished she'd never asked.

"For us to get to know one another."

She held back a sigh, too afraid to let her guard down. Even more afraid to hope he would see the logic in this.

"And time for us to consummate the mating."

"That's not going to happen, so you can forget it." She grabbed the comforter from the bed and wrapped it around herself. Not because she was cold, but because she felt that the more layers she had between them the better.

"It is going to happen, so best you make peace with it." He sighed, his chin dropping to his chest. After a couple of seconds, he looked back up and locked eyes with her. "I'm not a bad male."

"You could've fooled me." It slipped out.

"I'm not!" he growled.

"Actions speak louder than words."

Cloud sucked in a deep breath. "You are right. I need to prove myself to you. I will feed you and you can take off your shoes because I'm going to give you a foot massage. I will look after you and we will get to know each other and then we will consummate this union. I said take off your shoes," his voice turned gruff.

"No." She could feel herself frown.

"I thought that human females liked foot massages. Dragon shifter females do, very much so." His eyes clouded in what looked like pain. She couldn't figure him out. His emotions were all over the place. Angry and sad in equal measure. Haunted. He had such a sad, haunted look. That was it, the look in his eyes. Despite everything, Tammy felt sorry for him. Maybe she was a bit crazy as well.

"I'll take the food, please," she quickly added, not wanting to anger him. "Don't worry about the massage. I'm good."

"You need to grow used to my touch, Tamara. You need to know that enjoyment can be found in my arms."

She shook her head. "Just the food."

His jaw tensed. "Food now, touching later."

She ground her teeth. *Forget it!* She didn't respond though. It wouldn't do any good.

Cloud hadn't left in search of food like she'd hoped. She knew she wouldn't get very far if she tried to escape, but she had to try. He had to have supplies towards the rear of the cave because he emerged shortly with bread, ham, olives and a tossed salad. Despite her frayed nerves, Tammy found that she was starving and wolfed down a whole plate.

Then she proceeded to fall asleep. Like she didn't have a care in the world. Like everything was okay. *As if!* It was the sheer exhaustion of the whole thing. Firstly, waking up to find out she was deep in the mountains and that the shifters were dragons and not wolves like they had all thought. Heck, up until then she'd thought the guys would be vampires. It was all too much.

She'd battled to sleep last night. Who could blame her? Then the hunt itself. A grueling five and a half hours of hiking through rough terrain. Then this, abducted by a crazy guy.

A really sad, really lonely and all at the same time really angry person.

"Are you sure you don't want a foot rub?" Cloud sat at the edge of the bed.

"No, thank you," she quickly answered, rubbing the sleep from her eyes.

"A backrub?"

She shook her head, pulling the blanket tighter around herself.

"Something to drink? Something more to eat?"

"No. Why not take me back to your—"

"Not going to happen," Cloud frowned.

"Why not? You seem like a really nice guy." Nuts but nice. Maybe. She hoped he was nice. *Try not to think about it.* She sucked in a deep breath and willed her heart to slow back down. "We could date the normal way . . ." *Shit!* She didn't want him to get the wrong idea. He wasn't a bad looking guy but he wasn't her type. Kidnappers turned her off. "We could be friends and then maybe . . ." she shrugged. She hated lying to the guy. There would never be a future for them but she needed to get out of this situation.

He looked at her like she was the crazy one. *Go figure!* Then he shook his head. "Dragons do not date. I would not be permitted to spend time with you. Thunder and the others wouldn't understand," he snorted. "They couldn't possibly understand. No! How can I convince you that I am the male for you? I am one of best warriors in my kingdom. I am strong." He flexed his biceps, which were tree trunk-like. Then he bounced his pecs. "I'm a good listener and an even better lover. Please give me a chance."

What the hell did she say to that? She had a feeling that 'No, you idiot!' would not go down well.

When she didn't answer he moved closer to her. Tammy flinched back. *Please be a nice guy. An off the rails yet nice person. Please!*

"I'm not going to hurt you. Tell me something about yourself."

"It's not going to make any difference."

"Humor me," Cloud said.

Tammy had to fight not to roll her eyes. "Fine," she huffed. "I'm a server in a diner."

Cloud nodded. "You take people their food and drinks."

She nodded.

"That is a very busy job, running up and down with people's food. You're on your feet for hours on end. I have often felt sorry for the females at the Rusty Shack."

She frowned. "Oh yeah! Roxy mentioned that you guys go into town every couple of months, only, the Rusty Shack has been closed for a couple of years."

"Oh really? I wasn't aware."

"Don't you go on those . . . sex runs?"

Cloud sort of smiled. "Stag runs, not sex runs."

"Same thing, you head out there for sex, don't you?"

Cloud nodded, his whole expression became pinched,

his eyes clouded in thought. "I haven't been on a Stag Run in a while."

"Why not?"

He clenched his jaw and his eyes seemed to glint. He looked upset, about to cry. Then he gave a shake of the head and cleared his throat. "It doesn't matter," he said, his voice gruff. "I just haven't. It's been six years since I last went on one of those things."

Tammy got the distinct impression that something had happened in that time. Something bad. She needed to know what it was if she was going to get out of this situation. "We're sharing here, aren't we? You can tell me."

Cloud held out a hand to indicate that he didn't want to speak about it. "Take off your shoes and socks." He rubbed his hands together.

"I said I'm good. We were talking."

Cloud narrowed his eyes, icy blue bore into her. "We can talk and I can massage you. I'm a good multitasker. Take them off, I insist," his voice deepened.

"No, thanks." She stood her ground.

"Do it," a vicious snarl. It reminded her that she wasn't safe. Not one little bit. He closed his eyes and breathed deeply. "Please, just do it." His voice was even and calm but he looked like he was barely keeping it together.

Shit! What choice did she have?

Her hands shook as she undid a shoelace. "I'll do as you say, just take it easy." Her voice shook a little as well.

CHAPTER 5

Thunder forced himself to fly faster. He'd checked six of the eleven caves in his territory. What if the male had gone to a cave in one of the other three territories? He knew the location of one or two. Maybe Cloud did too. It was forbidden but Cloud didn't seem to have any regard for the rules at the moment. He prayed that wasn't the case.

The male was one of his best warriors. He knew that Cloud was struggling to come to terms with things but this was ridiculous. Never in a million years had he expected this. Not from a male like Cloud. Upstanding, kind, brave, gracious . . . he could go on. Grief did strange things to people though.

Did the male take the female in order to send a message? Was there more to it? Thunder tried hard to figure out what was going on in his mind but all the answers he came up with were not to his liking. Hopefully Cloud could be reasoned with. Thunder bristled at the thought of anything happening to the female. He had better not have harmed her in any way.

As he got closer to the next cave, Thunder had to slow down to keep the noise levels to a minimum. It would be best if he surprised Cloud. The last thing he wanted was to kill him, unless of course he had harmed the human, then all bets were off. If he could help it though, he would move in, incapacitate Cloud and take the human back to his lair. She was his top priority.

It used up more energy to flap slowly. His dragon form was strong, yet cumbersome. His beast was enormous, his wing span a good eighteen feet. He could hear voices coming from inside the cave. His heart leapt in his chest. She was here and she was still alive.

"We're sharing here, aren't we? You can tell me," the female said.

"Take off your shoes and socks," Cloud responded, he could hear that the male was rubbing his hands together.

They sounded calm. Two heartbeats, one slightly elevated. Had Cloud heard him approach? It was possible.

Despite his bulk, he landed without making a sound, his years of practice kicking in. He took a step towards the cave opening, careful not to allow his shadow to fall across the space.

"I said I'm good." The female's voice held a hint of panic, her heart-rate picked up a bit more.

"Take them off, I insist." Cloud sounded irritated. Thunder was sure that the male had no idea he was there.

"No, thanks." The female sounded more confident this time.

"Do it," a snarl. Thunder had to work to keep from

rushing in. "Please, just do it." Softer this time, sounding more like the Cloud he knew.

He could hear the female moving, obviously complying. "I'll do as you say, just take it easy," her voice shook. Her heart-rate was all over the place. The female was scared.

Thunder forced himself to stand down even though everything in him told him to rush in and rescue her.

Once Cloud's attention was on the female and the task at hand, he would enter and stop this madness. He really didn't want to harm the male. Cloud had been through enough.

"How is that?" the male asked.

The human didn't respond.

"Don't be angry. Please lie back and try and enjoy it."

"I don't know you," the human sighed. "You abduct me and then expect me to enjoy a foot massage." She muttered something under her breath that Thunder didn't catch.

"I'm not crazy," Cloud growled. "Stop saying that."

The female whimpered. "You're hurting me."

"Say it," Cloud ground out. "Tell me I'm not crazy."

The human moaned, the sound laced with pain. "Please . . ."

Enough.

Thunder crashed into the cave. Thankfully Cloud sprang backwards and onto his feet, moving away from the human. It was something that Thunder had banked on. All of the participating males within the four kingdoms had received intensive training running up to the human hunts. One of the things they practiced tirelessly was moving away from females prior to battle.

Even when instincts, adrenaline and emotions ran high, they moved away before commencing with any combat activities. They had used dragon shifter females during training.

Cloud reacted exactly as Thunder had hoped. The human shrieked and moved away from the both of them, sensing that her life was in danger. Her eyes were wide and the scent of her fear permeated the space.

Thunder snarled a warning at Cloud. He needed the male to stay the fuck away from her.

Cloud looked at the human, his whole demeanor changed. Now that he was thinking things over again, now that the element of surprise was over, the idiot planned on going after her. Thunder could see it. He growled low, another warning and the last one that Cloud would get.

Cloud's whole stance tensed. *Fuck*. The male wasn't listening to him.

It worried Thunder that the male showed no sign of fear. He also didn't show any sign of changing into his dragon form. Why not? The male would be on the back foot unless he changed. It would be impossible for Cloud to win in his human form. It made no sense. What was going on?

CHAPTER 6

The dragon was huge. Bigger than the others she had seen. His chest glinted bright gold, almost too bright to look at.

His deep growl filled the cave, his lip pulled away revealing a row of sharp, glistening teeth. Tammy had to squeeze her legs together to keep from peeing herself. She'd never been more afraid in her life.

Cloud kept his eyes on her. It was like he didn't care about the dragon. She moved backwards, one step at a time until she finally hit the cave wall. Shards of rock bit into her back but she didn't care. She was surrounded by dark shadows and even though she knew her vision was impaired, she knew that the shifters could see her perfectly. The beast had narrowed eyes, its tail swished from side to side in agitation. It looked beyond pissed. It looked like it wanted a piece of Cloud. One positive in all of this, at least.

Although the guy was clearly deranged, she found herself hoping he didn't get hurt, or worse, killed. For whatever reason, she didn't think he was a bad guy. Not really. Having said that, she wanted out of here and nothing to do with him ever again.

It all happened so quickly. One second, they all stood still, the only thing that could be heard was the sound of her rasping breathing, overly loud in the small space, and the next moment, all hell broke loose.

Cloud came at her, moving quicker than she thought possible and then in the blink of an eye, he was hurtling backwards into the dark recesses of the cave. She heard a loud, sickening thud.

The beast turned to her, its purple gaze bore into hers. She recognized his eyes, which softened as they landed on her.

"It's you," she whispered.

The dragon seemed to melt before her eyes, there were loud cracking noises. Within seconds a man stood before her. Not a man, a shifter. Him. Thunder.

He reached out and cupped her chin. His hand was warm and calloused. "Are you okay?" His eyes were filled with tenderness.

Tammy swallowed hard, she nodded.

"You are safe. I'm going to take you back to my lair." He took another step towards her and she couldn't help but feel relieved. More than just relieved, she felt completely safe.

She nodded again. "What about . . ." she tried to peer over his shoulder but he was too big, "him . . . Cloud?"

Thunder pulled his hand away. "We need to go now. I'm going to change back into my dragon form." He frowned deeply. "Cloud will be fine. I will send a team after him. He can't hurt you anymore."

Tammy nodded. The guy had abducted her and could've really hurt her. She shivered at the thought. "Are they going to harm him?" She didn't like the thought.

"Cloud needs to be apprehended. He is a threat to you, to the other humans as well. That cannot be tolerated." There was an edge to his voice.

"Please don't kill him. I don't think he's really bad. Off his rocker, yes but bad . . . I don't think so." From what she had seen of these shifters, they operated on instinct. They got into bloody fights so she wouldn't put it past them to kill one another as well.

The frown deepened even further and his purple eyes turned dark and turbulent. "Why do you . . . ?" His whole body jerked and his eyes widened, then he jerked a second time.

Thunder spun around, he gave her a light shove, pushing her back against the wall of the cave and away from him. Lightning cracked across the roof of the cave. It was beautiful, curving along the roof. For a second she was mesmerized by its sheer beauty. There was a crackling sound and all the hairs on her body felt like they were standing on end. It felt like raw energy rushed through her. The sensation wasn't entirely bad. In fact, it felt good. Raw energy rushed through her, around her. Yet, instinctively, she knew that there was danger in those streaks of lightning. One of the bright curves lanced out in a direct line across the cave.

There was a loud yelping noise that cut off the instant the lightning hit. It sounded like a wounded animal. Had to be Cloud. Thunder slumped forward onto his stomach. She could make out a dark shape to the rear of the cave. Smoke wafted from his chest. She could smell burnt flesh, it made her gag. There was no movement. Even his chest remained still. He looked dead. Thunder had somehow caused the lightning. He had directed it to Cloud.

Thunder moaned and she looked down at his naked body, noticing for the first time that he had two small wounds in his back. They leaked blood. The wounds didn't look that bad but they seemed to be affecting the big shifter.

"Oh no," she whispered, kneeling beside him and touching a finger to one of the wounds. It really didn't look too bad. Maybe it wasn't the wounds that were causing his current state. Maybe he was just tired from expending all of that energy. She was certain that making lightning had to be damned tiring. She pulled her hand back, blood on the tips of her fingers. It was almost hot to the touch. Thunder flinched and growled. He struggled to get up but kept falling back down in a crumpled heap.

"Let me help you." She tried to wrap her arms around his shoulders to help him up but Thunder roared. It was deafening. So loud she heard a whistling noise in her ears. She let go and moved back. Moments later he began to change. Cracking, stretching and popping. Then he seemed to melt back down before stretching and popping again. This happened several times. Thunder was struggling to change himself back into his dragon form.

He growled, his half-transformed face grimaced. It took what felt like an age before he finally got it right.

Once he was in full dragon form, his strength seemed to come back to him and he rose onto all four legs. Thunder walked to the opening of the cave and turned back to stare at her before taking another few steps. He turned back and gave a low growl. The sound was commanding. He wanted her to follow him. She glanced at an unmoving Cloud and then back at Thunder. There was no way she was staying here. Tammy followed the beast. She didn't exactly feel like another dragon ride, but what other choice did she have?

Once they were out in the full sun, she noticed that the wounds were bleeding more heavily. The blood streaked down his back. Cloud had hurt Thunder. The dragon shifter began to beat his wings. Her hair whipped about her face with each wing fall. He slowly lowered and gripped her round the waist. "Are you okay to fly?" If it weren't for the dire situation she might have laughed at the stupid question. It wasn't like he could answer her. His grip on her tightened a fraction and he rose into the air

Ten minutes later . . .

Tammy cried out as his grip on her loosened. Thunder flapped his wings, then fell a few feet before flapping madly again. He was struggling to stay airborne. Struggling to maintain his grip on her.

Like she had done earlier with Cloud, she grabbed ahold of his scaly talons. Hopefully she would maintain a grip if Thunder dropped her. His clasp on her loosened even more and she cried out in frustration and in fear.

They weren't nearly as high as she had been on previous flights, but she would die if he let her go, so high enough. *Don't look down, Tammy. Do not look down.* Instead, she concentrated on holding on even tighter. Thunder was breathing heavily. There were loud snorting sounds with every breath. Like he was struggling to take in enough air.

What was wrong with him? Had Cloud stabbed him with something? It was all a blur. She couldn't recall the other shifter getting close enough but maybe she was wrong. Thunder had shielded her view so it was possible. That had to be it. The two bleeding wounds were affecting him really badly. She had seen blood drip from his back a couple of times. Some of it had even splashed onto her. It seemed strange that such small wounds would bleed so much. Maybe they were deeper than they looked.

He lurched forward before falling another few feet. Tamara jerked in his grasp, making his scaly grip loosen a bit more. She shrieked. The great beast groaned and beat his wings a bit harder.

"Take us down!" Tammy shrieked, praying he would hear her. "You need a rest," she added when he didn't react.

His legs began to shake. *Shit!* His entire body quivered with what she could only imagine was fatigue.

Thunder made a howling noise. He sounded like he was

in pain.

"You need to rest!" she shrieked a second time. He lurched and she gripped harder as he fell. She screamed as he rolled head first in a clumsy somersault while plummeting to the ground. Within a few seconds, he gave an almighty flap with his giant wings. Unfortunately, it caused him to move upwards while she was still on a downwards trajectory. Try as she might, Tammy could not hold on and his grip finally gave out as well.

She felt herself pick up substantial speed. *Free-falling!* God help her but she was free-falling. The ground rushed up to meet her. It was amazing how quickly tiny objects became small objects and then not so small objects. She tried to scream but was frozen with fear. Her heart felt like it was somewhere in her throat. She had the most irrational thought—the earth was beautiful from up here. Truly, utterly beautiful. There was so much to see and do. So much more living to do. If only she wasn't about to die. She would grab hold of her second chance with both freak'n hands. Both of them. She'd even use her nails, dammit.

Talons gripped her around the waist. Thunder had her. No, he didn't. They were falling together now, although, not quite as fast as before. Those objects were getting rather big. The ground too damned close for comfort. Then they began to fall slower and slower.

She sucked in a deep breath. Her whole body trembled. So did his. At least they were moving in a lateral direction instead of a downwards one. Tamara released the pent-up breath she didn't even realize she was holding.

He groaned as they picked up speed. His talons gripped her a little too tightly and she struggled a bit to breathe. Tammy wasn't complaining, at least he had her this time.

They flew like this for close to an hour. It felt like forever. His grip never loosened. Thunder growled loudly and they began to rise. She could feel his body stiffen. The tremors that had racked him seemed to ease. Maybe he was getting better. Dragons – all non-humans for that matter – had super-human healing abilities. Most people knew it. Besides, she'd done some research when she knew she would be spending some time with the vampires. Roxy had also briefed them on dragon basics and Tamara distinctly remembered the queen mentioning that little detail.

They rose slowly, a sheer cliff directly in front of them. Maybe they needed to scale this particular mountain. Or maybe this was where they were headed. Was this his lair?

They reached a ledge, it was a couple of meters wide. Thunder flew forwards. *Please don't drop me.* The ledge was at an angle and covered in loose rock. She might just tumble to her death if he dropped her here. That would be so unfair considering all she'd just been through. He kept on moving forward towards what looked like a solid wall. As they drew closer, she realized that it wasn't solid at all but two overlapping walls with a space between them. An entrance. Thunder dropped her as they reached it. She felt herself sliding. Tamara screamed, trying to grab onto something, anything, but only found loose rocks. She dug her feet in, which helped some.

Thunder grabbed her. Not a talon but a hand. He gripped her around the wrist and pulled her back. Next, she was being hoisted into the air. He picked her up and despite the loose rock and sloping angle, he walked to the left and then through the overlapping wall. The space would have been too small to accommodate his large dragon frame, definitely while carrying her.

"Are you okay?" the asked, her voice sounding croaky and small. It echoed against the walls of the vast rock structure.

Thunder ignored her. She noticed that a sheen of sweat covered his face. His cheeks were flushed, his eyes fixed ahead of them. He kept walking, there was a loud crunch of gravel and rock beneath his feet. The light slowly dimmed as they walked into a gaping hole which was just as vast as everything else. Pitch black darkness swallowed them as they turned a corner. Tamara wasn't sure she'd be able to see a hand in front of her face.

"Where are we?"

His only answer was heavy breathing. She noticed that his tremors were back. She could hear his teeth were chattering.

"Hey, are you okay?" She gave his arm a squeeze to try and draw his attention.

Nothing but crunching footfalls.

"You can put me down you know. I can walk." At least she hoped she could. Her legs might be jello. "I can't see, but I can hold your hand or something."

He grunted, adjusting his hold on her. For a second she thought he might be doing as she had asked but he kept on walking. Then he seemed to kneel, but not all the way down to the ground. He put her down onto a soft surface. If she didn't know better, she might say it was a bed. Why the hell would there be a bed in the middle of a cave?

She was reminded of the previous cave she had been in, that had had a bed in it as well, so maybe it wasn't so farfetched after all. He crouched over her.

She couldn't see, but she could feel his heat above her, could hear his labored breathing. He pulled her backwards, so that she was more in the center of the bed.

Then he pulled away slightly. By the way the bed dipped on either side of her, she would say that he was on his knees which were splayed on either side of her. He seemed to be leaving. Thunder made a strange noise. Something between a strangled moan and a growl. Everything went still for a split second. She didn't have time to deduce what it all meant before his weight came crashing down on her.

CHAPTER 7

The first thing she did was panic, trying to push him off of her. He was completely unconscious and therefore a dead weight. A crushing weight. She couldn't move, couldn't breathe. Had to get free. Had to do it now.

After ten seconds of useless panic, she forced herself to calm down. To take small, sharp breaths. It was damned uncomfortable but she wasn't going to die.

Thunder had passed out. That much was for sure. She could feel the slow rise and fall of his chest. He was still alive, just out cold. It took a minute or two to free her left hand. If she pushed that hand against him and wiggled, she would eventually get out from under him. She had to take frequent breaks though. Her breathing eased up when she made it to the halfway mark, making it easier to keep going. It took about ten or fifteen minutes to finally free herself.

Once out, she just sat there, breathing heavily. She shivered. It was freezing. She hadn't felt it while under his warmth or while exerting herself, but she could sure as hell feel it now. Her teeth began to chatter and she rubbed her hands together, remembering her lost gloves. She only hoped that Claire was having better luck than she was.

Besides being cold, her other problem was that she couldn't see a thing. For all she knew, she could end up walking off a ledge or into a hole or something. If she listened carefully she could make out a dripping noise deeper in the cave. It would be dangerous for her to wander blindly through a hole in the side of a mountain, but what choice did she have? She needed to do something. Thunder was in trouble and she might just freeze to death if she just sat there.

Cloud had walked into the back of the cave and brought back supplies. They had probably come from a backpack he had brought with him but she had to look around. *Look around* . . . If only that were possible. There might be something in this place though that would help them. If only she could bloody see.

Tammy tried one last time to wake Thunder, who was still slumped in the same position, his breathing deep and unchanged. It was no use. Moving slowly and carefully, she let her legs slide off the bed until they hit the floor with that same familiar crunch. She felt along the edge of the bed, feeling for the headrest, and then proceeded in that direction. She shuffled rather than walked, with her hands outstretched in front of her. After a few seconds of shuffling, her hands hit a cold damp wall. She moved along the wall, trying not to trip over rocks as she did. She was concentrating so hard that when the wall suddenly disappeared, she tumbled forward, landing on a pile of hard objects. Small, long and brittle.

A fireplace. She was in the middle of a fireplace. Someone had prepared kindling and wood, maybe they'd left something to light the fire as well. A girl could only hope.

She worked her way back out the space along the next wall. It didn't take long to encounter another pile of wood. Thick pieces. Loads of them. This was one gigantic pile of wood. Then she had a terrifying thought. Did snakes live in dark caves? She sure as hell hoped not because this would be the perfect hiding place.

It took a good couple of minutes to navigate her way around the base of the large pile and she came up empty-handed. Tamara went down on all fours and slowly crawled back towards the fireplace. She was beginning to get a feel for her surroundings, a mental picture. She found the fireplace easily and took up a kneeling position, inching her way up the stacked wood, slowly feeling her way to the top of the pile. Then she worked her way across until her knuckles nudged something cold and the item fell to the floor with a clatter.

A lighter? Maybe. Hopefully. It had to be!

Her heart-rate sped up as she got back down on all fours patting the floor to try to find it. It didn't take long as her hands closed around something metal. It was icy cold. Yes, a lighter! Tamara couldn't help but grin like a fool. After a couple of failed attempts, a flame illuminated within the darkness.

Yes!

She quickly made her way back to the fireplace and put the lighter to the kindling, which burst into flames. It took her a couple of minutes to get a blaze going. She put her hands to the roaring fire, closing her eyes and allowing the warmth to seep into her body.

Once she was sure the fire wouldn't go out, Tamara tucked the lighter into her jeans pocket and looked around the cave.

There was what appeared to be a chest on the other side near the furthest wall. Tamara prayed that there were items of use inside of it.

The chest creaked open and she breathed a sigh of relief. It was certainly no gourmet meal but the chest was half filled with what looked like vacuum sealed digestive biscuits and several packs of beef jerky. There was a large serrated knife, a box of fireproof matches, a flat, cast-iron skillet for grilling meat, an empty water bottle and a medium-sized pack of sorts. It had to be a first aid kit, which would come in handy for those wounds on Thunder's back.

She grabbed the kit and went to the sleeping shifter. Tamara gave him a small shake. "Thunder! Wake up!" She gave him another shake, harder this time. There was no response. She put a hand to his brow, he felt hot to the touch. Was this normal for dragon shifters? Did they run at a higher temperature? It was impossible to tell. He looked completely normal. It worried her that he wouldn't wake up though. It could be that this was how shifters healed.

The small wounds on his back still oozed blood. Surely they should have healed by now? Then again, it would take a human at least a week – if not two – to heal from wounds such as these so maybe this was normal. It was impossible for her to tell.

There was a folded woolen blanket at the foot of the bed. It took some work but she finally managed to ease it out from under Thunder's legs. She pulled it up over his thighs and kept going until his ass was covered. Much better. Tamara opened the first aid kit.

What the hell?

It wasn't a first aid kit but a toiletry bag. The bag contained things like toothbrushes, toothpaste and deodorant. There was even shower gel, shampoo and dental floss. Why the hell would they fill a bag with toiletry items and not have a first aid kit? It didn't make sense.

She needed to find something to clean the wounds and something to bandage them. There was nothing else she could do with such limited supplies. Hopefully he could sleep it off. Tamara looked around her surroundings, at least as far as the light from the fire would allow. She took stock of the situation. They had enough supplies to keep really clean, to stay warm and enough food to last at least a week, probably more. What they didn't have was water. Anyone knew that a person couldn't live more than a few days without that very basic requirement. Then she recalled hearing the dripping sound. If she listened, it was still there, further back in the cave.

She slid from the bed and walked to the edge of the

light, peering into the darkness. From there the sound of dripping was much louder. She reached into her pocket and pulled out the lighter, which was one of those old-fashioned, refillable gas types. She flipped open the lid and flicked a finger to ignite the flame. Walking slowly and carefully, she made her way further into the cave. It didn't take long before she arrived at a beautiful, crystal-clear pool of water. She dropped to her haunches and cupped a handful of the icy cold liquid. The only question was, was it safe to drink?

Unfortunately, there were also no cooking utensils, other than the flat skillet, within the chest she had found. The best thing to do would be to boil the water but that wasn't an option. *Shit!* Tamara cupped her hand, filling it with water and brought it up to her face, giving the liquid a sniff. She didn't detect any odd odors. Next, she touched her lips to the cool water, taking a tentative lick. Cool, refreshing, the water was good and she suddenly realized how thirsty she was. It would be stupid to allow herself to gulp down a whole lot of the stuff, so she took a mouthful, allowing the rest to trickle back into the pool. She would have to wait a couple of hours, and if there were no adverse effects, she would know for sure that it was okay to drink.

Using the light to guide her, she walked back to the chest, fetching the water bottle and knife, which she tucked into her jeans. After filling the bottle she went back to Thunder. Tamara pulled the knife free and unsheathed it. She pulled out the edge of the sheet and carefully cut a strip about the length of a bandage. She did this a couple of times, cutting several pieces from the cotton fabric. The knife was damn sharp, she'd need to be careful when using it. She sheathed the blade and stuck it back in the top of her jeans.

Wetting one of the pieces of cotton, she used it to clean Thunder's wounds. It looked like they had finally stopped bleeding. He moaned softly as she ran the cotton directly over one of the wounds. It was the first reaction he'd given since passing out. Hopefully it was a good sign. There was no way to wrap the bandages around his chest so she ended up folding them into squares and placing them on top of the cuts. At least this would offer some protection. She wished, not for the first time, that she had some sort of disinfectant, but this was the best she could do.

Once done, she noticed that the woolen blanket had slipped down while she worked. The edge lay half-way across his ass. She swallowed thickly, allowing her eyes to trace the wide expanse of his back and shoulders.

She'd never seen a guy that was this well-built or this good-looking. Even his eyelashes were long, thick and dark. Tamara felt her cheeks heat. The fire was doing its job. She was feeling seriously hot, and all over. She quickly pulled the blanket up, carefully allowing the fabric to settle over his back. She yawned, suddenly feeling tired.

She looked about the space. There was no other furniture aside from the bed and the chest. The bed looked to be an extra-length king-size, which seemed pretty small considering a huge, dragon shifter guy was sprawled out, smack bang in the middle of it.

Tamara shrugged, what the hell, she'd kissed him already. Not that she wanted to be reminded of it. The guy was a first-class kisser. Of course he was. All she had to do was look at him to know he got plenty of action. A hunk like him would have women throwing themselves at him. He had tons of practice. That much was clear. She need not feel bad about reacting to the kiss. It was normal and didn't mean anything.

The kiss didn't matter right now, she reminded herself. It was exhaustion making her mind wander to unimportant things. She needed sleep. The floor was hard and damp and really not an option. Tamara lay down next to the shifter, on the tiny bit of bed left beside him. Since there wasn't much space to begin with, even though she faced away from him, her back still ended up touching his side. His warmth seeped into her. His breathing deep and rhythmic. The fire crackled every so often. Within minutes she was fast asleep.

Minutes, hours, days, she'd no idea of the time that passed when she finally opened her eyes and arched her back, stopping herself mid-stretch, she realized that her belly was flush against him. *Thunder.* She had wrapped one of her legs around his body, somewhere in the vicinity of that magnificent ass.

"Shit!" she muttered, under her breath, as she peeled herself away from him. A girl couldn't help it if she was a snuggler now could she? It was something that Chris had hated. He said it made him feel claustrophobic and sweaty. *Bastard.* Never trust a man who can't express his emotions or enjoy a good cuddle. Why was she even thinking about him? Maybe because he was the reason she was in this predicament to begin with. *Stop!* Moaning, even internally, wasn't going to solve the situation.

She looked around. The cave was dark, the fire reduced to glowing embers. She'd definitely got a couple of hours of sleep in then. Tamara rekindled the dying fire.

Thunder moaned, drawing her attention back to the bed. He was moving one of his arms, it looked like he was trying to get up.

Tammy rushed over to him. "Thunder."

His eyes were open. They were wide and had a glassy look about them that she didn't like. There was sweat on his brow and his cheeks were flushed. He grit his teeth, moaning as he tried to push himself up.

"No, don't!" she said, not wanting him to hurt himself anymore. "Stay still."

He moaned again, this time the sound came out like more of a word.

"What is it?" She leaned in a bit closer, trying hard to understand him.

He made the same noise only this time it came out sounding more like 'help' and then 'out.' She couldn't be sure though, he was half out of it.

Then again, maybe he was trying to tell her something. She couldn't dismiss it. Maybe it was important. "Out where? You can't go anywhere." She was beginning to sound panicked. Beginning to feel panicked.

"No," he groaned the word, his breathing labored.

"No?" She sounded bewildered. "I don't understand." Tammy wasn't sure what he was trying to tell her.

He looked agitated and tried to get up again. "Help . . ." He was definitely saying the word. Did he think that she still needed help? Did he feel that they were both still in danger, maybe? Or, was he asking her to help him? The latter seemed the most likely but she couldn't be sure.

"Help how? There is no first aid kit. We're out in the middle of nowhere," her voice was shrill.

"Out," he growled.

"Out?" she repeated, feeling frustration welling. Tamara frowned, rubbing her chin, her mind racing a mile a minute. She still had no idea what he needed or wanted. Maybe he was delirious.

She soothed the damp hair from his forehead. Thunder felt like he was burning up. He was definitely hotter than before. "Shhhhhh. Lie still." She rubbed the top of his shoulder that was closest to her. "I'm going to fetch you something to drink. You need to stay hydrated."

"Out!" he half yelled, half growled. "Get out. "

"I'm not going anywhere. I'm going to help you," her voice was shrill. "We'll get through this." He was clearly not thinking straight. Tamara retrieved the water bottle and headed back to the bed but by the time she got there, which was less than a few seconds, he was already asleep.

She spent the next couple of minutes trying to rouse him, but to no avail. His face looked really flushed and he was sweating profusely, so, she did the next best thing she could think of and grabbed one of the cotton pieces of material. Tammy poured water over the fabric and wiped his brow. Thunder was running a fever. There was no doubt of that. Worry churned in her gut. He seemed to be getting worse. Then again, maybe this was part of the healing process.

Tamara carefully lifted the blanket, pulling it down and looking under the makeshift bandages. She gasped when she saw his wounds. They were both red and raised. They looked like they were becoming infected. *What now?* They were in the middle of nowhere with no supplies, no means to contact the outside world. Thunder was delirious. *Think, Tammy, think!*

Wait a minute. There was something in the toiletry bag that might help. She rushed back to the chest. Her hand shook as she opened the zipper. Mouthwash, there was a bottle of the stuff inside. Good thing these shifters were meticulous about hygiene. She turned the bottle around and true as nuts, most of the contents of the peppermint-flavored liquid was alcohol. She could use it to disinfect his wounds. It was a long shot and one that most probably wouldn't work, but there were no other options available. They were in the cave in the top of a mountain just off of a sheer cliff.

Her hand shook as she grabbed the bottle. Tammy didn't want anything to happen to Thunder. Couldn't bear the thought of him dying. Her eyes stung. *No!* She needed to stay positive and to stay calm. He was not going to die.

Tammy swallowed the lump in her throat and chewed on her lower lip. This had to work. *Please, let this work.*

Tamara spent the next while painstakingly cleaning his wounds. He moaned and thrashed every time she tried to pull the wounds open in order to pour the mouthwash into them. She used one of the cotton swabs to catch the liquid. What Thunder really needed was an IV bag full of antibiotics, a trauma specialist and a hospital. He needed professional care. This was not going to cut it.

"Please work. Please work," she muttered a couple of times. "Don't you dare die on me. You're supposed to be a strong dragon shifter. A high and mighty king." Her voice cracked a little when she thought about how this could end. "Prove it. Get better dammit."

Once she'd done all she could, she redressed his wounds with clean, newly cut bandages and forced herself to eat and to drink, taking just a little water. Hopefully it wasn't contaminated in any way. She was going to find out soon enough.

This time she would be ready when he woke up, she had the water bottle and he was going to drink whether he liked it or not. Tamara needed to keep his temperature down so, for the next couple of hours, she kept reapplying wet cotton wipes to his forehead and replenishing the water.

She must have fallen asleep, because she awoke a bit later, still in her half sitting position slumped against the headboard. Her hand rested against his cheek and it fell from his face as he moaned and thrashed, trying in vain to get up.

His moans grew more insistent and again began to sound like words. "Help!" He repeated this several times while clawing at his back. His eyes were wide and glassy. His face was no longer flushed. It had a pale, grey tinge that she didn't like. The sweat poured off of him. One of the makeshift cotton bandages fell off and again, she couldn't help the gasp that was pulled from her. The wound was raised and red, so angry looking. So much worse than before. Only a few hours had passed. A few measly hours. Why was he getting so sick? She didn't understand it. He was supposed to have super-human strength, wasn't he? *Shit!*

Panic coursed through her. "I don't know what to do. What's wrong with you?"

"Out!" he yelled.

"I don't understand!" she shrieked back at him. "Say something else. Tell me how to help you."

By some miracle, Thunder managed to push himself up. His eyes locked with hers, they had a wild look like he wasn't quite there anymore. "Dying," he groaned.

No, she'd heard him wrong. Had to have misunderstood, surely? Yet, deep down inside she knew it was true. He was dying and if she didn't do something soon, it would be too late. Thunder would be gone.

"You need water." She felt like an absolute idiot for saying it. Water was not going to help him. The problem was that she didn't know what would. Panic welled. She had to stop herself from shaking him, from begging him for answers.

He grimaced, looking angry. "No. Help! Get out!" His eyes rolled back in his skull and he slammed back down onto the mattress, the last of his reserves leaving him. "Get . . . it . . . out," he whispered, his left hand clawing at his lower back one last time before he passed out.

Tamara was breathing heavily. She could feel that her eyes were wide. Her heart raced and adrenaline coursed through her. Everything in her told her to act, to do something to save him and to do it now. But what?

Then it dawned on her. She was an idiot. There had to be something in the wounds. That's what the whole 'get out' thing had been about.

She was right earlier, Cloud had never approached them, which meant that the two bleeding holes had to have been made by something. Bullets or . . . No! She hadn't heard an explosion or gunshot. If she dug around in his already infected wounds, she might just make things worse. She might end up finishing him off if she was wrong.

What if she was right though? What if some foreign objects were lodged in his back causing this infection? He should've healed by now or at the very least been well on his way to recovery. She had to do it. It wasn't like she had anything to lose. Thunder kept clawing at his back, as if trying to reach something. His last three words were '*get it out.*' *It*. She had to try. He would die if she did nothing. She pulled the knife from her jeans and unsheathed it. It suddenly looked really big, felt so heavy in her hands, which now felt incredibly clumsy. Could she do this? Did she have a choice?

CHAPTER 8

No. There was no other choice but to act and her gut told her that she was onto something. Right, first things first. Light. She put the knife away, rekindled the fire and got it burning as fiercely as possible. Tamara unsheathed the knife again and poured some of the mouthwash over the blade. Then she took a deep breath. "Here goes nothing," she breathed as she positioned the knife over the first wound. Her hands shook, so she forced herself to loosen her hold on the handle ever so slightly. It helped, but not by much.

"You can do this," she muttered to herself. "You can." She'd given this some thought. Granted, not a whole lot. Time wasn't on her side. She wished she could Google how to perform a procedure like this. Did she stick the knife in and dig around? Or, did she make the wound wider and open it up so that she could take a look inside? On the one hand she might push the object further into him if she wasn't careful and on the other, she might make things worse by making his wound bigger.

She stuck the tip of the knife into the wound and then removed it. Then she stuck it back in again. She sighed. This didn't feel right. The knife felt huge. Her grip clumsy. If there was something in there she was sure to push it in further. If only she had a scalpel and a long set of tweezers. At the very least, a set of kitchen knives. A hunting knife was not the best tool for the job. It was all she had though, so best she get busy.

She chewed down on her lower lip, feeling sweat drip between her breasts. Damn! That left option two which meant cutting him open. Just the thought left her feeling queasy and light-headed. She had to do it. If she didn't, he was going to die. Bottom line.

She swallowed hard, trying to get her nerves under control. "Here goes nothing." And everything . . .

Tammy put the knife back into the wound and pushed sideways. His flesh parted easily against the sharp blade. Fresh blood welled and began to run from the wound. She grabbed some of the makeshift bandages and used them to mop up the flow. Now for the fun part. With the help of the knife, she pried open the wound.

Thunder groaned. An agonized noise.

"Sorry!" Tammy whispered, trying to see into the wound. Her stomach did a flip flop. There! Something glinted. Something shiny. Something made of metal. What the hell was that thing? Not for the first time, she wished she had a set of tweezers. Anything, even eyebrow pluckers might work. Suck it up. All she had was this huge ass knife, but she would make it work.

Tammy would need to stick her finger into the wound. There was no other option. She was breathing hard. Using her sleeve, she wiped at her brow and sucked in another deep breath. "Come on! Don't be a chicken," she chided herself. "You can do this dammit!"

She pushed her index finger into the wound and pushed down, moving slowly and carefully. Thunder moaned again. Softer this time.

"Aaah!" she cried out as pain lanced through her. She yanked out her finger, which was bleeding. Something had sliced it open. Just a small nick.

"Knife," Thunder growled, his words barely recognizable. "Cut," he groaned. "Out."

"Okay. Okay." She wiped her finger on the bed linen which was beyond salvaging anyway, and picked up the knife. "This is going to hurt."

She bit down on her lip and dug her way into the wound using the blade. Aside from a couple of short, sharp breaths, Thunder didn't make a sound. Tammy sliced the wound open some more, digging around until the tip of the blade touched against the object.

"There!" she said, feeling excited. It wasn't easy but she somehow managed to pry the thing out with the tip of the knife. One thing was for sure, she was no surgeon.

"A ninja star thingy," she muttered. It wasn't very big, or very deep. She couldn't understand how it had caused him to deteriorate so quickly.

Thunder gave a sigh. "Other one," he said, his words ground out through clenched teeth, but he sounded stronger this time.

"I'm on it." She leaned over his back. "I'm so sorry. This is going to hurt."

Thunder grunted in response. Tamara went through the same motions of slicing the wound open to give her more room to work and then slowly pried the star out. They were small and razor sharp.

Thunder sighed as the second one came out. Tammy was careful how she handled the ninja stars. "Asshole, got you in the back." Talk about a cowardly move.

She shook her head. The second wound was still bleeding. The first had stopped already. It was probably her imagination but the wound looked less inflamed than it had been. Nah! Had to be her imagination. It was too soon.

She reached for the mouthwash and poured some liberally over the wounds.

Thunder moaned and arched his back.

"Really? You don't make so much as a sound while I'm digging around in your back with a knife but you can't take a bit of disinfectant?" She had to smile. His coloring looked more normal and he had stopped perspiring. He looked so much better already. Relief washed over her.

As expected, Thunder didn't answer. He was fast asleep. His broad shoulders rising and falling with each deep breath. "I sure hope you don't scar." She let her hands trail along the hard ridges of his muscled back. "That would be a shame."

Tamara stopped mid . . . feel. She was copping a feel on

an unconscious guy! Since when had she sunk so low? To take advantage of someone who was out cold. One who wasn't even her type, even if he was seriously yummy.

She grabbed the one remaining clean cotton wipe and used it to finish cleaning the dried blood. Then she got to work making more bandages, this time on the other side of the bed, before redressing his wounds.

Something warm wriggled beside him . . . and on top of him. It clutched him around the neck. Not an it. A she. The human. The female had both a leg and an arm wrapped around him. Her plump breasts were squashed up against his side.

The last thing he wanted to do was startle her but he had to see her . . . had to . . . he turned his head so that he was facing her. Her face was right there, inches away.

Even in the throes of sleep she was a beauty. Her mouth was slightly parted. She made soft snoring sounds. Her hair hung loose around her shoulders. There was a light smattering of freckles across her nose and cheek bones. Not easy to spot in passing but up this close, impossible to ignore. *Mmmmm, melted chocolate.* His stomach growled.

Her eyes moved rapidly under her lids, her lashes fanned her cheeks. Her nose was slightly upturned and her mouth generous and sweet. Oh so damned sweet. He couldn't wait for another taste.

She latched her leg tighter around him and pulled herself even closer, her hand curling almost possessively around the back of his neck.

If it weren't for the burning on his back and the feeling of weakness, almost to the point of paralysis, he would've turned his whole body to face her, pulled her against him.

In his current state, he couldn't lift a finger, let alone any other parts of his anatomy.

He felt her breathing pick up. Her body tightened. The human, Tamara, slowly opened her eyes. Fucking amazing eyes. Dark and gorgeous. Eyes a male might lose himself in if he wasn't careful. In this instance, Thunder wanted to throw caution to the wind.

She blinked a couple of time. Those beautiful eyes widened, her mouth rounding up into a startled 'O.' She sucked in a breath as she pulled away from him, moving faster than he thought possible for a human. "Shit! Damn! Sorry." She swallowed hard. "I'm a cuddler. I can't help it. I was asleep so technically I didn't know what I was doing. I had no idea." She held up her hand. This female was so damned cute. "It had nothing to do with you . . . nothing at all. Nothing to do with your hotness or anything. I . . ." She seemed to catch herself. "Oh god! Forget I said that." She moved back to his side and put her hand on his brow. A strange move. Was this some sort of mating ritual he didn't know about? He sure as hell hoped not since there was nothing he could do about it, and that would be a crying shame.

"Your fever has broken." She leaned forward, seeming to examine his face. Next she looked deeply into his eyes. This was definitely a way in which humans flirted with males. Blast, pity he was unable to reciprocate.

"I'm sorry, human," his voice was croaky from disuse. "As much as I would love to rut you, I'm too weak right now. Give me a couple of hours and I'm all yours."

Her brows drew together right before her eyes narrowed. "I can't believe you! You almost died, are still half freakin' dead and yet you're thinking of sex?" She shook her head. "Typical male," she muttered to herself. Something he noticed she did often.

"My apologies." He had to smile at how flustered she was. "I thought you were initiating sex."

"What?" She turned her attention to his back.

"Touching my face, looking deeply into my eyes. You were flirting with me . . . don't deny it."

She cocked her head and gave him a look that could kill, or worse. "I was checking to see if you were still running a fever."

"Running a fever?" He frowned, not sure what she meant. "I can't run right now, I'm kind of out of it. Even walking would be damn near impossible."

She smiled, but then quickly packed that beauty away. A shame, since the smile lit up her whole face. One small dimple appeared on her right cheek, just above her mouth. She shook her head. "Running a fever means that your body temperature gets higher than normal." When he didn't respond, she carried on. "You get hot and sweaty. Your eyes become glassy and—"

"Sounds like sex to me."

"Stop with the sex already. You nearly died, for Christ's

sake. You need to get your head out of the gutter. I might start to think that you're perverted or something."

"I'm sorry!" He couldn't help it. It was his body's way of telling him that sex would help him. He was about to get horny as hell. Sex helped non-humans heal. The good news was that he was used to going without. The bad news was that he'd never been wounded so badly before, or been in such close proximity to such a ravishing creature before either.

He would deal.

No problem.

"I'm not perverted."

"Could've fooled me."

"I still don't know what a fever is or why you were looking at me like that if not to initiate sex."

"I was checking to see if you were still sick." A look of concern graced her features.

"I'm fine." He licked his lips. "At least, I will be soon enough. I'm going to need some time to get stronger," his voice was still hoarse.

She nodded. "Good! You had me worried. Let me know what you need, I would be more than happy to help out."

Thunder nodded. "Water would be good."

"Oh shit!" She jumped up. "You must be dying of thirst. I'm sorry."

"Tamara . . ."

She turned back towards him. "Yeah?"

"Thank you." He kept his eyes on hers, which softened.

"You saved my life. That took guts, serious courage. I'm indebted to you."

She moved back to the bed and sank down onto the mattress. "No problem," she shrugged. "It didn't really take guts. It was something that had to be done, so I did it."

"Don't downplay it, it took guts."

She nodded once. "I still don't understand how such small things could cause such havoc. They weren't even that deep."

"Silver," he croaked. "Non-humans' Achilles heel. It's why we choose to stay far away from humans."

"It's that toxic to you guys?" she said almost to herself, looking shocked.

"Yup. It's pretty much the only thing that will kill a non-human. That and decapitation. Oh and . . ." He felt a warm glow inside his chest. "A lightning bolt to the heart is also pretty lethal." Thoughts of Cloud entered his mind but the human clasped a hand over her mouth and made a sound of disgust. He smiled. "TMI?"

She nodded, looking pale. *So damned cute.* She had used a knife to dig around in his back, yet hearing him talk of death made her queasy. Humans were strange creatures.

"Point being, I'm pretty much fucked for the next few days. It'll be a while before I can change into my dragon form. Residual silver in my blood will make it impossible. I'm going to be as weak as a day-old lamb."

She nodded. "You'll be okay though, right? Given time."

"Yeah." It warmed him that she seemed to care so much.

"It's really interesting, the whole silver thing."

"How so?"

She shrugged and turned her eyes up in thought for a moment. "My best friend works for an Allergist."

He frowned and she smiled. "Don't look so confused. It's a type of doctor who deals with allergies."

"What is an allergy?"

"It's similar to what you guys have against silver. Some humans are allergic to certain things. It can be something small like dust or grass, the reaction need not be serious. But they can also be allergic to something more hectic like bees or seafood; these can kill someone who suffers from such an affliction. There are things a person can do. I don't know enough about it but Nadia has told me that there are desensitizing methods where a sufferer is exposed to small amounts of whatever it is they are allergic to." She licked her lips. "For you guys that would be silver."

"Are you saying we could be cured?" It would be an amazing breakthrough if that were the case.

She shrugged. "I don't know. All I'm saying is that there are treatments available. You guys should do some research. This could be curable or at the very least you could be desensitized so that your reaction isn't quite so severe."

"That would be something." Thunder would definitely mention this at his next meeting with Blaze. "Thank you for letting me know about this and thanks again for saving my life."

Tamara nodded. "Don't mention it." She began to rise from the bed. "You still look really tired. I'm here to take care of you. Let me know if there is anything I can do to help. We have plenty of food and drink, as well as firewood, but . . ." She sat back down, her teeth dug into her lower lip. "What about Cloud? What if he comes after us? It didn't take you long to find us before, so it goes without saying that he could find us just as easily." She pulled the knife from its sheath. "I'll fight him. Protect you." Her eyes blazed with determination.

Thunder choked out a laugh, which turned into a groan. "It hurts. Damn!" Any humor quickly evaporated as his thoughts moved back to Cloud.

Pain and disappointment coursed through him. "The male is most likely dead. If not dead, then gravely injured. If he is still alive, he'll heal more quickly than I will but he won't be able to find us. We are in Water territory, in a cave I accidentally stumbled upon years ago. He won't know of it. Finding this cave will be like finding a needle in a haystack." Thunder grinned. "You won't have to fight anyone."

She pushed the knife back into the sheath. "Thank god!" The female put a hand to her forehead. "Don't tell anyone, but I'm not much of a fighter." She frowned. "Cloud looked dead. His chest was smoking and it wasn't moving. You said this cave is in Water dragon territory? I thought that going onto each other's territories without permission is against the rules or something."

"Yeah, under normal conditions. This is not normal." Here he was, King of Air. Lying on his stomach, unable to move, together with a human, stashed away in a cave just within the border of Water territory. Normal didn't even feature.

CHAPTER 9

The next day . . .

"I'll whip us up a delicious breakfast. How does that sound?" Tamara said as she opened the chest. "What do you feel like, eggs, bacon?" she joked. "Or," she tried to make her voice sound as dull and boring as possible. "How's about a little fried jerky and a biscuit or two?"

Thunder chuckled. It was a rich, deep sound that echoed around the cave. "I think I'll go with the biscuits, dragons don't eat eggs."

"Why not?" She would kill for a couple of eggs right now. Scrambled . . . no, a cheese omelet. Her mouth watered at the thought.

"Fire dragon females lay eggs so," he pulled a face, "egg eating is a bit of a no, no."

Oh shit! "Okay! I get it. You mean they literally lay an egg as in, that's how they have babies?"

He nodded. "Yup."

"What about you guys? The rest of you?" Not that she

was thinking of a relationship with him, with any of them for that matter.

Thunder gave a half smile like maybe he was misinterpreting her question and seeing it as just that. "Both Air and Water dragon females, including humans, give birth to live young. We're not too sure about the Earth dragons. They are a secretive bunch. Keep pretty much to themselves."

"Interesting." She grabbed a couple of the biscuits and a pack of beef jerky and walked back to the bed. "How are you feeling this morning?" She looked down at the food items in her hand, trying hard to will herself to forget about how she woke up this morning, yet again. Why couldn't she just sleep on her side of the bed? Why did she have to end up on top of him, hugging him closely? Although he kept his hands and every other part of his body to himself, he seemed to quite enjoy it, giving her a huge grin and a bright 'good morning' as soon as she opened her eyes. Asshole was lapping it up. It wasn't her fault. It wasn't like she did it on purpose. It was an unconscious thing and not something she had any control over. His grin just grew bigger when she explained it to him.

Thunder was still on his stomach, even though the wounds on his back were much better. They were no longer swollen and raw but they still had to properly close. He pulled the front half of his body up, coming to rest on his elbows, making a grunting noise as he did. "I'm still weaker than a whelp, but otherwise great." He turned to look at her, seeming to stare from under those long lashes of his. It was a strange look he had in his eyes and his gaze dropped to her breasts. *Shit!* He was totally checking her out. She swallowed thickly, the walls of the cave suddenly feeling too close. No! She had to be wrong. She estimated that they had been there for two days, so it was three since she'd had her last shower. Her clothes felt like they were sticking to her. Her hair was starting to get that greasy look, she didn't have to be able to see it to know that it was true. On a positive note, at least her breath was minty fresh.

Hunkboy looked like he had just stepped off the pages of a health magazine. The front cover at that. His hair was mussed but it still looked great. He had thick stubble on his jaw but it only added to his rugged good looks, and would you believe it, he didn't smell bad. Not even a little bit. That musky scent of his was more pronounced but she liked the way he smelled, so if anything it made him smell better. *Not fair!*

She tore open one of the packs and handed it to him. "Here you go. The breakfast of champions. I'm not sure how good eating biscuits from morning till night is, but hey," she shrugged. "At least we won't have to for much longer, right?"

The sides of his mouth quirked up. Oh yeah, definitely ready for the front cover of one of those magazines. "We call them life cakes even though they are more like a biscuit. They're perfectly balanced, whole foods. A person could live forever on just these things." He took a bite, chewed and swallowed. "But no, you won't have to live on them forever. I figure another three days, four tops and I should be able to shift."

She couldn't help the disappointment and it obviously showed on her face because he frowned. "It's only a couple of days. Like you said before, we have everything we need and we're safe. I'll have you out of here in no time."

"It's just," she didn't want to complain. "Never mind. You just concentrate on getting better."

"What's going on? What's wrong?"

"I noticed that this cave has all of the basics but those basics are really limited. I can't believe that people actually live in these things," she gestured around the cave. "Or vacation in them, or whatever you guys do. Firstly," she gripped her thumb. "there are no cooking utensils." She grabbed the next finger. "No first aid kit." She grabbed the third finger. "No clean clothing and no clean bedding." She looked down at her rumpled, dirty appearance and crinkled her nose at the thought of how her pits must smell.

Thunder took another bite of his biscuits, taking his time chewing and swallowing. "These caves are used for rutting."

Her cheeks heated immediately. Make that, her whole body ignited. He must have noticed because he smiled. "Dragon females don't go into heat very often. When they do it's intense and usually lasts several days. This is where a female will come to ride it out, either alone or with a mate. Clothing is not required. Food and everything else is all secondary." He looked to the rear of the cave. "No one really thinks about anything but sex."

"Oh. I see." She cleared her throat because her voice sounded a tad squeaky.

His grin widened. "You can bathe in the pool. You can even wash your clothes if you want."

"That's our only drinking water. I would hate to contaminate the water with my stench."

"The pool is very deep. It would take a lot to contaminate the water." He smiled. "I wouldn't call your scent a stench." His nostrils flared. "You smell good to me." He sucked in another breath through his nose. "Really good."

She ignored the flirty comments. "If I did wash, I would have to get back into these clothes since I don't have a spare set."

"You can wash those," he gestured to what she was wearing with his eyes, "and hang them up to dry."

She felt her jaw drop.

He chuckled. That same deep baritone that had her panties . . . *Not going there.* Thunder's nostrils flared again, and he stopped mid-laugh, turning serious. He cleared his throat. "Use this." He fingered the woolen blanket that covered the bottom half of his torso.

"What about you?" She asked, the air feeling a little thin. She didn't like the idea of him naked. It wouldn't be right. She didn't like the idea of just wearing a blanket either but the thought of staying in her dirty jeans and undies any longer was also not an option.

Thunder shrugged his massive shoulders. "I'm not one for modesty. None of us shifters are. It would make shifting hellishly difficult."

She had to smile as she thought of a whole bunch of shifters trying to preserve their modesty while shifting. He was right, it would never work.

"You don't look comfortable. Go and bathe. Here, take the blanket." He began to pull it off.

"No!" she half yelled, putting both her hands up. "I don't need it just yet." Seeing him half naked while he was wounded and unconscious was one thing, seeing him half naked—her mouth dried up – whilst very much awake was another entirely.

He paused, letting the blanket go. "Okay. Just say the word and it's yours."

She nodded. "Maybe after breakfast."

He gave a nod. "I need to ask a favor." He pulled a face, looking pained.

"Sure." She could hear the uncertainty in her own voice.

"I need you to help me get to the mouth of the cave."

"Right now?"

"Yeah, right now would be good."

"Um, ok. I thought you couldn't shift and I'm not sure that moving around will be good for you at the moment," she frowned, not liking the idea at all.

He gave his head a scratch. "I don't really have a choice. Dragon shifters have huge bladders but mine is getting seriously full. I need to go to the bathroom."

Flip! Of course he did. He might be a dragon shifter but he still had the same bodily functions as anyone else. *Duh!* She felt like slapping a hand to her forehead. "Right! Sure. I can help out. You'll need to excuse the BO though."

"BO?" He raised his brows looking clueless.

"BO stands for body odor."

"I like your BO, so don't worry about it."

Tammy had to giggle.

"Did I say that wrong?"

She nodded. "Yeah. When someone refers to BO, it means that they think they stink. So by you saying that you like my BO means that you like the way I stink."

"I like the way you smell. You don't stink." He winked at her.

"You're nuts," she shook her head. "How can you like the scent of my perspiration? It's not normal."

"It's very normal. You like the way I smell."

"I do not," she said too quickly. "That would be just as nuts."

"Why were you sniffing me last night then?" he smirked. *The bastard smirked!*

"No, I . . ." she nipped her bottom lip and squeezed lightly. "You were supposed to be sleeping. You *were* sleeping dammit."

"Shifters sleep with one eye open. You sniffed me and by that little sigh you gave I'd say that you liked it." His smirk grew bigger. *What an asshat!* He was loving every minute.

She shook her head. "I was checking to see if you needed a sponge bath." She tapped her nose. "You know, checking your level of BO."

He nodded, looking smug. "What was the sigh for then?"

"I was upset to learn that you did need one and rather badly." She shook her head, slowly trying to look put out. "I sighed out of frustration because it's the last thing I feel like doing. I wasn't even going to mention it." She shook her head. "I didn't want to embarrass you."

"I'm not embarrassed. If I stink then I need a bath," he shrugged.

"Sure, once you've . . . you know . . ." she gestured to the front of the cave. "I'll help you to the pool." She glanced to the back of the cave.

Thunder shook his head, looking serious. "I'll be lucky to make it to the front and then back again. Hell, I'll be lucky if I stand upright long enough to piss. I'll take that sponge bath you so kindly offered."

"I didn't offer you a sponge bath. I said you needed one." The thought of washing him from head to toe left her feeling a little out of breath."

"You said you would care for me and get me anything I needed."

Oh god! He wasn't going to make her do that. *No way!* He would be an absolute prick if he . . .

Thunder burst out laughing, the laugh turned into a low groan. "That hurts. You should see your face. I'm only joking. We both know that you think I smell good. As awesome as a bath sounds, particularly a sponge bath, it can wait. I'm sure I'll be strong enough to bathe tomorrow."

Tammy couldn't help but smile. "You're an asshole."

Thunder frowned and grit his teeth for a few seconds. "An asshole who's about to wet the bed," his voice sounded strained.

"Oh, shit, sorry!" She rushed over to him. Thunder pulled himself into a sitting position. He moved slowly and carefully. A sheen appeared on his forehead from the strain it took. The sheet pooled around his waist. "What do you need me to do?" Her heart-rate went up and her hands felt a bit sweaty.

"You have a deer in the headlights look," Thunder gave a half smile, he was breathing heavily. How was it that he looked so damned good despite being out of breath? For one, his chest was a thing of utter beauty. Those abs were impressive. They were *let me glide my tongue along that ridge* impressive. Stop!

Okay so he was hot, insanely good-looking . . . no need to get all weak in the knees and gaga over him. He was too darned hunky. Liable to break her heart. Stomp all over the pieces and move on in an instant. He might seem nice, they *all* seemed nice. He had charming down pat, as well. A sure sign that he was *not* nice. *You've been there and you have the t-shirt. Stop ogling him. Stop!*

"I've never played at nurse before. You're a big guy, I'm not sure how much help I can be."

"Give me a hand. Help me up and then maybe keep me

from falling over."

"Okay." She nodded, pushing out a breath.

"Okay then." He put out both his hands and she took them. Warm and calloused. Big, generous hands. Really nice hands. He squeezed hers, bringing her back. "You ready?"

She nodded, bending at the knee so that she could take his weight better. "Oh and, Tamara . . ."

"You can call me Tammy." *Why did she say that?* He was going to get the wrong idea. "My *friends* call me that," she put emphasis on the word 'friends.'

He looked her in the eye with those mesmerizing purple irises. *Stop!* She needed to find herself a life raft already. There would be no drowning in those babies. He licked his lower lip. *Don't look! Don't! Arghh!* She bloody looked. At his tongue, dammit . . . and just like that his smirk was back. "Tammy."

"Yeah?" a sigh. A damned sigh. "What?" she added a bit more harshly.

"You might want to keep your eyes on mine."

"Why? Stop your shit, Thunder. Just because you have really beautiful eyes does not mean that I want to sit and stare into them all day." *I do! I really do . . . not!*

He frowned for a moment. "No, I mean you should keep your eyes on mine because I'm about to lose my—" He gave the edge of his blanket a small tug. She wanted to panic at the thought of him naked but there were dark circles under his eyes and he was beginning to look really tired even though they hadn't set out yet.

"Just tie it around your waist or something."

He shook his head. "I can't get my ass up and tie the thing and stay upright." He shook his head. "Just keep your eyes on mine and we'll be golden," he smiled. One of his shit-eating grins. "Not that I mind you looking at my cock or anything."

She gave him a whack on the side of the arm and he almost fell over. Tammy grabbed him by the biceps. Huge, hard, really awesome biceps. Not that she noticed since she was busy trying to keep him upright. "I don't think this is going to work." She pulled him against her. Thunder gripped her outer thighs. She managed to keep him up . . . just.

"It will. It has to. I haven't wet my bed since I was a whelp and I don't plan on doing it now."

"Fine."

"Let's do this then. I'm ready." His breathing had almost normalized but he still looked dead tired.

"On three?" She took back his hands. Thunder nodded.

She counted down. "And up we go!" She leaned back, using her body weight to give him a lift. He made it up about an inch or two and fell back down.

"Fuck!" he growled. "I'm useless. Can't even stand up."

"I'll grip you under your arms and lift you."

"I weigh a ton."

"I doubt it."

"No really." It didn't look like he was joking. "Let's try the arm thing." He lifted both his arms. Only got about half-way up before his brow glistened and a grimace took residence on his face.

Tammy reached around him, careful to avoid his back. The position put them cheek to cheek. *Shit!* He really did smell good.

"No sniffing," he growled. "It's a come on, in dragon talk."

"I wasn't . . ." she let the sentence die. "I'm not a dragon."

"I am." Another low growl that she felt all the way down in her panties. Right to her clit, to be precise. She needed sex and sooner rather than later.

She ignored her body. Ignored him even more. "On three . . ." she counted down before she could give the whole thing too much thought. When she reached three she lifted and he seemed to rise for a few moments before falling back down. Wouldn't you know too, he fell all the way down. So did she, landing right on top of him.

He groaned, his face a mask of agony. "Oh my god!" She cupped his cheeks. "Are you okay?"

He gave a small nod.

She put one of her hands on his chest. "Are you sure?"

"I'm great! Perfect. Except that you're kind of sitting on my bladder."

Tammy scrambled off him. She hadn't realized that she was straddling him. Thank God the blanket stayed put.

Thunder pulled himself up onto his elbows. "Let me take care of my little situation and you can sit on top of me all you like. I'll even let you bounce," he winked at her. He was good at it too. Some guys looked like they had something in their eye and others like big, fat assholes wanting to score. Thunder looked hot, oh yeah, and sexy . . . and funnily enough, he looked sweet. It was all a façade though. She wasn't buying it for a second.

"Yeah, right!" Tammy snorted. An honest to God laugh snort. It sounded ridiculous. Not as ridiculous as her cheeks heating. She felt like a silly schoolgirl again. "You can forget that," she added, with a serious note to her voice. "I think we might have to come up with a Plan B here."

"Plan B is wet the bed and I hate that idea," he frowned. It took some effort to get himself back into a sitting position. Thunder groaned.

"No really. Maybe you could pee into the water bottle or something."

He shook his head. "No! I'm a male in my prime. It's a few measly feet. Just have to get up. Besides, I still have to drink out of that thing." He pulled a face of disgust.

"It's far."

"You're not helping. I have a plan."

"What did you have in mind?"

"Get on your knees." He pointed to the ground at his feet.

"I'm not sure I like where this is going." She narrowed her eyes and folded her arms. It was silly of her to make a joke at a time like this, but she couldn't help herself.

It was his turn to blush. A huge, gorgeous hunk of a man was blushing because she was insinuating he wanted a blowjob. She never expected it, not for one minute. "I didn't mean it like that," he said, still blushing. It was endearing. It made her warm to him. *No, not happening! Christopher Collins.* She reminded herself of her good-looking, successful, charming dickwad of an ex.

"You didn't mean it like that? That would be a first," she made an attempt at humor and failed. This whole thing felt awkward. No wonder she was cracking ridiculous jokes. May as well get this over with. Tammy knelt at his feet. Even his feet were beautiful.

"You might want to turn the other way." He twirled his finger and gave her a wink – one that reminded her just how charming he could be, even if he did blush on occasion. "Unless of course you want to look at my . . ."

"No!" she blurted. "That's okay," she added as she turned around to face the cave wall across the way.

Thunder chuckled at her reaction. *Ass-hat.*

"I'll get up using your shoulders for support. I'm heavy, so brace yourself."

"I'll be fine, just don't fall onto the floor or you'll be stuck there."

"What a tragedy that would be. I wouldn't get to cuddle with you tonight." She could hear that he was smiling.

"How many times do I have to tell you that it's by accident? It doesn't count when you're asleep."

"Still feels good. I'd definitely miss your arms around me, your lush . . ." She could hear that he was definitely smiling.

"Okay . . . enough of that Prince Charming."

"I'm a king."

"Whatever."

"Is that not important to you? My status?" His voice held an edge. It sounded like he was being serious. Like he cared either way. Maybe he saw himself as being high and mighty or something, just because he held a title. Again, she'd been there and done that.

She glanced back over her shoulder. He was frowning. "No," she said. "It's not important. Everyone is equal. We are all born and we all have to die one day. We all shit the same too. Do you think you are better than everyone else just because you have a golden chest?" *Oops, maybe that was going a bit too far? Tough luck!* He'd asked and she'd answered.

Thunder grinned. It was so wide that she saw his pearly whites. He looked like he liked her answer, which was weird since she had pretty much dissed him. "I have more responsibilities, more privileges . . ."

Of that she had no doubt.

"but I'm no better. Let's do this thing," he gave a nod.

She nodded as well, facing back the other way. This time, after Thunder finished counting down, it felt like her shoulders were about to be crushed to the ground. Like they might break at any second. He hadn't been lying when he said he was heavy. In fact, it may have been a bit of an understatement. Her legs shook. She felt the gravel press into her knees. Thunder grunted and then gave a shout of triumph as he made it up.

Tammy fell forward as his weight lifted off of her. She put her hands out to stop herself from plowing headfirst into the ground. Her hands were still a bit tender from their previous abuses so she cried out.

"Are you okay?" Thunder's voice was laced with concern.

"Yeah." She had to stop herself from turning her head. Tammy got back up, glancing at Thunder. At his face . . . no lower.

His eyes had a dazed look and he was swaying on his feet.

"Shit! Here . . ." she put her arm around him. "Are you sure you can do this?"

He grunted. "Give me a second—" He was breathing heavily. "Dizzy," he added.

He was leaning on her quite heavily but it wasn't anything she couldn't handle. She only prayed that he didn't fall because she hadn't been joking earlier, there was no way he'd be able to get up again. Not today anyway and maybe not tomorrow either. He would have to try to make himself comfortable on the ground until he was strong enough. The bed would be cold without him. She didn't just think that. *Argh!*

"I'm ready," his voice was stronger.

They began to walk. Small, shuffling steps. Tammy focused on the path ahead. It was littered with the odd bigger rock. She'd do her best to navigate around them.

She glanced at Thunder who looked like he was barely holding on. Sweat poured off of him, but he kept on walking.

"Thank fuck!" he muttered when they finally made it to

the walled section of the cave. He put one hand against the wall and leaned in.

"I'll leave you to it then," Tammy said, but the moment she let him go, he almost toppled over. Then, he overcorrected, nearly falling the other way. She grabbed ahold of him again. "Easy!"

Thunder chuckled. "I think I might need you to stay."

"Oh no! No way," she shook her head.

"Please, Tammy," a whispered plea. "I wouldn't ask unless I was desperate. I'm too off balance. I'm so damned weak . . ." he sounded exasperated and frustrated and desperate.

"I can't hold you up while you pee. It wouldn't be right. It's private and . . ." *Shit!* He was in a bad way. Too weak to be able to handle this solo. She'd pretend she was a nurse. "Ok, I'll do it."

"Thank you," he sounded relieved.

"Sure."

"Tamara . . ." She didn't like the way he said her name. Her full name. The corners of his eyes were slightly crinkled at the edges even though he looked serious.

"Yes?"

"If you don't want to hold me up, you could hold my cock instead if you would prefer. I'll lean up against—"

Cheeky bastard! She gasped in horror and he laughed. It was soft and weak sounding. "Stop your shit!" She moved to stand behind him, with both hands around his torso to balance him, again being careful of his injured back. By the whiteness of his fingers, she could see that he was leaning quite heavily on the wall.

Thunder did his business. She tried hard to think of other things. To sing songs inside her mind but all she could think of was his cock in his hand. All she could think of was his cock, period.

Who's the pervert now, Tamara?

You are. You! The poor guy is half dead and peeing against a wall. Hardly romantic and yet . . . Argh! Think of other things dammit.

It went on for a long time. Too long for her liking. Then again, this was the first time he was going to the bathroom. Once he was done, Thunder gave a little shake and a small circular thrust of the hips. Tammy licked her lips. The guy sure knew how to thrust. *No! Don't go there, Tammy.* She cleared her throat, feeling her cheeks burn.

"Thanks," he sighed. "That's so much better."

"No problemo," her voice had an edge that gave her nerves away. "Let's get you back to bed."

"Sounds good."

She glanced at him and he winked at her. Tammy rolled her eyes. *So full of shit!* She had to laugh. By the time they made it back to the bed, he sounded like he'd run a couple of miles instead of shuffled two dozen or so feet.

Keeping her eyes on his, they slowly shuffle turned until his back was to the bed and then he tumbled backwards, grunting as he landed.

She 'forgot' not to look and . . . *Boom!* There it was and in all its long, hard glory. His cock. His erect, engorged member. It was a very good-looking cock. Of course it was. Her mouth fell open.

"I told you not to look," Thunder smiled. It was a tired smile.

Tammy realized that her jaw still hung open. She spun around. "I can't believe you. Please tell me that wasn't erect. How could it be? You're still half dead for God's sake. You can hardly walk let alone . . . that."

"It isn't erect." She heard the sound of the bedcovers rustling. He sounded serious. One hundred percent serious.

Tammy turned back and gasped, averting her eyes. His groin area was hairless. He had heavy sacs and a large jutting penis. *Jutting, dammit!* The thing sure as hell seemed to face upwards and it was too darned big not to be erect. Her mouth opened and closed like a fish out of water and she turned back the other way.

Thunder chuckled. "I didn't say you could turn around yet." There were more rustling sounds. "Okay, you can look."

He had a 'cat that got the cream' smug look on his face. He didn't look in the least bit worried that Tammy had seen him naked. No modesty indeed.

Her cheeks were flaming. Her nipples were tight, other places wet. As soon as she got out of this place she was going to a bar and getting herself laid. Nadia had been after her for months about it. Her best friend said that it wasn't healthy for a person to be celibate for so long. Tammy finally believed her.

It was like her eyes had a life all of their own because they drifted to . . . well, there . . . between his legs. There was a definite bulge beneath the blanket. It took some effort to look him back in the eyes. Thunder was lying on his back, his hands folded behind his head. His brows were raised and there was a glint in his eyes. One she didn't like.

"You were joking, right?"

"About what?" he cocked his head slightly.

"About that." She pointed in the vicinity of his groin. Tammy couldn't understand why she continued along this path. It was rocky and dangerous but she couldn't help herself. She had this thing about knowing when she was right about something and not being able to back down.

"That what?" he was enjoying himself.

"Your thing . . . your erection. You were joking about not being . . . you know . . . hard." She felt a little flustered as well as a little out of breath. She felt hot and if she was totally honest with herself, a little bothered as well.

He shook his head. There were two frown lines on his forehead. "A male should never joke about his cock."

She swallowed hard.

"I do not have an erection. Maybe a semi at best."

Her eyes darted back to the bulge. *Couldn't be. It got much bigger than that? No way!* Her eyes narrowed.

"Would you like to see it again? Examine it? I wouldn't mind."

"What?" she might have yelled the word. Couldn't be sure because she was panicking. "No way. No!" She huffed out a breath. "Keep that thing covered please," she nodded, pointing at his dick.

Several moments later, she was still pointing at his dick

but couldn't seem to stop herself from doing it.

"Sure thing, but let me know if you change your mind," he winked at her. It somehow managed to break the spell and she snapped her hand back.

"Stop that."

"What?"

"Winking at me. I don't like it." She didn't. Although Chris never winked, it was just the kind of thing a charmer would do. One of the many tricks in his arsenal. Then again, it was better if he did wink. It would remind her that he was not her type. The polar opposite to be exact. "On second thought, wink all you want."

He frowned. "You are a strange female, Tammy."

Good! He wasn't interested in her. He found her strange. This was good.

"Good thing I like 'strange,'" he added, turning to his side, grimacing as he did.

Argh! She couldn't win. She definitely could not win with this guy. He was just looking for action. It was what charmers did. They told a woman what she wanted to hear so that they could get into their panties. Chris was a typical example. Thunder was another. They were all the same. Once a player got into your panties, he'd move on to the next one. Or worse, the charmer would actually start a relationship with you. One he couldn't possibly commit to, and then what?

She'd be left with a broken heart at the end of it all, or worse. Tammy knew firsthand how much worse it could be. Oh, so much worse – like 'ruin your life' bad.

CHAPTER 10

Hours later...

He couldn't believe she was still holding out. Was getting naked in the same space as him so bad? It wasn't like he'd actually look . . . much. No, he wouldn't look. Since when did he need to sneak glances at a female?

Tammy was attracted to him. She was just as attracted to him as he was to her. She was also skittish. The only thing on his side right now was that there was nowhere for her to run or he had no doubt that she would've taken off for the hills.

If there was one thing he had learned over the years, it was patience. Especially where females were concerned. He only got to be around them twice a year. That was it. Although he'd never had to learn how to apply patience when winning one before, he figured it couldn't be that hard.

Thunder watched as Tammy tried to smooth the sweater she was wearing. How she readjusted her undergarment through her clothes. The one that wrapped around her breasts. She looked distinctly uncomfortable. He noticed that she'd brushed her teeth twice since waking up. She was trying to get clean and it wasn't working. He'd meant what he said, he didn't mind either way, but she clearly did. "Hey, take the blanket and go and bathe."

Tammy had just been throwing some logs onto the fire. She looked his way and shook her head. "Maybe later."

"What difference does it make? Now, in an hour from now, tomorrow? It'll be cold but you'll feel a lot better."

"So you *do* think I have BO then?" she pulled a face.

"I didn't say that. You smell fine to me. You look even better. I would lick you from your head to your toes – maybe concentrating on somewhere in the middle – if I had a bit more strength."

Her eyes widened and her mouth dropped open. "Not happening, mister!" She looked flustered and her scent of arousal wafted over to him. He had to fight to keep from sniffing the air. *Oh, so damned sweet.*

"Go and do what you need to do. I'm about to take a nap anyway."

Interest sparked in her eye. "You are?"

"Yep," he yawned. It wasn't a real yawn but it ended up being real in the end. He was pretty tired come to think of it. "Go bathe. Hang your clothes in front of the fire and they'll be dry in no time."

"You won't look?" She sounded like a total innocent. For a second he was inclined to believe that she might even be a virgin but that was impossible. She'd talked earlier about a broken heart and virgins weren't included in the program. So she'd been with at least one male then.

"I won't look," he half growled.

She looked at him like maybe she didn't believe him or something.

It got his scales up. "I've seen plenty of naked females. They all willingly took their clothes off for me. I'm not about to start peeping through holes in the wall anytime soon. I don't have to."

"I'll bet," she mumbled under her breath. "Fine," she said the word like she was angry. Then she gave a small sigh and paused for a beat. "It would be great if you could lend me your blanket."

Thunder smiled to himself.

"Just make sure that you cover up please." He noticed that she had averted her gaze, as if the sight of his dick might make her turn to stone or something.

"You've already seen me naked." He decided to toy with her because it was so much fun and she made it so easy.

"Just..."

Completely flustered. He had to suppress a smile. *Fuck it!* He smiled anyway.

"No... it's... keep it covered." She wagged a finger. "Just keep it covered, okay?"

He laughed. "I'm just screwing with you. I won't look and I'll keep it," he paused, "covered." He winked at her.

She blushed a whole lot more, so adorable that it almost hurt to look at her. Thunder grabbed a pillow and used it to cover his dick. "It's safe, you can come and fetch your blanket now."

"Thank you." She tried to take the blanket without really looking down. Her cheeks were redder than an overripe tomato in the sun. "Wait just a . . ." She looked down at him over her nose, her eyes narrowed, her embarrassment forgotten. "That's my pillow!" She pointed the object covering his dick.

He gave a single-shouldered shrug. "You can have it if you want." He pretended to lift the pillow.

Tammy took to looking outraged. She put her hand on the pillow in question. It was clearly a reaction. She hadn't given the action much thought though it seemed. "Don't you dare!"

Oh fuck! There was a pillow separating his cock from her hand. A case of cotton and some duck down. That was it. His dick decided it was happy and began to harden up.

Tammy suddenly realized what she was doing and snatched her hand back. "Behave! I can't believe you actually run a whole kingdom. You're in charge of people and stuff," she huffed and stormed to the rear of the cave.

He didn't understand her. Not even a little bit. Normally when people were attracted to one another, they rutted. The sexual tension in the cave was so thick that you could cut that sucker with a knife. If they just rutted, it would make things easier. It would clear the air. Human females could be a little strange about sex though, they attached a lot of feelings to the act. He'd had females ask for his number after sex or beg for a date, or a relationship. This, despite the fact that he was clear that it was just about the sex. A 'one night stand' as humans called it.

He got the feeling that Tammy would put a lot of feelings behind sex. That she wouldn't see it as just rutting. With a female like her, he would definitely see it as more as well. This was not a stag run. This was serious. She attracted him and intrigued him. He was desperate to learn more about her, to find out what made her tick. So, as much as he hated to admit it, she was right to avoid sex right now. He needed to stop teasing and flirting. As much as he wanted to explore things with her, he had no idea how Blaze would take him changing into his dragon form. According to the rule book, he would be immediately disqualified. Tammy would need to decide if she wanted to go home, or stay. If she stayed, the other unmated, highest ranking males would get a chance to fight for her. If he allowed himself to become attached to her, maybe even fall in love with her and he had to watch her go it would break him. He needed to be sure that she could stay before he took her to his bed. It was as simple as that.

Simple.

Tamara gave a sharp intake of breath. Like something had happened to her. He instinctively looked. To check on her, not because he was some spying freak.

He was fucked if staying away from her would be simple. It would be anything but. She had made the noise because the water was cold. The pool was further down the cave. There was very little light but he could see clearly. The silver hadn't affected his vision. Not in the slightest. One of her feet was in the water. She stood facing away.

Her hair cascaded down her back. It was her ass that took his breath away though. Two globes of perfection. It was an ass a male could grab and squeeze. An ass that would have some bounce during rutting. His mouth watered and his dick hardened up into an erection that physically hurt. The tip of his dick throbbed in time to his heartbeat and his sacs drew up in preparation for shooting off.

Perfect!

Just fucking perfect. Thunder turned onto his belly and willed his dick to go down. He put her pillow back on her side and then thought better of it and exchanged his pillow for hers.

Tammy gave a yelp. He could hear by the sound the water made that she had entered the pool. *Not looking.* "Are you okay?"

"I thought you were going to sleep," her voice sounded strained. Her teeth chattered. He could hear the lapping of the water as she frantically washed herself off in the frigid pool.

"I would be if you stopped making so much noise," he lied. His boner throbbed against his belly. There would be no sleeping any time soon. If Tammy saw this sucker she would crap herself.

"I'll try." More slopping about in the water. He could hear a scrubbing noise. "It's freezing in here. My feet feel like ice blocks."

He smiled. "Let me know if you need help getting out."

A louder splash. "No, thanks," she answered through chattering teeth.

He was supposed to be behaving so he bit down to stop himself from asking if she was sure. It wasn't like he could actually go over there or anything. He doubted he would last through even a quick bout of sex. More throbbing. *Fuck!* He needed to think about something boring. Sheep jumping over a hedge. *Yup! That would do it.*

Instead, he listened to Tammy as she lifted herself from the pool. How she muttered a curse when she stubbed her toe. How she got to work cleaning her clothes . . . still naked. *No, don't think about it.* At long fucking last, she wrapped the blanket around herself. It took an age before she finally finished. Then he listened to her hanging her clothes up. She began to hum softly to herself and finally felt himself calm. His breathing turned more rhythmic. He was so damned tired. He willed his muscles to relax. Willed his mind to calm. He was halfway to sleep when he heard her soft intake of breath. Her heart-rate picked up.

Tammy was standing next to the bed. She was looking down at him. At his ass. She was aroused. Her sweet scent engulfed him and his cock sprang back to life in an instant. "See something you like?" Why couldn't he keep his big mouth shut and just pretend to be sleeping.

"I thought you were asleep," her voice was high-pitched.

"I told you, dragons sleep with one eye open. Shall I turn over, give you something to really look at?"

"Don't be an asshole."

He *was* being a dickhead. He had no idea how to act around her. He wanted her. Wanted to get to know her but he had no idea if a future was possible. If it was, he wasn't sure she would want him as well. Outside of the bedroom anyway. Sexual compatibility was one thing, compatibility as mates was a whole other matter. He turned his head towards her and opened his eyes.

Fuck!

Mistake!

Her hair was still damp. It was freshly brushed. Her eyes were big and wide. She had that deer in the headlights look. Spooked and ready to run but nowhere to go. Her nipples were hard through the thin woolen blanket. She'd tied the blanket just above her left shoulder. The other shoulder was bare. "You're beautiful," he blurted. It was the truth.

He hadn't meant to say it though, it just slipped out. For a moment she got a faraway look. Like the compliment meant something to her and then she straightened her shoulders. Her eyes narrowed on his. "I'll go and sit by the fire while my clothes dry."

"What did he do to you?"

"What? Who?"

"The male who broke your heart. The one who left you jaded."

He watched her shut down even more. "It happened a few years ago. It's not really something I want to talk about. I've put it behind me."

He shook his head. "You haven't."

"You don't know me. And for the record, I have talked about it . . . twice. To two different people. Friends of mine. I've worked through it and I'm over it. What can I say? I trusted the guy and he abused that trust. I left him, thinking that we could still maintain a business relationship but I was wrong on that note as well. Bottom line, I fell in love with a guy who was all wrong for me. I won't let it happen again."

"So, you're not interested in a relationship?" He needed to know.

"I didn't say that. I'm not interested in being in a relationship with the wrong guy. I'm careful . . ." she raised her brows. "Yes, and jaded too, but I still hope to find love one day . . . maybe. I prefer not to talk about it"

Thunder decided to drop it. She'd said more than he had hoped. "I'm glad you're over it and that you've talked about it. If you need to talk more I'm here. Not going anywhere," he tried to defuse the situation with a smile.

In her defense, she tried to smile back. "Get some rest. I'll bring you your blanket back as soon as possible."

"Take your time, it looks better on you."

She blushed. *So cute*. She nodded once and was about to turn to leave when he said, "He was an asshole not to realize what he had. He should have taken better care of you."

"Yeah, he should have." She gave him a small, really sweet smile. "Get some rest. You look tired."

"I'm not sure I'll manage all by my lonesome, but I'll try."

"Argh! You're too much," she groaned, but at least she was smiling, one big, wide smile. He'd do anything to see her smile some more.

CHAPTER 11

The next morning...

Sleeping was becoming her new favorite pastime. Not just sleeping, but sleeping next to Thunder. Snuggling up close with him. Not him *per se,* just a warm body.

"Why aren't you pulling away as quickly as your human form will allow?" Thunder asked, his voice still thick with sleep.

"I figure I've pretty much slept as close as I can get to you the whole night, so why run away now? I need a minute or two to wake up properly. So if you don't mind..."

He made a sound of affirmation. "Not at all." He began to play with her hair, threading his fingers through the strands. It felt so good. How could such a small thing feel so good? "Don't get any ideas," her voice sounded a bit on the husky side. *Nah!* She was still half asleep. "It's not personal or anything. It's just that I don't get much human contact, so this is nice."

"Non-human contact in this case."

"Same thing."

"Not really."

"Yeah, it is."

"Nope. Non-human contact is better every time," he sounded deadly serious.

"Oh my God, your ego might just be as big as your . . . feet." She almost said cock. What the hell was wrong with her?

"This has nothing to do with ego," he chuckled, his chest vibrated, sparking interest from her nipples which were pushed up against said chest. "Non-humans have better senses."

"So?"

"We can pick up on subtle things like heartbeat, breathing. You probably didn't realize it but you actually let off a scent when you're happy, aroused, in pain."

"Wait a minute . . ." She had to look him in the eyes. "You know when I'm aroused?"

He smiled and gave a nod. "Yes, I do."

That sucked. It sucked a whole damn lot since she'd been aroused a ton of times in the last few days.

"Hey," he touched her cheek, which was feeling distinctly hot. "It's nothing to be embarrassed about. Being aroused is normal. We are a male and a female sharing a small space. You can deny it all you want but we are attracted to each other, so your body's reaction is normal."

She couldn't deny it. Tammy decided not to say anything more on the subject instead. She gave a small nod and tried to pretend it didn't bother her. Like it was nothing.

He continued to play with her hair. "We pick up on these changes and know if what we are doing is effective or not. We can feel it as well." He touched the side of her arm. "Even the tiniest of goosebumps or where a female is most sensitive. That way we can find the most pleasurable spots . . ."

"Okay, I get it," she mumbled, trying not to let his words affect her body. It was time to change the subject. "How are you feeling?"

"Much better. I think I might be able to manage that walk on my own today."

"That's good news."

"I think I might even go and take a bath," he sniffed at himself. "I think I may have that BO you were talking about."

He still smelled really good to her. She lifted her head and sniffed at him. "I don't sm . . . what is it?"

His whole body had stiffened. His eyes had a strange look. "You shouldn't do that."

"What?"

"Sniff me. We discussed this yesterday, you may as well ask me openly to fuck you because it means the same thing in our dragon culture." He clenched his jaw.

Hearing him talk about fucking her made her clit do that zing thing. Like a tiny electric current suddenly burst through her. She got this heavy, not unpleasant feeling in her lower belly. In short, she was horny as hell. "Oh!" A croak. "Sorry!" She moved away from him and he let her go.

"Just don't do it again." He gave her a pinched smile as he turned to face the other way and then moved onto his belly. "I might take you up on your offer next time."

She started to laugh. "As if!"

"I will, Tamara." His eyes bore into hers. "And if I start touching you, I can guarantee you that you won't ask me to stop."

No, she wouldn't. Yes, she most certainly would. No, no she wouldn't.

No sniffing him. No ogling him and no more getting aroused by him. He was not her type. Once they got back to dragon land she was headed home. Surely after all she and Thunder had suffered, they wouldn't make her stay her full two weeks? She sure as hell hoped not. She couldn't take it anymore. She made her way to the fire and threw on a couple of logs, preparing to blow on the embers, when she heard him groan. Thunder was on his feet, his blanket tightly clutched around his waist.

"You okay?"

Thunder nodded. "Why? Want to come along?" He bobbed his eyebrows up and down.

She smiled and shook her head.

"Sure you don't want to hold my . . ."

"No!"

"I was going to say hand, you pervert," he grinned.

"Sure you were," she shook her head and grinned back.

"Okay," he bobbed his brows again. "I was totally

going to say cock."

Flip! Her throat closed just hearing him say the word. *Cock.* He was right, they were attracted to each other. She was attracted to him because, well, you only had to look at the guy to understand why. He was attracted to her because she was the only woman there. Men were horny bastards. Thunder was no exception. His brow furrowed and he narrowed his eyes for a moment. "Are you okay? I was only joking. I'm more than capable of doing this on my own today and please do me a favor and throw me down a cliff if I can't hold my own cock to piss."

She managed a semblance of a smile.

"That's more like it, although not quite there. Hell, you can throw me down a cliff right now if it'll bring back that gorgeous smile of yours."

He was a really sweet guy. Even though he was just trying to get into her pants, she'd take it. Tammy couldn't help the grin that was unleashed.

Thunder grinned back. Man alive but he was a hottie. Blanket riding low on his narrow hips. His abs, chest . . . he even had those muscles that ran along the sides of his ribs. Not to mention a face that was holy hotness on steroids. A face for TV, a voice for radio and a body for the bedroom. *Yeah baby!*

She caught herself licking her lips. *Stop!* She had allowed her brain to wander off again. Her eyes to wander. She cleared her throat. "Maybe killing yourself is a bit extreme."

He shrugged. "It would be worth it. Besides, I'd come

back and rejuvenate unless I somehow managed to decapitate myself on the way down."

"Good to know, and for the record, I wouldn't smile if you threw yourself off of a cliff."

"Mmmm," a deep murmer. "So you like me after all."

"*Like* might be pushing it a bit."

He laughed, and then swayed a little on his feet but managed to catch himself. "I'd better get to it." He pointed in the direction of the exit.

She nodded, watching as he carefully made his way to the mouth of the cave. After a minute or two she couldn't see him anymore, could only hear his footfalls.

Tammy busied herself with getting the fire going properly. It was good to see Thunder back on his feet. Another day, two tops and he'd be able to change into his dragon form again, which meant that they'd be able to return to his lair. She looked forward to it even though she'd miss the big guy. As a friend. Someone to have a laugh with and to cuddle at night. Hey, it wouldn't take her long to get used to sleeping alone again.

"Penny for your thoughts."

Tammy jumped, she hadn't heard him sneak up behind her.

"Nothing important, just watching the flames. As a little girl, my dad would take me camping. He could only get leave once, maybe twice a year, if we were lucky. I loved those trips. We fished and slept in a tent. I loved watching the fire at night . . . come to think of it, that's where I learned to make one even if I never did it myself.

Anyway, it was great, we'd toast marshmallows." She had to smile as the memories came back. "We didn't have much money but we had each other." It sounded like a cliché but it was true.

"What about your mom?" Thunder leaned his big frame up against the wall.

She shook her head. "I don't have a mom."

"I hate to break this to you, but everyone has a mom."

"I don't." She was over her mom not being in her life. It was something she had made peace with. "She left when I was three. To be more precise, she left just before my third birthday, so no mom in my life. I don't even remember her. My dad has been amazing. The best." She missed him so much. "When I was six, he showed up to 'Mothers and Daughters Day,' much to my delight and my teacher's horror. He even took me to buy my first bra. He's always been there for me."

"Sounds like a great guy." He folded his arms. *God, even his forearms were hot.* "Like he's a really nice person."

She lifted her eyes to his. Those purple-colored irises glinted in the firelight. His face was shadowed with stubble.

"Yeah," she nodded. "Really nice. He finally remarried three years ago and retired to Florida. I haven't seen him since but we talk often." She gave a laugh. "I told him I was going camping and that there'd be no signal." She gestured around the cave. "So maybe this is karma getting back at me."

"It could be worse."

She thought of Cloud and shivered. "Yes, it could have been."

"You are safe now."

"I know. I have my knife." She pulled the blade from its sheath in her pants.

Thunder shook his head, he looked solemn. "That won't save you. It's stainless steel. He'll heal too quickly. Don't worry though because he isn't coming."

She nodded. "You looked sad when we were talking about him the other day. You knew him, didn't you?"

Thunder gave a nod. "Yeah, he was once one of my best warriors."

"What happened to him?"

"His mate died. Part of him died that day. He hasn't been the same since."

"That's awful." She looked down at the ground for a moment.

"She was pregnant, already quite far along."

Tammy gave a sharp intake of breath. "Poor guy. No wonder he looks . . . looked so lost, so haunted. He blames you. I don't know whether to refer to him in the past tense or not." She couldn't help but frown. "Why would he blame you for his loss? It doesn't make sense."

Thunder sighed. "In a way, it is my fault. I push all mated couples to procreate. It is my duty as the king of my people to see another generation born, moreover, to see female dragons born."

"Yeah, Roxy mentioned that humans only seem to be able to have boy children."

"And we are grateful and love our human mates." His eyes burned with such intensity that she could feel it. For just a moment it felt like he was referring to her but she wasn't his mate. She wasn't even dating the guy so it was crazy thinking. The way he looked at her still gave her a warm fuzzy feeling though, which she couldn't explain.

"Thing is," Thunder went on, "we need female dragons. It would be a shame if they died out completely."

"Terrible." She couldn't imagine it. What if all human women died out? As in gone forever. She wouldn't be there to see it since she was a woman but heck, it would be just terrible.

"We push mated couples to have whelps." He was frowning heavily. In that moment, his eyes looked just as haunted as Cloud's had been. "I even teased him about having weak seed. It was stupid since we both knew he wasn't the problem," he shook his head. "That's when he asked my advice about whether his mate should take the herb." For a long while Thunder didn't say anything.

"What herb?" It didn't sound good.

"Aside from very few females being born, many of the females we have do not go into heat and therefore cannot become pregnant. It is what forced us to seek fertile females elsewhere." He put up a hand and his eyes widened. "Do not misunderstand we . . . we are greatly attracted to humans. We are highly compatible as a species. It is not a hardship but an honor to accept your kind into our fold."

Charmer.

"There is an herb that forces dragon females into heat. It works every time but only fifty percent of the females who take it actually give birth. The rest go into labor early . . . they hemorrhage out before the baby can be born. It is the reason why so few females use the drug." He shook his head, his eyes hard, his jaw clenched. "We don't understand it. We don't normally die from such a thing. It's a slow death. An agonizing death. He asked my advice and I didn't dissuade them. I should have."

Tammy's eyes welled with tears. "I take it that you didn't encourage them either."

He shook his head. "I didn't tell him not to do it, so . . ." he widened his eyes. "I may as well have encouraged them by default. I wish I could go back. I'd tell him not to do it. I have since banned the use of the herb."

Tammy already knew the answer. She needed to hear it anyway. "What about the baby?" A whisper. Her lip quivered.

Thunder shook his head. "Too young to survive."

"Cloud lost both his wife and his child?" A tear fell.

Thunder nodded. "Yeah. Six months ago. He's been in a bad way ever since. It's why I couldn't believe it when he asked to take part in the hunt. In the end, I couldn't deny him. I guess I did feel like I owed him something."

"You didn't." She wiped away the tear. At least he would be in a better place now. With his family.

"I have days where I feel like it's my fault, I should have told him . . ."

"It wasn't your decision to make." She stood up and took a step towards him.

"Cloud blamed me, kept asking me why I didn't stop him. Asked me why I pushed so hard for whelps. Why I made childless couples feel inferior. I never realized I . . ."

"That wasn't fair of him. You didn't force his mate to take that stuff. Don't do this to yourself. He's not all there. Wasn't all there," she pointed to her temple. "He told me that I was his mate, that you owed him so he was taking his payment in the form of me," she pointed at herself. "A human being. That's nuts. He thought he could rub my feet, give me a massage and that I'd fall in love with him. I'm sad that he might be dead. He wasn't a bad guy – at least I don't think he was – but he also wasn't entirely sane. I can understand how the death of his family would do that to him, but you can't blame yourself."

Thunder stepped closer. He gave her a half smile before threading some loose hair behind her ear. "You're right. Thank you. I feel a bit better about the whole thing. I felt like I pushed him over the edge. I also felt responsible for his death as a result – if he is dead that is."

"He almost killed you. He would have forced himself on me." She shivered again. "He had serious mental issues."

Thunder nodded. "I'm going to kiss you on the cheek now. Don't kick me in the balls, okay?"

Before she could respond, he leaned forward and kissed her on the cheek, right next to her mouth. It was somehow better than a real kiss. It almost felt like he meant it. Why hadn't he tried to kiss her though? Why the chaste peck? Then she realized what he'd just said and that he'd said that to her before. "Why do you keep saying that? About kicking you in the balls?"

"On the last hunt . . ." Thunder's cheeky grin was back. "Blaze and I decided on which female we were each going to each take. I went for Roxy, unfortunately, she had decided that Blaze was her man right from the start. I guess I'm not used to a female saying no because I didn't even notice that she wasn't interested. I just leaned in for a kiss. Next thing, she kneed my balls a shot. It was hands down, the most painful minute of my life. Not one I want to experience again."

Tammy couldn't help but laugh. "So poor old you ended up womanless? That had to hurt your ego."

"Actually. There were two females."

Ouch! It hurt to hear him talk about another woman. She was an idiot for caring. *He's too hot, too charming, he's wrong for you, Tammy. Stop it!* "What happened?" she asked. "With the other woman?"

He gave a small shrug. "She turned out not to be my type."

"Hmmmmm," Tammy folded her arms. She was a sadomasochist. She had to be for asking the next question. "What's your type then?"

Thunder looked her deep in the eyes and she felt her heart beat harder. "I like a female who enjoys the simple things."

"Like?" What the hell was wrong with her? That

sounded just like flirting.

"I don't know, a female who enjoys toasting marshmallows and staring into a fire. A female who would enjoy taking a walk in the rain and making love under the stars."

Her heart sped up. She bit down on her bottom lip.

"Do you enjoy walking in the rain, Tammy?"

Yes! Yes! Yes!

He is a charmer. He wants to get in your pants so bad he'll say anything. "I'm not sure," she stammered. "I've never tried it."

"What about . . . ?" His eyes had that mischievous glint.

"No!" she blurted. "Never tried that either. Did she not enjoy the simple things then? That woman from the last hunt. Was she complicated?" She decided to change the direction of the conversation. To direct it back to the other woman. Not that she was *the* woman.

"Nope, she wasn't complicated at all. She was here for the money. She didn't really care about me, only this," he rubbed his golden chest markings.

Shit! Oh shit! Tammy was here for the money too. She was a bad person. A terrible person. *Don't panic! You're not staying.* Not falling in love and not staying. She had been honest about not being here for love. "Oh. That sucks. I'm sorry. She obviously made you believe differently"

"It's okay. It wasn't meant to be. She wasn't right for me. I enjoyed her company for a while . . ."

"I'll bet." It just slipped out.

"But when I really got to know her . . . What did you

say?" He narrowed his eyes and his mouth gave a twitch.

"Nothing."

"Nothing, my ass. You said 'I'll bet,' and if I didn't know better I'd say you were jealous."

She shook her head. "I'm not, I mean, we're not even together."

He turned serious. "No, we're not." Thunder pushed himself off the wall. She had to look up even higher to maintain eye contact. "I'm going to jump in the pool."

Disappointment coursed through her, which was really stupid. He turned and headed for the back of the cave. He walked really slowly and carefully but it was clear that his strength was returning.

Why hadn't he played the relationship card? All charmers did it. They made you believe in forever so that they could sleep with you, or even worse, they actually seriously dated you while continuing to screw around. Thunder wasn't doing it though. "Okay," her voice sounded light and breezy even though she didn't feel it. "Enjoy!" she added as he was swallowed by the dark.

Was it her? Maybe he wasn't attracted to her after all. Maybe he was only referring to her arousal earlier – as in one-sided. Maybe all of the remarks and taunts were only teasing, like he had said, and not flirting like she'd believed. She should be happy. Thrilled that he didn't have feelings for her. It's what she wanted. Join the program, stay for the minimum period and hightail it out of there. No falling in love. No letting a guy fall in love with her – the easy part – and make a bit of money in the process. No harm no foul. Just enough to start over. She'd been toying with the idea of moving to Florida. It would be nice to be closer to her father. He wasn't getting any younger. Point was, she should be happy he felt nothing for her. She should be happy Thunder wasn't attracted to her, yet all she felt was disappointment in the first degree.

It sucked. It totally sucked.

CHAPTER 12

The water was refreshing. His body felt so much less heavy and cumbersome than on the land. He could feel remnants of the silver still running through his veins. It made him feel slow and weak. It wouldn't be long now. Maybe by tomorrow they could head back. He could send a team to collect Cloud's body or to apprehend the male if he was still out there. More importantly, he could face Blaze and fight for a future with his female.

His mind kept returning to the human. Tamara was beginning to trust him more. To open up to him. The more he learned of her the more he wanted to know. The more time he spent with her, the more he wanted.

Despite the temperature in the pool, his dick still made an appearance. Just the thought of that female did things to him. Just the thought of peeling her clothes off and tasting all the treasures beneath. There was also the thought of sinking into her tight, wet heat that almost had him coming in their drinking water. Not a good idea.

Thunder forced himself to breathe slowly. He forced his mind away from the lush beauty. Sheep jumping, deer running, his brother's mate pregnant with their first child. Jealousy surged through him. Cloud, dead on the cave floor, smoke billowing from his chest.

That did it.

Thunder needed to get back to bed. He needed a whole lot more rest today. He had to be strong enough by tomorrow. Aside from needing to get the human back to the comforts she was used to, he needed to send that team out just in case Cloud had somehow survived his lightning bolt. Tammy had been right, he'd reacted out of pure self-preservation. The silver wedged in his back and a female to protect, he'd thrown the full force at the other male. Still, there was a chance he still lived and a chance he might come back from whatever dark place his mind occupied. Thunder could hope.

He climbed from the water, his arms shook a little as he took his weight onto them. Thunder shook his head. *Blast, but he was a weakling.* He hated the way it made him feel. At least he had managed to take himself to the bathroom this morning. He joked and teased Tammy but the truth was, he was embarrassed about needing so much of her help. He could not wait to give her a taste of his true strength. To prove to her that he was a strong male. One of the strongest of his kind. Thankfully, such things didn't seem important to her. Not his status and not his power. She seemed to genuinely be interested in him. She had shown him glimpses of herself. Was opening up and starting to trust him. It made him happy and excited and worried and in equal measure. What would Blaze say? It wasn't something he would dwell on now.

After waiting a few minutes to air dry – for the most part at least – Thunder wrapped the blanket around himself. His hair was still damp and he felt a few droplets run down his back. He walked slowly – his top speed at the moment.

It took a while and he was out of breath by the time he made it back. Tammy was throwing logs into the fire. He sat heavily, the mattress dropping under his weight. Then he pulled his legs onto the bed and made himself comfortable.

Tammy was tidying up around the bed. He moved onto his side, tracking her movement. Her presence relaxed him. He enjoyed her company. He could feel himself calm, his heart-rate slow. Yes, a nap was exactly what he needed.

Wait just a second.

Tammy wasn't wearing her sweater. She was in a powder blue t-shirt. Come to think of it, from the way her breasts looked in the shirt, he didn't think she was wearing her coverings either. His gaze settled on the sharp points of her nipples as they speared the fabric. On how her breasts swayed as she walked.

Fuck! His cock twitched. Thunder moved onto his belly and turned to face the other direction. It was the first time she'd taken her sweater off, aside from when she'd bathed. She was right to call him a pervert because he was a pervert. A serious pervert. She really was starting to trust him and starting to relax around him and all he could do was stare at her and imagine what it would be like to slide his hands under her shirt. All he could think of was squeezing her flesh, of sucking on her nipples.

He tried to get comfortable but a hard dick was not conducive to a comfortable position. Or sleep for that matter.

Unfortunately, Tammy moved into his line of vision. She bent over to pick something up. *That ass. Oh, that ass.* It was what dreams were made of. The dirty kind.

Thunder groaned and turned his head to face back the other way. She was such a sweet female and he was such an asshole.

"Are you okay?" Her voice was laced with concern. "Are you in pain?" The bed dipped as she got onto it.

Great! She was in bed with him. It was just the three of them. Him, Tammy and his raging hard-on. He wanted to groan again but knew she would get the wrong idea. Somehow he managed to hold back a low growl as well, one that would speak of his extreme arousal.

He couldn't get the outline of her breasts out of his mind, or her plump nipples, or her sweet heart-shaped ass. He couldn't shake the image of how her hair would looked spilled over his pillow. He was sure her eyes would darken with pleasure as he plunged into her.

"I'm good," he finally managed to croak. "I need to sleep," he added, as he closed his eyes. For the first time he found himself hoping she would leave. That she would go and sit by the fire or . . . just go. Somewhere else, anywhere else. His attraction for her, coupled with his body's need to heal were a powerful combination.

He groaned again . . . softer this time.

"You're so tense," she half whispered.

He jumped when she put her hands on him. *It's just your back, dickhead! This doesn't mean anything. Down boy. She's not coming onto you, so take it easy and calm the fuck down.*

"Wow!" she exhaled. "Really tense." Tammy began to massage his tight muscles. She started at his shoulders. "Your wounds are looking so much better. They're properly closed." Her voice sounded strange. She ran her hands down his back and back up.

Fuck!

His dick throbbed beneath the weight of his body. It wanted freedom. It wanted her.

"How does that feel?" Her voice was soft and tentative.

He grunted a sound of affirmation. It did feel good. Far too fucking good. As far as his body was concerned, it was game on.

"I'm glad, but you're still so tense." Her hands stopped moving for a second. Part of him screamed out for more while another part – the logical, rational part – screamed for her to stop.

"Um . . . it would be easier if . . ." She swung a leg over him and straddled his ass. *Mother fucker!* As in, she put her pussy on him. Granted, said pussy was covered in jeans but still. His mind went into overdrive. His eyes widened and his dick gave a lurch. Her hands were back on him, massaging, kneading. Working some kind of magic. He growled. It couldn't be helped. His chest vibrated something fierce.

By Claw and by Scale. By all that was green and winged.

All he could think of was turning around. Of putting her onto her back and . . . not a good train of thought. Not good at all. She moved to his lower back. Her touch firm and rhythmic.

What the fuck!

He growled again. Softer and lower this time. What was she doing? This felt like . . . this felt . . ."Maybe you should stop," his voice was thick with desire.

"Doesn't it feel good?" Her voice had a nervous edge.

"It feels too damned good. It feels like . . ." he let the sentence die, like she was coming onto him.

Her hands kept moving.

"What's going on?" he had to ask. This wasn't like her. Her MO was to flirt a little and then to run. To fuck the hell out of him with her eyes and then blush just as hard. This was different. This was a definite come on. It had to be.

She gave a deep sigh. "I just . . ." She stopped massaging him, pulled her hands away. After a few more seconds she got off of him and sat next to him instead. "It was a stupid idea."

He looked up at her. Her cheeks were heated. Thunder turned, scrunching the blanket over his dick so that she wouldn't see how seriously turned on he was. Not that she was looking at him. She was looking everywhere but at him. "Were you coming on to me?"

A tiny nod, almost undiscernible. "Um . . . I'm sorry. I shouldn't have. I . . . you . . . me . . . we . . ." She made a groaning noise and put a hand over her eyes. "You said it, we're two adults, I just thought that . . ." She shrugged. "I guess I assumed that you were just as attracted to me as I am to you and . . . it was stupid," she rolled her eyes. "I thought maybe we . . ." she gave a laugh. "Never mind. Forget this happened."

"It's not stupid."

"It was." She pulled a face. "I'm really embarrassed now. I just . . . please forget it." She looked everywhere but at him. Her cheeks blazed. *So damned adorable.* "I'm such an idiot."

He had to fight his instincts, the ones that screamed for him to take her up on her offer and to do so immediately. He could think of nothing better than to strip her naked and to sink into her glorious heat. Of making her come a multitude of times and in a multitude of ways.

He wanted it so badly, he gripped the blanket to stop himself from reaching for her. Tammy scooted to the edge of the bed, a look of embarrassment etched on her face.

"I *am* attracted to you," he growled. "But it's more than just an attraction. I have feelings for you, Tammy."

She sucked in a breath and those stunning eyes met his. "I don't understand why we can't . . ." She narrowed her eyes like she didn't believe his admission. "Let's just forget it okay?"

"I broke a couple of rules when I came after you. The main one being that I shifted. I changed into my dragon form after claiming you. It is grounds for an immediate disqualification."

"I don't know what that means." Her eyes looked so big. Her skin so pale.

"It means that there's a good chance we can't be together. You will most likely be sent home once we return to my lair."

"But that's crazy. You had to shift otherwise you would never have made it in time. You came after me, rescued me." Her gaze was raised to the ceiling in thought. "You had to change." She gave a shake of the head.

"I'm hoping that Blaze will understand and that he will give me permission to pursue this . . . us."

She frowned but nodded. "Okay, well, I'm not sure how I feel about a relationship. You didn't seem interested in me at all, earlier when we were by the fire. Never mind that, I just thought that maybe we would relieve some of the . . . tension . . . you know . . ." She looked down at her hands which were folded in her lap.

"Still jaded?" He gave a smile.

Her frown deepened. "Something like that. I guess I struggle with trust."

"That dickhead really pulled one over on you." He touched the side of her arm, not trusting himself to do any more. "Look," he paused, considering his words carefully. "Let's get back and first ensure that this can actually go somewhere and then we can look at taking the next step."

She gave a nod. "I need to be honest with you. You're not really my type. I'm not sure I want more than just a physical relationship but we can talk about it in a couple of days." She seemed to notice how her admission affected him because she touched his arm, looking worried. "It's not you, it's me . . . I just don't know that I want to take that step with you . . . or with anyone for that matter," she quickly added.

Disappointment was a big, bitter pill to swallow. That asshole had really hurt her. "Well, that's something you need to figure out then because I like you." He grabbed her hand. "I really fucking like you. Don't freak out but it wouldn't take much for me to fall for you. Just in case you misunderstood me earlier, you're exactly my type." He didn't believe her when she said that he wasn't her type. It wasn't him being arrogant. There was definitely something there. It had to come from both sides. She was just afraid. Thunder was sure of it.

She chewed on her lower lip.

Thunder squeezed her hand. "If we get the go-ahead, we can take it slow. One thing is for sure, we are not having a purely physical relationship."

"We're not?" Her cheeks reddened up all over again. Then she shrugged like it was no big deal. "It's probably for the best anyway."

He disregarded the comment. Thunder shook his head. "Don't misunderstand me, I want to be with you in that way. You need to let me know if it's what you want too because I don't want to fall for you and end up hurt. Be sure, Tammy. You need to be very sure."

She nodded. "Okay. I'm really scared though."

"Life isn't always easy. It sometimes takes courage. You need to be willing to take a chance and to be brave. We can do it together."

She wanted to say something else but he put a finger over her lips. "Think on it." Thunder couldn't help it, he leaned forward and kissed her. Her lips were so soft. It took everything in him to pull back, especially when her eyes drifted shut and her breathing kicked up a notch.

A musky scent hit his nostrils. It was a scent he recognized. Adrenaline surged through his veins. His scales scratched beneath his skin and his nailbeds tingled but he was still too weak to shift.

He heard the flap of wings. One pair of wings to be exact.

There was also heavy beating of a beast's heart. A dragon.

No! Fuck no! It wasn't possible. How had Cloud found them? Thunder pulled Tammy behind him. The female had a bewildered look, not sure why he was manhandling her in such a manner.

There was a cracking noise.

"No!" Tammy whispered, as she realized what was happening.

"How touching," Cloud said as he walked towards the foot of the bed. For a moment, Thunder was tempted to leap to his feet. To fight. To flee. To do something – but what could he do against the male?

Remnants of the silver still ran through him. He was still weak. They didn't stand a chance.

"I can see by the look of shock on both of your faces that you thought you had killed me. Sorry to disappoint.

Your aim was off. Not by much, you almost ended me."

"How did you find us?" Thunder asked.

Cloud smiled. "It took me a while to heal and then I followed the trail. Thanks for that by the way. You bled most of the way here."

Thunder felt like an idiot for not realizing that he had bled, that he had left a trail.

Cloud looked about the cave. "Then again, I guess I have myself to thank for making you bleed in the first place. Although, I should have made you bleed a bit more since it took me a day or two to scout the area." His eyes focused behind his shoulder. On the female. His female.

"Don't do this." Thunder had to try.

Cloud locked eyes with Thunder. He had that look about him. Tammy had described it as haunted. It was the best description he'd heard. The male laughed. "If only you had told me that. Don't do it. No. If only, my king." He gave a sweeping bow, a mocking bow. "You didn't say any of those things. You gave your blessing." His face twisted in anguish. That female . . ." he pointed to Tammy and Thunder growled. Cloud ignored him. "Is mine. I will get her with child as soon as possible and take back what was ripped from me. The time for being patient is over."

"I'm so sorry Wind died."

Cloud visibly blanched.

"I should have dissuaded you. I wish I had but, in the end, it wasn't my decision to make. It was yours. Both of yours. You knew of the risks and chose to follow that path."

"Chose," Cloud spat. "It was never a choice. I went to you so that you could tell me that I was being stupid. I had to talk her into it," his voice choked up. "Did you know that? She didn't want to take the drug, but I . . . she wanted it too in the end." His eyes filled with tears and he squeezed them shut for a beat. When he opened them, they were hard and fixed on him. "Childless couples are made to feel inferior. We are made to feel like losers. I am a warrior." He beat his chest. "I didn't feel like one," his voice came out softer. "You," he pointed at Thunder, "made me feel like less . . . like nothing."

"I'm sorry that you felt that way. It was never my intention to make you or any other male – couple for that matter – to feel that way." Thunder wasn't perfect but he had always treated all of his subjects as equals. Yes, they encouraged mated couples to have young but it was a given that not all would manage it. Females were rare, a fertile pair was almost unheard of. He felt sorry for them. He would never ridicule them. Tammy was right, this was the way that Cloud saw things. It wasn't necessarily the truth though. "I should've dissuaded you that day. It is something that I must live with but that was my only form of wrongdoing. At the end of the day, it was ultimately your decision, both you and Wind's decision to go ahead. To take the chance. I'm so sorry that it didn't work out. That the cost was so great. I will do anything to help you through your suffering."

"You can't help me!" Cloud spat, his face red with anger. "You can't bring her back. What you can do is take responsibility for my mate's death and hand over that female," he pointed at Tammy who whimpered, pressing herself against his back, trying to hide away from Cloud.

"She isn't mine to give."

"It's only a matter of time before you win her. The mighty king Thunder. She is mine now." He sniffed the air. "You haven't claimed her fully yet." He smiled. "I'm glad . . . not that it would have made any difference."

"Don't do this, Cloud. I might be weak now, but it won't last for forever. If you take her now, I will end you." He could see that he was not getting through to the male. Cloud was too far gone. Too angry, too sad, too crazy to see things any way but his own way. He was going to hurt his female. Force her into mating him. He would justify his actions to himself.

It wouldn't do much good but he would fight. He had to try to stop Cloud. The male had a bag slung around his shoulder. The strap was loose and the bag rode low on his body. It would pull tight when he changed into his dragon form. He saw a blade sheathed there. A silver edge, he was sure. If only he could get his hands on it, he might just stand a half a chance. He knew the bag would be filled with more weapons as well. Thunder needed to proceed carefully.

Cloud smiled. It was the smile of a crazy man. His eyes turned wild. They even glowed. "Hand her over and I'll let you live."

"I can't do that."

"Suit yourself." He lunged at Thunder, moving almost

too quickly for his eyes to register. *So damned sluggish.* The backs of his fingers touched the handle for a split second. He was too slow.

Cloud backhanded him. It took a moment to register that he was flying through the air. Thunder crashed against the far wall. Pain exploded through his shoulder. The room winked in and out of focus.

Thunder shook his head to try and clear it. He staggered to his feet, trying hard to summon his power. *Too damned weak.* As Cloud came at him, he realized his mistake. Maybe it wasn't too late to change tactics. The other male punched him square in the nose. Blood gushed from the broken appendage. It ran down his throat, feeling hot and thick. He staggered backwards, his back hitting the wall. Screams flooded the cave. Pain flared.

CHAPTER 13

Tammy screamed as Thunder's nose crunched under Cloud's fist. *Blood. Oh Lord but there was so much blood.* It ran down his face. Splattered on his chest. His eyes looked dazed. He staggered backwards, hitting the wall hard with his back but somehow managing to stay on his feet.

"She is mine!" Cloud roared. He clenched his left hand and pummeled Thunder on the side of his head, using his arm like a club.

"Nooooo!" Tammy screamed as Thunder went flying. His body actually lifted off the ground for a second or two. She was sure she heard something else crunch. His jaw maybe. His body crumpled in a heap somewhere in the shadows, she could barely make out his motionless form.

She had to do something. Cloud was going to kill him. "Noooo!" she screamed again, as the shifter pulled a long, sharp looking blade from a sheath in a bag on his back. It glinted in the firelight.

Silver.

Poison.

Deadly.

Thunder wouldn't survive another run-in with silver. She just knew it. He was in no position to defend himself either. She had to help him.

Cloud smiled. The guy was even crazier than she had first thought.

"Let's go," she said. "I'm here and ready to become your mate." She added the last when he didn't look her way.

Cloud's eyes flicked to her for a second before moving back to Thunder.

"Leave him," she shook her head. "We're wasting time."

"I need to make sure he doesn't disturb us again," Cloud growled.

"No!" she cried. "You're wasting time. Come to me." She opened her arms.

Cloud took a step towards her, then another and another. Just when she began to relax, he turned back towards Thunder. A look of pure hatred on his face.

It was then that she realized he would not be able to leave Thunder alive. His feud ran too deep. His madness was taking over. Tammy jumped to her feet, still on the bed. She launched herself on the shifter, landing on his back, her arms around his neck, her legs around his body. "Run, Thunder, run!"

It was hard to tell. The cave was just so dark back there but she was sure she saw movement.

Please get away. Please. "Run!" she shouted as she

tightened her arms. "Leave him alone, you bastard."

"Get off." He tried to peel her off of him but she held on tight. "Let go," he growled.

"Stop this!" she shouted. "Go away. Leave us alone."

"Last chance." He stopped trying to pry her off. "Let go, female, and do it now."

"Fuck you!" she shouted.

Cloud began to walk. It was like she was a tiny, inconsequential bug. It was only at the last second that she realized what he had planned. "No!" she barely managed to get the word out when he slammed her up against the wall.

Pain rushed at her. It ran up the whole of her spine. It blossomed on the back of her head.

He was going to do it again. Maybe this time he would injure her badly. He might even render her unconscious. As it was, lights flashed across her vision. She was halfway to unconscious already. Tammy let go. She slid down his back, landing hard on the ground below. She pulled herself into a ball. Blackness danced on the edge of her vision. Lights flickered in and out. She was sure that it was only the sharp pain that kept her from passing out.

Cloud was moving again.

"No!" she whispered the word. Her lips felt dry. Her mouth felt like it was filled with cotton wool.

There was a bright flash as the light caught the blade. He had it hoisted above his hand, both hands on the hilt. Utter horror consumed her as Cloud brought it down in an arc. He hefted and slashed a second time. This time sparks flared in the dark as the blade hit rock. The blade must have rended flesh and bone. "Nooooooo!" she tried to scream but it came out in a hoarse whisper. *Don't think about it.* Tammy made a squeaking noise. Her whole body felt frozen with disbelief.

"It's done," Cloud growled as he sheathed the blade. "I am your mate now. There is no denying it. No one to rescue you. Accept your fate, female." He closed the distance between then and gripped her by the wrists, hauling her to her feet.

"You bastard." Tears slid down her cheeks. Thunder was gone. *No!* Her throat felt clogged. Her chest hurt. "You bastard!" More firmly as she beat against his chest with her fists. It was like hitting a wall. Then there were scales and claws. Cloud had shifted into his dragon form. He nudged her towards the entrance with his head. She staggered a few steps and fell, stones digging into her side and one of her knees. He growled in her face. His hot, fetid breath accosting her. He nudged her again, harder this time.

Tammy rose wearily to her feet. She realized that she was still crying. She couldn't stop. Using the back of her hand, she wiped the tears away but more took their place. The dragon nudged her and growled more fiercely. She stood back up and he nudged her again. Her head hurt. Her back flared with fresh pain every time he pushed her. At least she was alive.

Poor Thunder!

Her sobs echoed around the cave. She couldn't believe

it. He nudged her again, causing her to take a couple of quick staggered steps in order to stay on her feet. Nudge. Stagger. Nudge. Stagger. When she realized his intention, she tried to dig her heels in, but it was no use. Next thing she was sliding down the incline. Rocks and dirt loose at her feet. Downwards . . . downwards . . . then she was falling. Cloud caught her, her breath catching in her throat as his claws closed around her.

Bastard!

White hot anger burned inside her. It churned and grew. She ground her teeth and looked up at the beast. The strap was tight, a bag flush against his belly. It looked small against his dragon frame. The sword was sheathed next to the bag. It was the same sword he'd used to kill Thunder. More anger flooded her. She reached up and clasped her hand around its hilt.

Tammy swallowed thickly. They had barely left the cave entrance. She looked down. Sweat beads seemed to form across her entire body. This time both fear and anger coursed through her. This was most likely her one opportunity to get away. There might not be another. If she took this opening, there was a very good chance she would die. If she didn't . . .

The other option wasn't even comprehensible. Cloud may have been a good man once upon a time but that was no longer the case. He had killed Thunder. Her throat clogged with emotion. He was going to hurt her. Force himself on her until she became pregnant with his child. She shivered at the prospect of all she would have to endure. A fate worse than death?

No one was coming. It was up to her to save herself. She also wanted to do it for Thunder.

He flapped his great wings and they lifted higher. It was now or never.

Tammy pulled the sword from the hilt. The dragon seemed to tense midflight. Without thinking about it, and with no hesitation, she slashed the blade across his belly. It was much easier than she had expected. Like a hot knife through butter, the knife sliced the beast wide open. Intestines and gore slid from the gaping wound and all over her.

She expected him to let her go. Or to plummet to the ground. Or all of the above. He screeched. The sound so loud it hurt her ears. He did fall a few feet before righting himself. For the next few seconds he continued to flap his great wings like nothing had even happened. Then he began to lose altitude. Down . . . down . . . down . . .

They began to tumble head over tail. Cloud didn't let her go. Not once did his hold falter. Tammy squeezed her eyes shut. Her stomach lurched with each hard roll. Any second now. They were about to hit the ground. There was no way she would survive the impact.

Bang!
Darkness.

CHAPTER 14

Bright light. Pain. Eyes grainy. More pain. Her mouth tasted metallic. Blood. Tammy blinked a couple of times. She wasn't on the ground. She knew this because she was looking down at it. Her brain felt foggy. Her body stiff and sore. She was lying on something soft. Something squishy.

Tammy turned her head. *What the . . . ? Intestines.* Tammy's stomach lurched. She suddenly felt hot and sweaty. She turned to the side, gagging hard. By some miracle she managed to keep her stomach contents down. Maybe she didn't puke because she hadn't eaten. Tammy couldn't remember. *Why was she here? What had . . . ?*

Memories surfaced causing her to moan. Thunder. He was gone. Murdered. The body beneath her shuddered. Cloud was still in his dragon form. He was still alive. She needed to get away. With effort, she managed to move the fingers on one hand and then one of her legs. A couple of minutes later she slid off the dragon, landing on her feet. She managed to stay upright.

Cloud was lying on his back. His eyes were closed. His

wings a broken mess. His body broken and bleeding. He had broken her fall, whether unintentionally or on purpose she did not know. He shuddered again. Blood dripped from the slice across his belly. His innards hung out in great coils. The beast was dying. He had to be. There was no way he could survive this. The fall together with the silver was too much. Tammy couldn't muster any sympathy. She only hoped that he died quickly. No one deserved to suffer.

Her head hurt. Her back hurt. Her chin felt raw. Her knees throbbed. She was covered in blood and slimy stuff that Tammy would rather not think about. It made her feel ill to do so. In short, she was bruised and battered but very much alive. She shuddered to think how this could have ended. She was lucky to have come off so easily. Tammy concentrated on putting one foot in front of the other. It was cold but not as cold as when she and Claire had been hiking together. *The hunt.* It seemed like a lifetime ago. The sun shone brightly warming her back.

Twenty minutes later and she was at the cliff wall. It was just as tall and just as sheer as she remembered. There was no way in hell she would be able to climb this.

She sat down on an outcrop of rocks and put her head in her hands. She wasn't sure why she'd come back. Why was she torturing herself like this? Thunder was gone. Going up to the cave to see his body wasn't going to bring him back. Not that she would make it up there.

She had to try though. What if by some miracle he had survived? What if he was up there broken and bleeding?

She let out a sob and rose to her feet. Tammy gripped the closest rock and looked for a foothold. *There*. She put her foot on the small ridge and hoisted herself up. Then she looked up a few feet, looking for the next handhold. *There*. She stretched up and gripped it. Her hands felt smooth and slippery but she ignored it and gripped tighter. Then she looked down for a higher foothold. *There*. It was tiny but she could do it. She put her foot flush against the rock and pushed up. Both her hand and her foot gave way at the same time and she fell down, managing to stay on her feet. She tried a second and a third time, falling on her ass and landing hard.

Her teeth gnashed together. The grazes on her hands opened up when she used them to break her fall. She pulled her knees up and hugged her legs. Tammy cried with frustration. She cried because she was dirty and hungry and tired and sore. She cried because . . . she was a woman and a woman had a right to cry sometimes, dammit. She cried despite the fact that she would become dehydrated quicker. Right now, she didn't give a shit. She cried because of Thunder. For what might have been. If only she was bolder, she could have told him that she had feelings for him too. It wouldn't have changed things but at least he would have known.

Then she stood herself up and dusted herself off. She was going to give this cliff one more go. Chances were she wasn't going to make it but she had to try. Maybe if she tried a little bit further to the right. There seemed to be more handholds. Maybe this would work better. Tammy shaded her eyes for a second before reaching for the closed ridge of rock.

"You're going to kill yourself!" a voice boomed. It seemed to come from above her. She held her breath for a few seconds. Maybe she had imagined it. She was overly tired or had hit her head harder than she thought.

She reached for the handhold again.

"Don't," an amused growl. *Amused? Really?* "Stay there," the voice boomed again. Closer this time.

She recognized the voice. *No!* Tammy rubbed her temples. She was hearing things.

"I'm on my way down!" Thunder shouted. "Give me a minute. Just stay there."

"Thunder!" she shouted, looking up.

There he was. Naked and climbing down the side of the sheer cliff. He was moving quickly, so gracefully. "You're alive!" she shouted. "Oh, my God!" She covered her mouth and realized that she was grinning. "I can't believe it."

He kept on climbing down. "Cloud didn't kill me," he said as he descended a small outcrop.

"I can see that," she laughed.

His muscles rippled and bulged as he made his way down. His thigh muscles were thick. His ass clenched and released. "I don't understand it," he said, breathing heavily. "He pretended to kill me." He was close enough now for her to make out his facial features. One of his eyes was puffy and his nose was bloody. Thunder grinned. "I think he did it to make you submissive. If you thought I was dead then you wouldn't fight him." His breath continued to come in loud pants, as he continued to descend. When he was about twenty feet from the ground, he let go, landing in a crouch at her feet. "He fucked up."

"Yes, he did."

"He pissed you off." Thunder rose to his full height. "Remind me never to piss you off."

Tammy threw herself into his arms. "You're alive."

He pulled a face and fell back, landing on his ass with a grunt.

"I'm sorry," she laughed when she caught him smiling. "I can't believe you're here."

"And you're . . . a sight for sore eyes. I can't believe you got away." He cupped her cheeks, examining her. "I saw him fall. I was sure . . ." he frowned, his mouth pulling together. His eyes filled with concern.

"I cut him, he's dying," she spoke quickly, looking into those amazing eyes of his. Her heart felt like it was swelling in her chest. "I'm so happy you're alive," she breathed the words rather than said them, her voice hitching at the end. Tammy gripped him tighter around the neck. She leaned forward and pressed her lips to his. She pushed her whole body against his. Against that magnificent chest. Tammy gave a small sob as she thrust her tongue into his mouth. Next, she threaded her fingers through his hair, loving the way it felt between her fingers.

She'd almost lost him. There was so much to say, so much to do. One thing was for sure, she was done with being afraid. Okay, maybe not totally done but close enough.

CHAPTER 15

Her core was pressed against his belly. Her mouth was on his. He deepened the kiss, groaning into her mouth. Her breasts were mashed against him. He loved the feeling of her hands on him, kneading his scalp, pulling softly on his hair. He swallowed up her whimpers and moans. She tasted like he might never get enough of her.

With great effort, he pulled away, putting his forehead against hers. "Hold that thought," his chest rumbled with a low growl. He'd never been more turned on in all his life.

"What . . . ? Why . . . ?" Her eyes were unfocussed, her lips slightly swollen from their kiss. She pushed herself more firmly against him. Rubbed herself against him.

"You need to show me where you left him."

That sobered her up. "He's finished. There is no way he could have survived."

"He was bleeding?" Thunder kept his arms around her. "When you cut him, it was across the belly?"

"How do you know?" She frowned.

"You're covered in blood. If I'm not mistaken," he pointed at the smears of gunk caked to her t-shirt, "that's . . ."

"Don't say it," Tammy wrinkled her nose. "Please, I'll vomit." She touched her cheeks, her eyes wide. "Do I have any on my face?"

Thunder had to work not to smile. "A tiny smear."

She seemed to relax. "Just a smear." She touched her cheek – the one that was covered in dried gore. Her hair on that side was plastered to her scalp. She'd never looked more beautiful.

"You're so damned gutsy and courageous." He closed his mouth over hers for a second. Thankfully, it was one of the only places that wasn't covered in grime. He would've kissed her anyway.

"I did what I had to," she said as he pulled back. She frowned for a moment. "You didn't fight back earlier."

Thunder nodded. "You noticed."

"I did."

"I would've been dead if I had. I couldn't win in my state. I hoped he wouldn't be able to do it. We've always had a strong a friendship. I hoped it would keep him from killing me in cold blood, despite his mental illness, and I was right."

"He was going to hurt me."

"I know." Thunder held her closer, he put his cheek to hers for a moment. The dirty one. He didn't care, he could have lost her.

Tammy was the one to pull back. "I hate to say it." She looked pained for a moment. "It will be better if he is dead."

Thunder felt a deep sadness at the thought of the male

being dead. At the same time, he felt relief. They had grown up together. At one time he had been a good male, one of the best. He couldn't deny it though, Cloud was no longer that male. "I need you to show me where you left him. I need to be sure that he's dead." Thunder struggled to get up, he held Tammy close to his chest as he did. Then he put her down and she almost collapsed.

Blast! His own energy levels were running on low as well. Thunder gripped her tighter. He shouldn't have showed off on the climb down. "I will carry you."

"No way!" She touched his cheek for a moment. "You look really tired." Her eyes darted about his face. "I can walk. It's not too far."

"You sure?"

She gave a nod.

"I can carry . . ."

"I'll walk. I'm fine."

Thunder nodded back, he took ahold of her hand. "Lead the way." He needed to try to preserve his energy. It was difficult to kill a dragon. He doubted Cloud was dead.

"That way," she pointed to a break in the trees a couple of miles down a sloping hill.

"What happened to your blanket?" Her eyes stayed focused on the path ahead.

Thunder gave a grunt. He used one hand to cover his dick. It was still standing at full attention. "The blanket?" Thunder raised his brows. "I guess I didn't even think about it. I hightailed it after you."

She made a snorting noise. "I should've been miles away by now. Too far for you to run. Definitely too far to find me."

He let go of his junk. She'd seen him already. The flush of her cheeks gave her away. As did the hitch in her breathing. The scent of her arousal. Her hard nipples. "I meant what I said earlier. I told Cloud that I would come for you and I would have. I told him I would end him and I would have." He gave her small hand a light squeeze. "Turns out I didn't have to because you're a badass." Thunder shook his head and gave a chuckle.

She gave another little snort. "If you say so."

"I do. It's good to see that you're not afraid anymore."

She looked away, her cheeks burning up. "I'm getting there." She glanced back in his direction, only she didn't look at his face. She looked significantly lower and from under her lashes. His dick hardened up even more. The little human was totally checking him out.

"You can admit that I was right earlier . . ."

Her eyes snapped back to the horizon and she tripped on a loose rock. Thunder gripped her hand a little tighter to steady her. "Are you okay?"

She gave a nod. "Yeah . . . it was easier going up than it is negotiating the way down. I didn't realize this hill had such a rise."

"You didn't notice on your way up because you were so set on getting up that cliff and giving me lip-to-lip to save my life that you—"

She smiled. "It's mouth-to-mouth and I was not. Okay,

maybe I wanted to save your life but . . ."

"Hah!" Warmth flooded him. "I knew it. You like me. Maybe you should start by admitting it along with . . ."

"Fine," she half growled. It was cute on a human. "I've always had a thing for men with big dicks."

It was his turn to trip, only he didn't do it as gracefully. His feet skidded and he landed on his ass. *Damn his weakened state.*

Tammy giggled and put her hand in front of her face. "Are you okay?" she finally managed to get out.

Thunder tried to give her a dirty look and failed. Then again, at least half the looks he gave her were dirty . . . positively filthy. He got back up. They walked in silence for a few minutes. "I call bullshit. My big dick is a serious plus but it isn't the reason you . . . have a thing for me."

"I don't have a thing for you." She glanced up at him before looking ahead. Then she sighed. "Okay, maybe I do have a thing for you. A small thing. Not a big thing."

"And it has nothing to do with my dick?" She had more than just a thing for him.

She laughed. "Hopefully, at some point, it will have a lot to do with that particular piece of your anatomy, but . . . your dick has nothing to do with it outright. No." *Yes! Whoo hooo!* He felt like punching a fist into the air.

"Good." He could scent dragon. That and blood. It told him that they were nearing the site. He pushed Tammy behind him. "We're going to talk about this some more later . . . Fuck!"

"Oh no. I swear he was here," Tammy frowned, her

eyes darting around the clearing. "That looks like blood but maybe it was further over there," she pointed to the right. "Or maybe there." Tammy rubbed her forehead. "I could've sworn."

"You're right. Look at the indentation," Thunder indicated the ground. The blades of grass were bent. The weeds trampled. He walked to the site, bending over to examine the area. His chest throbbed. Thunder was sure that Cloud snapped one of his ribs earlier. Although he was healing much quicker than before, he still wasn't at optimum. There were still traces of silver in his blood. "He bled quite profusely. Those are drag marks," he pointed to gouges in the dirt. "Let's follow the trail." He grabbed Tammy's hand and together they followed the blood and the ripped earth. "He is staying in his dragon form."

"What does that mean?" she whispered.

"It means he's stronger than I had hoped. If he was gravely injured or dying he wouldn't be able to maintain his dragon form. It means he'll heal quicker as well. Let's hope we can find him. Are you okay to walk? I don't want to leave you."

She nodded. "What will you do if we catch up to him?"

Thunder clenched his teeth for a moment. "I should kill him."

"Should?" Her voice was soft. It didn't hold any anger or judgment.

"I should kill him. I *must* kill him. He won't stop."

"No, I don't think he will. You won't be able to kill him unless it's in self-defense though."

"I have to," he growled, picking up the pace. It irked him that Tammy was right. He would have to force himself to act. To take care of the situation and to kill the injured male whether he retaliated or not. Dragon shifters did not do well under incarceration. Besides, Cloud's actions were more than enough to warrant the death penalty. He only wished it could be different.

They continued for another twenty minutes. He noticed that the trail became less and less obvious. The male was already healing, hardly bleeding anymore and walking with more care. He snarled when they reached the banks of the river. The trial ended there.

"What's wrong?"

Thunder stared into the churning current. "He's taken to the water. I would have to track each side to find a point of exit. We wouldn't be able to do it quickly enough and I'm not leaving you. That leaves us with one option."

"I'm all ears." Her eyes were wide. Her face pale. For a second he was tempted to take the easier way. Easy would mean looking over his shoulder. Not leaving Tammy's side for a second. *Mmmmm . . . that he could go for.* It wasn't what he wanted for her though. She was a fiercely independent female who wouldn't take kindly to having him, or a few of his warriors, be her shadow. He also liked the idea of spending more time with her. Thunder wasn't ready to face reality.

"We're going to make him come to us."

"How will we do that?"

"We'll camp out right here," he opened his arms and

let his gaze track the clearing. It was beautiful. By the look in her eyes as she looked around them, he could see that she thought so too. He'd build a shelter, get a fire started and hunt for meat. There was plenty of fresh water.

"He will come . . . of that I have no doubt." Until he did, Thunder would grow eyes in the back of his head. He wouldn't let Tammy know that he was continually looking, watching and waiting, but that's exactly what he would do. When Cloud came, he would be ready for the male.

CHAPTER 16

"You're right," Tammy nodded her head. "He will come. He'll wait until he's strong again and then he'll blindside us."

Thunder flashed those gorgeous eyes her way. "I'm stronger than he is." He bounced his pecs. Not in a flashy elaborate way, but still . . . they bounced. *Boom! Boom!* If she was completely honest, it made her a little short of breath. He flexed his biceps next. Just a tad. Enough for her to notice but not so much that it was over the top. It made her look. It made her really look. Guns that could make a girl drool. Next he flexed his abs. *Boom!* There they were. *So ribbed. So sexy.*

Since her eyes were already looking down, she let them drift even lower. His cock wasn't fully erect anymore, it was back at half-mast. It had gone from being freakin' huge to merely really big.

"You need to stop looking at my dick," he growled. It gave a twitch. "At least for the time being. I need to think."

"Oh, so it's true that a man's brain is connected to his penis. Blood flow can either go to one head or the other, not to both?"

"What? I don't know . . . then again . . . maybe," he sighed. "You're making me lose my train of thought. As much as I would love to have this conversation with you right now, we can't." He kept on cutting her off. She was ready to take the next step. Ready to say to hell with it and jump in head first, but Thunder obviously didn't feel the same. Granted, he was right, this wasn't the right time. "Where were we . . ." his voice brought her back. "I will protect you from Cloud. I'm almost at optimum strength."

"You're forgetting," she paused, "he took that bag of tricks with him. He has all of those silver weapons. His bag wasn't in that clearing. Neither was the sword. It will have fallen close to the crash site."

"He's going to need his weapons," Thunder's voice was filled with such venom she felt a shiver race down her spine. "Every single one of them and more. He won't blindside me again."

❧

Thunder put a finger to his lips. The universal signal to be still. They were perched up in a tree. The branch was wider than many tree trunks she'd seen in her life. They'd been up here a long time, at least an hour by her estimation. Her ass was numb and she was cold – her jeans were drying somewhere back at the river. Thunder had assured her that he knew how to get back there.

She'd washed up earlier. The basics, stuff like cleaning her hair and washing her face and hands. Then she'd scrubbed her jeans. They looked like something from the set of a horror movie. That meant that she was left in her t-shirt and panties. Thankfully the shirt was pretty big. Unfortunately, her legs were unshaven but that didn't stop Thunder from looking at them and groaning. Like they were the best naked legs he'd ever seen. His 'you know what' had hardened up, so he really did find her attractive despite the hairy legs.

A noise from below drew her attention. Thunder put his finger back to his lips and pointed to the right of them. A herd of deer were making their way, one by one, down a trail. Thunder had explained earlier that the trail had been made by animals to get through the forest. They used it regularly to get down to the river to drink, as well as to move around from one grazing area to the next. The deer were bigger than she expected. They were so beautiful. She'd never seen a wild animal up close like this. She held her breath as they walked closer and closer. Her heart beat faster and faster. Her hands felt sweaty. She was no longer cold as adrenaline pumped through her veins. She was tempted to shout out. To warn the poor innocent creatures. Instead, she pursed her lips together.

She glanced up at Thunder who gave her a half smile. It was tender and held apology. He looked back down at the animals which were right below them now.

The next few seconds went by quickly.

Like a whirlwind. Thunder dropped down from the branch. There one second and gone the next. He landed on one of the deer. The rest scattered in a clatter of hooves. There was leaping, clumps of ground were thrown up, animals snorted loudly. The sound of hooves became softer and then disappeared altogether.

She looked down and swallowed hard.

"I'm sorry." Thunder wiped his brow.

She gave it nod. "I understand."

He smiled, his big thighs straddled the dead deer, making it look small in comparison. The poor thing's head was at a strange angle. It took brute strength to kill an animal of that size with only his bare hands. She'd offered her knife to him – it was still in the sheath in the front of her jeans – but he'd refused. He said he preferred to kill with his hands.

"We need to eat," he added.

"I know. I feel bad for the poor thing. It might have been pregnant or someone's mom or someone's dad. I don't know if I'm going to be able to eat it."

Thunder laughed.

"What's so funny?

He jumped to his feet, moving to just below where she was sitting. "This is a female." He pointed at the deer. "She wasn't pregnant and she wasn't lactating. I could scent each individual animal. There were four in the group that were pregnant and one with a calf. There was a young male who will be chased from the herd soon, as he is reaching sexual maturity. There was only one other male. There were two other females that were also not pregnant. This is the older of the three. Her meat will be tougher but at least she has had more of a life."

"Show off," she smiled. "I'm glad you let the younger

animals live. That's really sweet."

"I did it for you. If it was just me, I'd have succulent meat for dinner."

She laughed. "You talk such shit."

Thunder opened his arms. "Whenever you're ready."

"Seriously?" she raised her brows. "You're going to catch me?"

He gave a nod.

"That's really showing off. I think I can climb down." She glanced at the route in question. It looked a lot worse from up here than it had on the way up.

"Just jump already. I'll catch you," Thunder said. She looked at him. "Do you trust me, Tammy?"

'Yes," she half groaned. "I do."

"On three then."

She gave a nod.

Thunder counted down. On three, she slid from the branch and Thunder caught her. "That wasn't so hard, was it?"

She shook her head. Thunder kissed her on her nose and put her down. Then he hoisted the carcass onto his back. "Stay close and let me know if you can't keep up," he gave her a wink.

Such a show off. Tammy rolled her eyes at his retreating back. What a back it was. She'd never tire of looking at his ass either. Thunder stopped walking. "Stop checking me out."

"I . . . it . . ." she sighed. "Fine," she huffed. "It's just that I thought I saw something walking on your back. A spider, or a bug or something."

Thunder laughed. It was a rich, deep sound. "There are a lot of those in the wilderness."

"There sure are." Her eyes were back on his ass. She was a pervert. A total pervert. Thunder had turned her into one. She'd never found a guy more attractive. Not even Chris had had this effect on her. It excited her but it also scared her. Terrified her, but Thunder was right. She needed to be brave.

Tammy bit the last piece of meat off of the stick she was holding and threw it into the fire. "Oh my gosh!" She leaned back against the tree behind her. "That was the most delicious meal I've ever had. As in ever. I swear . . ." She looked over at Thunder who had just taken a bite out of one of the chunks of meat on his make-shift skewer. "You could take me to a fancy French restaurant and feed me five courses of food that look more like canvasses than meals and I would still prefer old-age deer."

Thunder chuckled. "It didn't take much to convince you to eat it."

"Are you kidding me, just hearing the fat sizzle as it dripped in the fire and smelling that wonderful scent of cooking meat . . . there was no way I could say no."

"Even after watching me gut it and helping me cut it up?" He smiled and took another bite.

She grabbed her stomach. "Don't remind me. I didn't love that part of the whole thing."

"You did well, Tammy." Thunder threw his stick into

the fire and rubbed his hands together. Then he turned his eyes on her and her breath froze in her lungs, despite the heat of the fire.

"What is it?" Her voice had turned husky. *Not now voice. It isn't what it looks like.*

"I'm trying to remind myself why we need to wait. We're next to an open fire, under a blanket of stars and you're the most beautiful female I've ever seen."

"You are too charming for your own good." Her chest still tightened at his words. He looked so sincere. "Um . . . we need to wait because we might not be allowed to be together and I'm a scaredy cat." Her voice had dropped about a hundred octaves. *Okay, maybe not that many but close.* "Because we're being stalked by a crazy guy, maybe even right at this very minute." She tried to look into the darkness that surrounded them but couldn't see a thing.

Thunder chuckled. "I am on my guard. Cloud won't get to within a half a mile of us. My senses are restored and I'm almost at optimal strength. You cut him with a silver blade, he will not be faring nearly as well. I think we have a day or two before we need to worry."

"Well that's one less thing then," she tried to smile but her muscles felt tense. Even the ones on her face.

Thunder looked really serious. "Sex would be a really bad idea."

"Yes, it would."

"When I asked you earlier if you were still afraid, you said you were getting there. How are you feeling now? Any changes?"

Her heart beat a little faster. *Was he suggesting . . . ?* "I wish I could say differently but I guess I'm still a bit afraid. More open to the idea of something but not quite there."

"You still think I'm going to hurt you?"

"You have a ton in common with my ex," she paused, watching as his eyes darkened. "Let me explain. Chris is very good-looking, he is hands-down the most charming guy I've ever met. At least, he was before I met you. I think that if he could wink and have the same effect as a wink from you, he would develop a tic he'd do it so much. Anything to be the center of attention and to get his way. I met him and fell hard, we were living together within a month. It was all too quick. It turned out he was a huge dick. So, I clearly am a really bad judge of character. I can't trust myself to make the right decisions when it comes to men."

"I remind you of him," Thunder's voice came out sounding flat. There was an underlying anger.

"Let me finish," she turned so that she could face him. His jaw was clenched. His eyes blazing. "You're even better looking. Way more charming and without even trying. All of those things pissed me off so badly. My attraction to you pissed me off even more . . . and don't get me started on the wink. It makes me feel weak in the knees. I never thought I would ever fall for a guy who uses his eyeballs as a means to flirt."

"You don't like my wink?" He looked distraught.

"I love your damned wink. You might be sexy and charming but you're also nice. You're sweet. You care,

Thunder. You're not the kind of guy who would fuck around while in a relationship."

"He fucked around on you?" A muscle in Thunder's jaw ticked and his biceps bulged as his body tensed. Oh, and those muscles on the sides of his neck pulled tight as well. Not that she was checking him out right now or anything. This conversation was too important for that.

She nodded. "Yup. I left for an appointment which cancelled ten minutes after leaving the office and ended up walking in on them," she swallowed hard, still feeling pissed off after all this time. Once thing she did notice though was that although she was still angered by his indiscretion, she was no longer upset by it. "He was fucking *our* PA on *my* desk. *My* damned desk. He didn't even have the decency to use his own. That was the kind of selfish prick he was. He couldn't believe it when I ended the relationship." She exhaled sharply. "In the end, he agreed that we would continue our working relationship. I helped build that agency," she tried not to sound bitter and failed. "We had a good thing going. I was about to be made partner in the business, or so I naïvely thought. I don't think he ever intended to give me that partnership." She realized that she was clasping her hands tightly in her lap and forced herself to let go.

"What happened? I have a feeling it wasn't good. He changed the lock on the door or fired you."

"Worse." She felt the humiliation flood her body. "I was arrested the next morning for theft and taken to the police station in my pajamas. They put me in handcuffs."

"What did the fucker do?"

"He staged a break-in at our offices. Made it look like I was the one who had broken in . . . or let myself in as was the case. You see, he and I were the only ones with a key. Whoever had trashed our offices let themselves in. Moreover, the security guy on duty swore that he saw me arriving and leaving three quarters of an hour later. Chris must have paid him off. The footage from our CCTV cameras had been mysteriously deleted. The police were suspicious because of the open and shut nature of the case but there was nothing they could do about the overwhelming evidence against me."

"What happened? You said that you were arrested for theft, what was supposedly stolen?"

She clenched her teeth. If she saw Christopher in the street, she would probably end up being arrested for assault. She knew without a doubt that she wouldn't be able to stop herself from punching him in the face. "Five thousand dollars was missing from the safe. He and I were the only two people who knew the code for that safe and I sure as hell didn't steal a cent."

Thunder growled low, his eyes were glowing slightly.

"I was lucky enough to have the charges dropped," she made her voice sound overly light. "But first, I had to agree to pay the money back and pay for the damages."

"I hope you told him to go and fuck himself."

She shook her head. "I wish, but I didn't have a leg to stand on. My lawyer advised me to take the deal. She said I would end up in jail if I didn't."

"Motherfucker."

She nodded. "I've never met a bigger dick in all my life." She choked out a laugh. "Although in his case it's about this big." She put up her pinky finger. "In that regard, you guys have nothing in common."

Thunder didn't so much as crack a smile. "Yet, I remind you of him."

She widened her eyes for a second. "Weren't you listening to a thing I said? Chris had a couple of really good qualities. Not many, but a couple. You have those qualities and it's what made me nervous of any kind of relationship with you." She squeezed her eyes shut. "It sounds really stupid saying it but I was afraid. I still am, although not nearly as much. You are nothing like Chris in ways that count. You're too sweet, too kind. You have a fantastic sense of humor. I enjoy being with you . . ." She paused for a second. *Be brave, Tammy. Be brave dammit.* "I would like nothing more than to see where this goes. To take a chance and risk my heart on us . . . on you . . . but we need to take it slow. I rushed head-on once and it was a mistake."

"You are in safe hands . . . I would never let anything happen to you. We can take this very slow. Slower than slow. Now," his eyes narrowed onto hers before dropping to her lips, "come here." He touched his lap. His very naked lap. "I want to touch you," His voice was thick.

"Um . . ." She moved closer, kneeling next to him so that they were facing one another. "I thought we were going to wait. You wanted to be sure . . ."

"Fuck being sure." He pulled her onto his lap. "I won't let Cloud or Blaze or anyone else take you away from me. Just let them try. I'll fight for you." He pressed his lips to hers. Soft, warm and insistent. She pushed herself against him, thread her fingers through his hair.

He felt wonderful, glorious, amazing. "Are you sure about this?" She could hear the hesitancy in her voice.

"Yes." He kissed her again. "Do you want me, Tammy? I sure as hell want you."

She pulled back so that she could look into his eyes. They'd almost died today. There was no way she wasn't doing this.

She nodded, looking down at his lips. Such kissable lips. "Yes." A sigh.

"Good." His hands cupped her breasts and she moaned. So did he. *Oh shit!* She remembered something important, something she would sooner forget. He didn't need to know. He would never find out. She had to tell him. Tammy pulled back.

"What's wrong?" His eyes were glazed over. They were so filled with desire that she was tempted to ignore the voice inside her head but she couldn't.

"There's something I have to tell you."

"You can't wait to scream my name?" He smiled and tried to kiss her.

"No, that's not it." She moved back so that he couldn't reach her. "It's really important."

"You," he gripped her hips, "enjoy multiple orgasms?"

"I've never had a multiple . . . no, that's not it. It's really serious, Thunder."

"Serious," he frowned. "Mmmm . . ." Then he grinned. "You have a really small, really tight pussy and you're afraid I'm going to hurt you?"

"You need to be serious."

"I am being serious. You are small and tight but I will fit . . . I promise. I'll hit both your G-spots and you'll love every minute. I'll make sure of it."

She frowned. "Women only have one G-spot."

He shook his head and made a sound of disgust. "Human males have no idea what the hell they are doing. Then again, most of them don't have the tools to reach that second one." His gaze dropped back to her lips.

She was speechless for a moment. Her mouth opened and closed. She really wanted him to prove that she had a second G-spot. Hell, she'd be happy if he proved she had just one of the things. She sighed. "I need to tell you something really important. I'm a really bad person and I'm so sorry. I feel terrible." She felt sick to her stomach.

"What are you talking about?" He cupped her cheek with his big hand. "You're not a bad person. Not even close."

"I am. Once you hear what I have to say you won't want anything to do with me."

"I seriously doubt that." He put his hand back on her hip and gave a squeeze.

"I'm just as bad as the woman from the last hunt. The one you sent packing."

She saw his lip twitch but he thankfully didn't laugh.

"Not a chance. I don't believe it."

"I am." She felt her eyes sting but blinked away the tears. Tammy looked down and spotted his very long, very thick erection. *Oh God!* She quickly looked up at the sky. *Wow! The stars were amazing.* Time to man up and confess. She looked at him dead-on. "I'm also a money grabber. The only reason I agreed to be in the program was for the money. I'm so sorry." She covered her face with one hand. "I haven't been able to find work in my industry. Not after what Chris did. Everyone believes him. They think I'm an office wrecker and a thief. I can barely make ends meet. I cleaned out my savings paying the bastard back for money I never stole," she sobbed. "I joined the program hoping to make a quick buck. I never once thought I'd meet a great guy, that I would meet you. I was . . ."

Thunder shook beneath her. His body jerked and vibrated. She was too scared to look at him. He was so angry he was shaking.

"Tammy," his voice sounded strained.

She had to face him. She looked up. His eyes were twinkling and he was smiling . . . scratch that, he was laughing. He was laughing hard.

"What's wrong with you? I just told you how I used you for money . . . cash. I wasn't here to fall in love or to find a mate. I was here for the daily allowance I was promised. I'm just like that other girl."

"You are nothing like her." In a quick move that had her breath catching, he turned her so that she was on her back and so that he was between her legs. Every delicious inch of him. This was no time for noticing things like the fact that his hard-on was pushing against her clit.

"I am exactly like her. I'm a horrible person."

"Are you here for the jewelry?"

"What jewelry?" His eyes were beautiful. His mouth, oh that mouth.

"That's my point exactly." She wanted to say something but he put his finger over her mouth. "I have lots of jewelry."

"Dragon shifter men wear jewelry? That's really strange but I guess I can deal."

He frowned deeply. "No. They are family heirlooms passed down from my mother and grandmother. They will belong to my mate one day."

"Oh. I see."

He looked at her throat and then inspected one of her hands, before inspecting the other. "You don't wear jewelry?"

"I'm not much of a jewelry person."

He smiled.

"But that doesn't mean that I'm not a money grabber."

"Do you like designer clothes and shoes?"

"I might," she shrugged. "I've never owned any so I wouldn't know."

"Are you telling me that you'd shell out a couple of thousand bucks for a bag?"

"Hell no! What a waste! That doesn't mean I didn't come here for the money though."

"You were also very honest about not being here to

find a mate and about being jaded in the love department. If I can recall," he raised his eyes. "You pointed that out to me almost immediately. You didn't want to mislead me."

She shook her head.

"When we get back to my lair, I'm writing you a check for the time you spent here. I'm paying you double what you were promised as a daily allowance, you deserve it."

"No way!" she yelled, even though he was right in front of her. "Don't you dare even think about it."

"Why not?" His brows pulled together.

"Because everything has changed. It wouldn't be right. I can't take your money now."

Thunder smiled. "I rest my case. You are the best. Is there anything else you need to tell me?"

"I take it you're not mad?"

"Not even close. Was there anything else? Because I would like to make love to you under the stars." Then he frowned. "Actually," he looked pained. "I'm going to fuck you first. It was a long couple of days holed up in that cave and I thought I lost you today." His chest heaved against her. "I promise to make love to you right afterwards though."

"Okay, I can live with that." She swallowed thickly. Her core tightened with need.

"Let's get you out of these clothes." His face had a pinched look. "Before I rip them." By the intense look in his eye, she could tell that he wasn't joking.

He helped pull her t-shirt up. It snagged on her head.

"Fucking hell!" Thunder growled.

Tammy squealed as his hot mouth closed over her nipple. "I've been dying to get my mouth on you." He thrust up against her, his erection snagging her clit. She moaned some more. Then she realized that the shirt still covered her face so she pulled it the rest of the way off. It was just in time to see Thunder suck on her other nipple. "So damned plump," he growled.

"Fuck!" he mumbled before sucking on each nipple one after the other, like he wasn't sure which one he wanted more.

Thunder cupped her between the legs, stroking her through her pants which had long since dried. "Holy hell," she managed to choke out between moans. It had been a long time. Normally when things got a little . . . tense, she'd take care of herself. It wasn't something she'd had a chance to do in a while though and things had been really, really tense inside that cave. He rubbed her some more, doing a stellar job considering she was wearing jeans and panties. Her moans grew louder. She was going to explode and really soon. She couldn't wait to come. Couldn't damn well wait. Rub, *yes,* rub, *yeeeees,* rub . . . Then he stopped to unbutton her jeans.

"I hate you!" she growled. "Hate. You." She was breathing heavily. "So much!" she added when she caught his smirk.

"Were you about to come?"

"You know I was." *Asshat.* He certainly smiled like he knew it had been about to happen. Like he'd stopped on purpose.

"I'll need to make it up to you." He pulled her jeans and her underwear off. "I'm not going to get you off dry-humping instead of on the end of my dick. I want to be inside you the first time we come. Also, we'll come together."

First time.

She flooded with wet. As in, if she'd been wearing panties, they'd be soaked.

His eyes stayed on hers. "Are you good with that?"

"Yes, good." She licked her lips. "Really, really good."

His cock jutted from between his thighs. Thunder gave her a feral grin before positioning himself between her legs. "I won't hurt you," his voice was deep.

She nodded. She could feel him hot and heavy between her legs. Right there. *Oh god!* She'd never been so turned on. Never wanted anything more.

"I promise I'll fit," another deep rumble.

"I know. Please just . . . please . . ." He pushed into her, stealing her words. Stealing her mind. "Wait! Stop."

He pulled out. There were sweat beads on his forehead. He was so turned on he looked angry. "What is it? Are you okay?"

"What about a condom? I haven't been taking my pill and it's a bit too soon for a baby, don't you think?"

"I would scare you if I answered that question," he paused.

Did that mean that he wanted a baby with her? It more than likely did. She waited for the panic to set in. For that icy fist of fear to tighten around her insides but it didn't happen. All she felt was warm all over at the prospect. What the hell was happening to her? It was too soon for feelings like these. That little voice inside her whispered that she was going to get hurt but she ignored it. *Be brave!*

"You're not in heat. You won't fall pregnant."

"Are you sure you don't have a condom on you?" she smiled. It was a stupid joke to make at a time like this. Roxy had mentioned that shifters could scent if a woman was ovulating. They couldn't give each other any diseases but it was ingrained in her to have the guy wear a condom. She'd never had sex without one before.

"Oh shit!" He fake-slapped his forehead. "I totally forgot, I keep a strip tucked into my ass for times just like this one." Thunder looked completely deadpan, then he grinned.

If she wasn't so turned on, so close to coming, she would have laughed. "I trust you," she whispered, then leaned up and kissed him. "We don't need a condom."

"You sure?"

She nodded, tightening her thighs around him.

"Very sure?" He circled her clit with the tip of one of his fingers. Tammy bit down on her lower lip and nodded. Thunder pushed back into her.

Lord up above. Lord! Oh God! Her hips rocked up like they had a life of their own. He moved slowly at first, carefully nudging his way in deeper with each stroke. He rested his weight on his forearms which were on either side of her head.

Her mouth hung open and her breathing was ragged. When he pushed all the way in, she whimpered. Another stroke and she mewled. Then she moaned. Then she mewled again.

"You feel amazing," he whispered it into the shell of her ear. Goosebumps popped up . . . everywhere. He was moving fast now. In and out in quick succession. Hard and yet controlled.

Oh. My. God.

Using one arm, he lifted her thigh higher. Much higher. "Oh God!" she choked out. Everything began to tighten. Every part of her body. Even her hair follicles. Everything and everywhere and all at once. "I love you! Fucking love you!" she shouted, as she went over the edge. After that, she couldn't talk, couldn't move or think, she could only feel.

Thunder groaned, his body jerked against her a couple of times. His movements slowed, his thrusts became more circular in motion. "I'm so glad you love me because being inside of you is my new favorite pastime."

Oh shit! She hadn't actually said that aloud had she? Damn, she had. She wished she could take it back.

CHAPTER 17

Her cheeks turned pink. She chewed on her lower lip for a beat and even squeezed her eyes closed.

So sexy. So his. Thunder had to stop himself from saying *mine*. Except he wouldn't say it as much as he would growl it or snarl it so he kept his mouth shut.

"You know I didn't mean it like that, right?" She spoke quickly, her eyes wide. "I told you earlier that I hated you so that was just . . ."

"You can stop the cover-up. I know you meant it."

She narrowed her eyes. "I didn't. I totally didn't . . ." Her cheeks went from pink to red.

"Mmmmm." He kissed her nose. "Just like you weren't snuggling up to me on purpose."

"I wasn't," she huffed. "I was asleep."

"I'm teasing you."

Tammy had her mouth open and a finger pointed at him which was some feat considering he was still on top of her. Still inside of her. His favorite place on the planet. He hadn't been joking about that. She closed her mouth and frowned. "You are so full of shit."

"You love it, just like you love me."

Her eyes widened and she sucked in a breath.

"I'm joking. Relax already." He nuzzled into her neck, kissing her on that sensitive patch of skin somewhere halfway between the base and her ear.

Tammy moaned. He loved the sound of her pleasure.

"One thing is for sure." He began to move, thrusting slowly.

Tammy pulled her legs up higher, she grabbed his ass and squeezed. "What's that?" Her voice was husky and breathy. "Oh God!" she moaned as he thrust a little harder.

"You're sleeping on top of me tonight and there will be plenty of cuddling. Even more snuggling and it will be on purpose."

She giggled, the sound quickly morphed into a moan. "I would love some purposeful cuddling with you," her voice was strained.

Thunder changed the angle of penetration, sure to hit both G-spots. Tammy made a mewling noise that drove him insane. She dug her fingers into his ass and ground herself up against him. He thrust back into her snug, wet pussy and she arched her back. *Fuck!* Sweat beaded on his brow. He kept his thrusts slow and steady, sure to hit those spots each and every time. He pulled back so that he could watch her. Her eyes were closed, her head back, her mouth was parted. Her breasts were moving in sync with their bodies. Bouncing even though she was on her back. Her nipples were dark and so damned plump. He groaned, trying to hold it together. She was the sweetest, sexiest female he had ever seen or been inside of. She felt so damned good. So right.

"Oh wow!" she moaned. "Oh wow!" All breathy. "I'm going to come again." She swallowed hard. Her eyes only managed to half focus on him. "Again." She said the word with such awe. He wasn't nearly done with her. Not even close.

"Do it," a low growl. He forced himself to keep the tempo slow. "Come for me."

Her pupils dilated. "Oh yes. Yeeeees." He could feel her pussy start to flutter around him. Her flesh sucked him even deeper. His own balls pulled up as she gave a long drawn out moan. She grit her teeth as she fell apart underneath him, on him.

Her wet sheath closed around him, soliciting a groan from him. She cried out as her pussy began to spasm. Thunder couldn't hold off any longer. He allowed the sensations to roll through him, to consume, but not entirely. He had to keep his wits about him. Being with her like this still rocked his world even if he couldn't completely let go. Not whilst watching out for Cloud. He growled her name, having to stop himself from proclaiming his love for her, even though he felt it so deeply that it was no joke.

Mine. He drew her closer, kissing her neck, trying hard to catch his breath.

"I do have two G-spots," she said, looking shocked. "And I think I might be addicted to sex."

"Good." He continued to kiss and lick. "Because I'm addicted to you and we're going to have a lot of sex."

The next day . . .

She stroked his chest, drawing lazy circles around his pecs. Tracing every indent of his abs. It felt incredible. Tammy felt incredible "How are you feeling? Maybe we shouldn't have stayed up quite so late." She sneaked an upwards glance. There was a smile on her face. "Four times was maybe going a little bit overboard. You are still healing."

"You didn't seem all that worried at the time."

"I couldn't really string much of a sentence together."

He couldn't help himself, Thunder smiled. "'Oh my God! You are fucking amazing! I'm about to come' are considered to be sentences."

"Smartass." She gave his chest a light slap.

"Careful. Slapping is considered to be foreplay."

Tammy giggled. "Everything is considered foreplay."

He had to chuckle. "You're catching on."

Her eyes glinted in the morning light. "So," she rested her chin on his chest, looking up at him. "How are you feeling?"

"I'm perfect." He cupped her butt cheeks and groaned. "You have an amazing ass."

"Thank-you. When you say perfect, do you mean perfect as in back to normal?"

"Yup." He rubbed his hand up and down her spine. "I'm back to normal." He was nearly there on his own steam but the sex had certainly helped.

"Do you still think we need to wait here to see if Cloud makes an appearance?"

He nodded. "Yeah, I do. Silver or no silver I will crush him." He moved to a sitting position, taking her with him. "You need to get out of the way if he shows up . . . when he shows up. Run, hide and don't look back. The only thing he can use against me is you." He cupped her cheek. "I'll come for you once it's over."

She nodded, looking really afraid. "I think it would be better if we went back. There would be safety in numbers."

"I don't want to run or to hide. I need this to be over. Besides, I want to spend a bit more time with you before we have to face reality."

"I'm sure they'll understand. Blaze is about to become a father. He's also in love . . . I mean, he's in love." Her smile looked like it was fixed on her face. All the color drained from her face.

Also. She'd said also.

Thunder wanted to hug her, kiss her, agree wholeheartedly with her but his female wasn't ready to admit her feelings yet. It didn't matter that she'd let it slip, that he knew deep down she felt the same way he did. She wasn't ready for such a major confession. There was still a part of her that was afraid. She'd only just agreed to date him. To giving them a chance. As much as he wanted to say something, he didn't. "I don't think Blaze being in love and mated will help. He's a tough son of a bitch. He is strictly by the book. I've never known him to bend a single rule."

Tammy started to say something but stopped herself. "You might be pleasantly surprised."

"I hope so." He tucked some loose strands of hair behind her ear. "I really fucking hope so. I'm not looking forward to going up against him, or punching him in the mouth, but I will if I have to."

She visibly relaxed. "I'm going to bathe in the river."

"The river gets deep quickly and there are vicious undercurrents. Let me find a spot for you. I'll be back in a minute." He dropped a kiss on her mouth before standing up. Thunder took a short walk up the bank until he found an alcove.

He made his way back, almost falling on his ass when he spotted her. Her legs were long for a human. Her t-shirt stopped just below her ass. Her breasts were outlined against the thin fabric. He was so far gone it was scary.

Her gaze immediately zoned in on his cock. Tammy was the most responsive female he'd ever fucked.

Fucked . . . with her even fucking wasn't really fucking. He still felt it deep. His thoughts drifted to the night before. The first time had been fucking, the second was making love, the third was definitely fucking. Once Tammy got onto all fours, it was game over for him. If he hadn't strummed her clit he would've come before her and that wasn't acceptable. The fourth was so slow and sweet, he'd worshipped her body. He'd drawn out her pleasure for a very long time. She was shaking when he finally let her fall apart.

He was afraid she might be feeling a bit tender this morning. He hoped to God he was wrong. By the greedy look in her eye, he was feeling more hopeful by the second.

"I'll wash your back," he murmured, his dick hardening up some more at the thought.

She gave a gentle shake of the head. "You're incorrigible. I'm sure you will."

"It's so you don't wash away in the current."

"If you say so."

"I mean it." He took hold of her hand. "I found a safer spot, just up this way," he paused for a moment and then sniffed at the air. No sign of Cloud.

The trees were enormous. They thinned out closer to the river. The grass was about knee high. There were plants here and there between the grass, they had the most beautiful purple flowers. Every so often, a plant with a red flower peeked up above the undergrowth.

They stuck to the bank, which was strewn with pebbles. The actual river bed looked like it was made up of them. The water was clear as crystal. "It's so beautiful out here. It's not as cold though. The weather is milder somehow." She frowned.

"Yeah, you're right. We're in Water territory. The Air kingdom is higher up in the mountains. It's colder up there." They continued to walk.

"I've always liked winter. There's something about the

snow and the chill in the air. I love how your breath fogs, and sitting by the fire."

"Don't forget toasting marshmallows and cuddling up to your lover."

She knocked her shoulder against his. "Sounds good to me."

"The air might be warmer but the water is freezing cold." He stopped walking and pointed to the alcove. "We're here."

"It doesn't look all that cold but I know it is." She smiled. "I may not have gotten all the way in but I washed in there yesterday, remember?"

He gave a nod.

"In and out." She slapped her hands together. "I can wash quickly."

He made a sound of affirmation. "We don't have any towels though but I'm sure we can make a plan."

She liked the sound of that. "I'm sure we can." She'd never been with someone as skilled as Thunder. He knew exactly what he was doing. She realized that it probably meant that he had been with a ton of other women, but it wasn't something she wanted to dwell on.

"Oh, we'll make a plan alright . . ." he didn't finish his sentence because she'd pulled the t-shirt over her head. His eyes zoned in on her boobs. He seemed to study them with such intensity. *Don't cover up. He's seen you naked. He's been inside you. Stop being an idiot.* Then he dropped his gaze down to her belly and to the overgrown landing strip between her legs before moving back to her breasts. He growled, seeming to like what he saw. Maybe. She hoped. *Oh God!*

Tammy knew it was stupid but she used an arm to cover her boobs anyway. She felt like an idiot but couldn't help herself. A guy like him had to be used to perfect women. "They're not as perky as they were. My best asset and they're . . ."

"Fucking amazing. I could stare at them all day."

She shook her head, feeling more self-conscious than ever before. It wasn't like her. She normally didn't care about such trivial things . . . *But look at him. Just look.* The guy was gorgeous. Beyond hot. "I wish. You shouldn't be able to hold a pencil under your boobs." She lifted one of her breasts, dropping it again. Oh flip, her boob actually wobbled like jelly.

"Fucking amazing!" He seemed to really mean it but maybe he was just being nice.

"Stop saying that. I could probably smuggle an entire pencil case under these babies."

"They're soft." He cupped them. "So damned soft," his voice croaked. "I love how they move when I'm inside of you. They'd look fantastic around my dick." She swallowed hard, feeling a zing between her legs. Another one deep inside her.

"So responsive. You like the sound of that?"

"I like your dirty talk. I always thought it would turn me off, I was so wrong." Oh so very wrong. It turned her on in a big way.

"You've never had a guy tell you like it is before? Open

and honest?"

"Raw and uncut?"

He grinned at her. "Yeah, raw and uncut."

"I guess not, but I like it."

"Good because there's a lot more where that came from." He gripped her waist and ushered her backwards a few steps. "How about, when we're done bathing."

"Yeah." His eyes looked like they darkened, her own breathing definitely picked up a few notches. She couldn't believe how ready she was for another round.

"I'll lick you dry." He walked her backwards a few more steps, until her feet hit the edge of the water. She sucked in a sharp breath. "Told you it was cold. I have a feeling that your pussy is going to be extra wet for me, despite the frigid temperature. It'll be in need of a ton of licking."

Her heartrate picked up. "Oh really now?" She raised her brows. *He was going to go down on her?* Chris had never gone down on her.

"Yeah, really. I have a feeling I'm going to love the taste of your wet pussy."

Holy hell! Holy freaking hell. All of a sudden, she felt really hot and a lot wet. He walked her backwards and her eyes widened as the water rose on her legs. Maybe not so hot after all.

He winked at her. "It's better to get it over with." Thunder let her go and dove in. It didn't seem to affect him at all.

He surfaced and swiped his hair back. "Come on." He opened his arms.

Tammy had her arms around herself. She gave a nod and slid in. It felt like the air froze inside her for a moment and then she yelled. "Oh my God, it's freezing!" Tammy estimated that she would only be able to handle this temperature for a minute or two and got to work. She dropped below the surface of the water. Her hands worked frantically, rubbing her scalp. She groaned as she resurfaced.

Thunder was back under, she couldn't see him. She washed all over, breathing like she was in a Lamaze class. The water was just that cold.

His arms banded around her and he surfaced in front of her. "Better?"

"Much." Her teeth were chattering and her nipples were freezing off.

He pulled her close, his heat warming her.

"Put your legs around me and hold on," he whispered into her ear, making her shiver and this time not from the cold.

She did as he said. Thunder was rock hard against her. Tammy pushed her chest against him, sighing as more of his heat bled into her. "You're not cold at all, are you?"

He walked out of the river. "Not even a little bit." His hands were on her ass. He paused, seeming to scout the area. She'd noticed that he did that a lot. He was probably keeping an eye out for Cloud. Then he turned his gorgeous eyes onto her and she couldn't think of anything but him. "Are you okay?"

She liked how concerned and careful he was with her.

Always checking to make sure she was happy. "I'm great." Even though she was wet, she was warm.

"Good." He walked for a few beats before putting her down on a mossy patch under one of the enormous trees. It was soft against her back, reminding her of the bed he had made for them last night. The snuggling had been amazing. Even though she'd only worn her t-shirt, she hadn't been cold at all.

Thunder stayed between her legs. "You're so wet." His eyes tracked her body. Droplets clung to every inch of her. Just like they did to him. His hair was sopping. Even his eye lashes held droplets of moisture. In short, he was so incredibly hot. By the way he was looking at her, eating her up with his eyes, he must feel the same about her. "I promised to lick you dry."

"You did," her voice was breathless.

Thunder started at her neck, slowly moving his way to her collarbones. By the time he reached her breasts she was arching her back. He nipped at her nipples. It felt so good. She'd never realized how good teeth against skin would feel. Her hands dug into his scalp.

He moved lower and lower. "Open your legs wider," Thunder growled. He stared at her between her legs. "I think I might be in love with your pussy."

More dirty talk. Tammy was resting on her elbows, her chest heaved. She watched as he lowered himself. Closer and closer. "So damned wet," Thunder licked his lips.

Tammy was wriggling. She couldn't help it. Thunder looked up at her, he gave her a feral grin and then lapped at her slit. Tammy grit her teeth. *So good!*

Then he closed his mouth over her clit and sucked. He sucked on her some more and Tammy groaned. He had been right about the whole clit sucking thing. She groaned again.

"I'm going to finger fuck you now," he mumbled against her clit.

"Okay," breathy and high-pitched.

Thunder moaned against her clit. "Delicious. I could eat you out all day." Another rumbling groan. The vibrations hit her clit and her eyes widened. He slipped a finger inside her and licked on her clit.

Tammy moaned, her breath was coming in solid pants. Thunder was sliding his finger in and out. He seemed to be rubbing up against the wall of her channel. She couldn't be sure because it all felt so good.

His mouth, his finger . . . make that two fingers. She began to rock against his hand and mouth. Couldn't help it. He gave her clit a nip and she gave a hard yell. "Oh God!" It had felt really good.

"Like that?" He lifted his face. His mouth was wet. It took a moment to realize that he was talking to her. His fingers still pumped into her. She could hear how wet she was as they slid in and out of her.

"Yeah," she choked out.

"A human who likes biting, I think I might be in love." She didn't have a chance to dwell on his words because he nipped her again, his teeth quickly replaced by his mouth. He gave a hard tug on her clit and then another. His fingers pumped.

That was her. Over and out. The end. Her back bowed, she made the most god awful noise as the rush hit. He kept up the onslaught, making her stay up there for a long damn time before finally slowing so that she could come down.

When she eventually came back to her senses, her throat hurt from the groaning. Her breathing was so heavy that she thought she might hyperventilate. She had her legs closed around Thunder's head. Her hands were fisted in his hair. "Shit! Sorry!" Tammy let go.

Thunder was smiling. "Feel free to come on my face any time. I like a bit of hair pulling and nothing says thank you quite like nails in the back," he winked at her.

"I'm sorry. It's just I can't remember when last . . ." she stopped mid-sentence.

"You haven't been with anyone since . . . the loser, asshole."

She shook her head. "No, I haven't but he never . . . did that."

Thunder's eyes turned stormy. "He's such a fuckhead. He didn't deserve you, Tammy." He gathered her into his arms like she was the most precious person in the whole world.

"He's so far in my past right now. I can't even remember what he looks like." It wasn't entirely true but for the first time since he'd burned her, she didn't feel quite as angry or upset. She would probably still punch him in the face if she ever saw him again.

"Good!" His eyes softened. "I'm glad you're moving

on."

She was moving on. It felt really refreshing. "Now." She moved so that she was straddling him. "I could do with a round number two and you look like you could do with some help with that," she gestured to his very hard cock.

"Are you offering to bounce on my dick?"

She tried not to groan at his words. Her clit was throbbing all over again and that heavy feeling was back. "I believe I am," her voice was husky.

"Be my guest." Thunder put his hands on her hips and lifted her. She positioned his dick at her opening and he slid in easily. Her mouth fell open and a breath was pulled from her as she bottomed out. *So full! So gloriously full!*

"Fuck," he growled.

He looked like he was in deep concentration. His jaw was clenched, his eyes focused on her. She gave a tight smile and lifted and then dropped. They groaned in unison.

Tammy put her hands on his shoulders. Thunder held onto her hips, guiding her up and down. He also thrusted into her from below. She let her head fall back. Slowly but surely they picked up the pace until her breasts were bouncing hard with every thrust.

Thunder was looking at her chest like it was the most fascinating thing he had ever seen. He was frowning deeply. Despite the fact that she was halfway to a spectacular orgasm, she felt her cheeks heat and not from the exertion.

Then his gaze locked with hers. She felt the same static

in the air as when he had thrown a lightning bolt. Every hair on her body stood on end as an unexpected orgasm slammed into her. If it weren't for Thunder holding her in place she might have jerked off of him. Her eyes rolled back and her back bowed.

Thunder put his head in between her breasts and jerked hard, grunting her name. He fucked her harder, his hands digging into her hips. It felt so good she didn't care. Couldn't care about anything other than what he was doing to her. Thunder finally slowed, his breath coming in ragged pants.

"So," she was out of breath. "You've been holding out on me."

He chuckled, his face still buried in her breasts, his breath tickled her skin. "I shouldn't use my power during rutting. It just happened," he shrugged.

She sucked in a deep breath. "Why not? It felt amazing. Feel free to do that any time. In fact, I'm nearly ready to go again."

"You are an amazing female. I would like nothing more than to use my power but you aren't my mate . . ." he paused, "yet. It's forbidden. I've never done that before." He looked unsure.

Oh boy! She wasn't sure what to make of that.

"I figured since we already broke a couple of rules." He lifted his head, looking her straight on.

"I guess."

"I won't do it again," he said, it was like he could sense her discomfort.

Tammy nodded. She could breathe easier again.

CHAPTER 18

Six days later . . .

Tammy got busy tidying the shelter. It wasn't so much tidying as it was reassembling. The wind had howled a bit last night. It had blown off a couple of the long leaves that made up the roof. Thunder had been extra jumpy, he'd leapt up several times during the night. She didn't think he'd slept very much over the last few days. She wanted to suggest that they go back but she didn't want this to end or to change. She had a bad feeling.

A branch snapped behind her and she jumped. "It's me," Thunder said. "I brought breakfast." He held up a fish.

"Is that . . ."

He nodded. "It's a salmon."

"Wow! You caught it?"

"Don't look so shocked," he laughed. "Yes, I did and with my bare hands." He stood taller. "Here." He threw the thing at her and she caught it, giving a yell as her hands clasped over its scales. She almost dropped it.

Thunder chuckled.

"It's not funny," she smiled, trying to hold onto the fish, it was heavy.

"You can put it down," he was still smiling. "I'll clean it when I get back."

"Where are you going?" She hated being left alone, even for a second. The back of her neck seemed to prickle, like someone was watching.

"He's nowhere near us." Thunder walked towards her. "I would scent him if he was."

"He might be downwind."

"I'd hear his heartbeat."

"He's snuck up on us before." Tammy had become a bit paranoid about Cloud over the last couple of days. She could sense that Thunder was on edge and it worried her. He could be lurking anywhere.

Thunder narrowed his eyes on hers. "I won't let him get within an inch of you." He took the fish from her and put it on the ground. "I'm going to be over there, just up the way." He gestured behind him. You're welcome to come with. I saw some wild spinach growing there. I thought it might be a nice accompaniment to the fish."

"Sounds yummy. I'll stay here, but . . ." she gripped his hand, "don't go too far."

"Never." He kissed her and her belly did a flip flop. Thunder pulled back, he kissed the tip of her nose before turning and walking away. He did things like that often. He kissed her nose and put his forehead to hers. He touched her as much as possible and not just sexually, he'd hold her hand, pull her into a hug or sling his arm around her. The way he looked at her made her feel special. Again, it wasn't just the lustful, desire-filled looks, it was also the tender ones.

Things were happening quickly. Thunder was filling a space she hadn't even known existed but they needed to slow down. There was no rush.

Tammy picked up the fish. It weighed a ton. She was going to clean it. She and her father used to fish on some of those camping trips and she'd watched him gut the fish. It had always made her feel ill, so she'd never actually done it herself. Thing was, Thunder was so damned sweet. She had to smile just thinking of him. He fetched them food. The deer, a rabbit, this fish. He foraged for vegetables. Mainly roots that tasted like yams.

She headed to the river's edge and set the fish down. Tammy pulled the knife from its sheath and sliced the fish open. Next, she reached into its belly and pulled everything out, trying not to breathe or to think about what she was doing. She worked quickly, allowing the innards to wash away. Then she rinsed out the cavity.

She'd watched a couple of those cooking shows on television and had seen how the guys sometimes scraped the scales off of fish. This salmon had a smooth feeling skin. It would probably be easier to cook if she left it on.

An arm snaked around her middle and she tensed up, preparing to scream if need be.

"You didn't have to do that." Thunder kissed her neck.

"I wanted to." Tammy put the fish down. She rinsed

her hands and turned slightly so that she could look into his eyes. "You built our shelter. You do all the hunting and gathering. You make the fires and cook the food. You keep me warm at night."

"It's my job to take care of you." His eyes took on that soft look.

It had been a long time since someone had taken care of her. A very long time. Probably not since she'd lived with her dad. "We're in this together, we're a team. It's a two-way street."

"Thank you." He kissed her cheek. "I was thinking." He kept his arm around her and pulled her up as he rose.

"Yeah, what's up?"

"Maybe we should head back. I'd love to hide out with you forever but my people need me. I'm sure they will be worried by now. Also," he cupped her cheek, "you deserve to sleep in a warm bed."

Finally, it was out. One of them had to say it first. They couldn't stay here. Having said that, she knew there was another issue to address. "What about Cloud?" It had to be said. There was a part of her that was thrilled they were going back to civilization and another part that liked being out here with Thunder.

He frowned. "I'm not sure why he hasn't made an appearance. I really thought he would've by now."

"We don't need to go back. I don't mind sleeping in our shelter. I don't mind either way." She sucked in a breath. "I guess what I'm trying to say is, don't make this decision because of me." She was worried about being sent home. She hated the thought of not seeing Thunder again.

"It's twofold . . . I need to let my people know that I am safe. I trust my second in command to handle things in my absence, but I'm sure that they are worried."

She nodded.

"And . . . I want you in my bed." He put his arms around her. "I don't want you to have to gut fish, although . . ." His arms tightened around her. "I found it sexy watching you do it. You are incredibly sexy, period."

"I smell like fish guts and you think I'm sexy?" She had to laugh.

"Yeah I do. I think that I will always find you sexy regardless of the circumstance. I'm going to miss seeing you in just your t-shirt though. You have very sexy legs."

"Hairy legs," she snorted.

"Sexy. I couldn't care less about a few hairs." He clasped the backs of her thighs. "And an incredible ass." He cupped her butt cheeks. "Come to think of it, I prefer you naked." He kissed her and squeezed her ass. One of his hands slipped between her legs.

Tammy moaned. From pulling out fish guts to so turned on that she could barely remember her own name in no time. He slipped a finger inside her as he deepened the kiss. God, but he was good with his hands and his mouth . . . he pushed one of his thighs between her legs, his finger slid in deeper. Thunder pulled back, his eyes were glowing. "I have to rut you one more time before we go back." He nuzzled her neck. "I'm never going to get enough," he whispered against her skin.

Tammy moaned again. Her heart hammered in her chest. "Are you worried that this will be our last time?"

He tensed, his hand stopping mid-thrust. Tammy wriggled against him, needing him to keep going.

"Not a fuck!" Thunder growled. "They will not take you." He crushed his mouth to hers, more urgent. His finger was more insistent. Maybe it was two.

Oh god! She was going to come soon.

"Hold on," he growled, against her lips. "Legs around me," another low growl.

Tammy hooked her ankles around his back. He began to walk, taking huge, quick strides. Then her back touched against something hard. A tree. Its surface was rough through her t-shirt.

Thunder sheathed himself inside her in one hard stroke that took her breath away. He didn't wait for her to acclimatize or to catch her breath, he began to move in hard, rough strokes. She was very wet, so it didn't hurt. His facial expression was tense. His eyes even more intense. His hands were still clasped around her ass. The bark dug into her back with each hard thrust.

She groaned loudly, the sound just as raw as their lovemaking. It was just as raw as the sound of his body slapping against hers. As the greedy sucking noise her body made as he pushed into her. Repeatedly. She couldn't take her eyes off of his. The coiling sensation had already started. Her clit throbbed, he was rubbing against it as he pushed into her. Over and over. Fast, deep, hard.

Thunder's eyes narrowed, his jaw clenched tight. His frown deepened as his body began to jerk against her. His eyes never left hers. He fucked her harder. So intensely beautiful as his jaw tensed, as he orgasmed. He groaned her name and all she could do was let go. Rushing to meet her own release.

She dug her nails into his shoulders and tightened her legs around him as blinding pleasure rushed through her. Thunder leaned forward, leaning his head into the crook of her neck. She cried out when something stung her neck. An even more powerful orgasm took ahold. She felt her eyes roll back and her back bow. It felt like the world slowed as her blood rushed.

Too. Much.

Too. Good.

Her body jerked with each hard spasm. Thankfully, the intense pleasure slowed as Thunder released her neck. *He was biting me,* she thought with a start. Thunder kept his head buried in her neck, his thrusts slowing. They were both panting heavily.

He finally pulled back slightly, using one hand to cup her face. "Are you okay?"

"Yeah," a pant.

"I'm sorry." He planted a kiss on her lips. "I was too rough with you."

"I won't break."

"You're human." He put her down, pulling out of her as he did. Then he lifted her shirt, inspecting her back. "Fuck!" he said harshly. "You are going to have bruises."

"I'll heal. It's not a big deal."

He swept the hair off her neck and shook his head. "I marked you. I'm sorry." He ran a hand through his hair. "I need to be more careful."

"Bullshit. That was probably the best sex I've ever had. So what if I have a bruise or two, or a hicky on my neck," she shrugged.

"A hicky?" He shook his head. "I bit you. I'm sorry, it's just that I got a little crazy at the thought of you leaving." He scrubbed a hand over his face.

"We'll convince Blaze. It will all work out." She could see by the look in his eyes that he wasn't convinced. Tammy put her fingertips against the tender spot on her neck and winced. It stung a little.

"I'm a dick. I'll be more careful in the future."

Tammy was reminded of something Roxy had said, that biting was mating behavior. The queen had also warned that shifter men could get really intense and possessive when they were experiencing mating tendencies. It was just a little bite in the heat of the moment. They were good. It was too soon for mating behavior. Far too soon. He had promised that they would take it slow. She needed for them to take it slow. There was no other way. One small step at a time.

"It's fine." She put her arms around his waist.

Thunder hugged her back. "Let me get you fed and then we can head out. The rest of your clothing should be dry."

"You washed my stuff?"

He nodded. "Yeah, it's much colder higher up in the mountains."

"You're incredibly sweet. Do you know that?"

Thunder kissed her softly. "Sweet on you," he winked.

CHAPTER 19

The Air Castle

The hall was enormous, both in width and in height. Fire blazed in all three hearths. There was a vast window looking out onto the mountain range. The sky was blue. The higher mountain peaks were snow covered. Painted with whites, blues and even purples. The valleys below were thick and green.

It had only taken an hour and a half to make it back, give or take a couple of minutes. They showered and changed. Thunder had checked to make sure she wasn't too tired before inviting her to attend a debriefing. He said that he needed to meet with his second in command. She had a feeling that he would've stayed with her if she had been too tired. He hadn't so much as left her side since they arrived here. Then again, that wasn't true. He'd left her for all of ten minutes but had positioned an army of warriors outside the entry points to his apartment. Needless to say, he was really protective of her.

Even now, he clasped her hand firmly in his. They sat

at the middle of one long side of a huge table. Tammy was excited to be in the Air Kingdom, in Thunder's castle. So far, she had only seen a few of his people. They had all been polite. They'd refrained from staring, even though she had looked awful and had probably smelled even worse.

Her hair had taken half an hour to brush out. She'd tried hard to keep it under control but there was only so much you could do using fingers as a brush. It felt so good to wash with actual soap and to condition her hair. The absolute best was brushing her teeth, instead of having to use ash from the burned out fire on her finger. Nothing beat the spearminty goodness of actual toothpaste or the bristles of a good ol' toothbrush.

The far door opened. A really tall, really built guy walked in. It was Thunder's second in command. Tammy noticed that his chest was golden. The guy strode towards them, his mouth broke into a smile as his eyes locked with Thunder's. "Brother. I heard of your troubles and am glad you are well. If I had known, I would've sent a search party."

Thunder nodded his head, he also smiled back. "It's good to see you, Storm. You could not have known. This is Tamara. Her friends call her Tammy."

Storm turned to her, his smile instantly evaporated. His eyes seemed to harden. They were the same color as Thunder's. "Hello, Tamara. I am Storm, Second in Command to the king and runner up to the Air throne. I am royal." He gave his chest a knock with a closed fist and then turned back to Thunder. "I am here to give you feedback on all that has happened in your absence."

Thunder nodded. "Yes. Take a seat. What are our reserves looking like? Winter is about to hit. I have a feeling it's going to be a bad one. Also, have we made quotas since—"

Storm looked at her and then back at Thunder. "Have you mated this female?" He didn't look happy.

Thunder frowned. "We are not here to discuss my love life. You may begin," his voice was clipped and in a tone she had never heard before.

"With all due respect, my king," Storm bowed his head. "I would prefer to give feedback to you and to you alone. This female is not Air . . . she is not even a dragon." It was probably her imagination, but his voice seemed to be filled with disgust.

Thunder dropped her hand and then he was on his feet. She hadn't even see him rise. "You will do as I say," his voice was soft yet delivered a punch all the same.

Storm took a small step back and then squared his shoulders. He narrowed his eyes. "I must insist. The messengers you sent have returned, Blaze has called for a meeting. This human will be made to return to . . ." Storm made a flourish one hand, "wherever it is she came from. Do you want her to have the information I'm about to impart? It's bad enough she knows of our existence."

Tammy got the distinct feeling that Storm didn't like her. She wasn't sure why. It couldn't have been something she did, or didn't do. The guy didn't even know her. She wasn't going to take it personally. "It's fine." She touched Thunder on the side of his leg. He was wearing a pair of cotton pants. They were black and rode low on his hips. Probably not something she should notice at a time like this, but hey . . . she couldn't help it. She had eyes. "I'll go back—"

"No," a growl. Thunder sucked in a deep breath, he turned to her. *Oh shit!* He was seriously pissed. He had that whole tight jaw, tense thing going on. His features softened when he looked at her. "You can stay. I would prefer it if you stayed."

"Are you sure? I don't mind . . ."

"I'm very sure."

He turned back to face his brother. "Tammy and I are together. You may continue." His jaw ticked. His hands were clenched at his sides.

"Together. You are not mated to her, my king. I can't talk of quotas, I can't possibly . . ." Storm looked flustered for the first time.

"You can and you will." Thunder sat back down. She noticed that he sat on the edge of his seat, that he was leaning forward.

She put a hand on his thigh. He visibly relaxed, but only somewhat.

Storm was breathing quickly, he took a step forward and sat down. After a few beats he rose back to his feet, the chair scraping.

"Enough of this!" Thunder boomed. "Tammy and I are together. It is serious . . . we are dating."

"Dating!" Storm made a noise of disgust. "Dating? Please be kidding me. You were dating the last one as well and look how that ended. Now you expect me to debrief in front of your latest plaything?"

Ouch! No wonder he didn't like her.

"I'm five seconds away from making you bleed," Thunder's eyes were narrowed, his face was red.

"Someone needs to keep their head in all this. She will be made to leave. Blaze will ensure it. Even if she was, by some miracle, permitted to stay, it's just a matter of time before this ends," he scowled as he pointed between the two of them. "You're so damned pussy whipped you can't even see it. It's just like the last time."

She felt Thunder tense. "No," she shook her head. "Please don't fight. I'll go." Storm was being a serious dick, but she still got the impression that it was because he was worried about Thunder.

"Listen to the female. At least she is rational."

"Her name is Tammy. She is not my plaything, she is my female. Mine!" Thunder snarled. He stood up, his eyes blazing. "I won't beat you for your insults because my female has requested it. Do not compare her to any other who has come before because there is no comparison. If it were up to me, we would already be mated. It is only a matter of time." Her heart beat faster. Thunder was just saying that to put Storm at ease. She forced herself to calm down.

"But Blaze . . ."

"Fuck Blaze! I don't care what he or any rule book says,

I will listen to my heart. Tammy is a good female. An honest female. I trust her with my life and with my kingdom. I trust her with every secret I have. She will never betray us," he paused, seeming to contemplate his words. "Something was off about Lily from the start. It was good to have a female in my bed . . . I won't deny that."

Double ouch! Tammy tried hard not to be jealous.

"It may have made me blind initially but not for long. Lily was only here for a week before I sent her away. I have been with Tammy for longer than that. Our relationship didn't start off as sexual . . . Why the fuck am I even explaining this all to you?"

Tammy also stood up. It felt weird being the only person sitting. "Maybe because he is your brother and if I end up staying we could be family one day."

"One day . . ." Storm muttered, looking disgusted. He even shook his head and pinched the bridge of his nose. He finally let go and sighed heavily. "I had hoped it wouldn't come to this," he looked Thunder head-on. "I did some digging while you were away. I found out which female you were with. There was only one missing and Granite had seen the two of you, so it stood to reason that you were together. I assumed that you were holed up somewhere. Tamara Schiffer is not who you think she is."

What the hell!

"She is a gold digger. Just as bad as Lily . . . No . . ." he sneered. "She's worse because she has you completely fooled. That female," Storm pointed at her, "was arrested for theft. Did you know that? She stole money from the male she was living with. She almost destroyed his business. She's poor and looking for a meal ticket. I'm sorry, I can see that you are taken with her."

"That's the only intelligent thing you've said."

Storm's jaw dropped open for a second or two before he clenched it.

Thunder turned to her. "I'm sorry." He put an arm around her. "I'm sorry about the things he said and sorry that my brother is a complete fool and an idiot to boot."

"He's not." She looked up at Thunder. "He cares about you. He went to all this trouble because he's worried. Your brother is a good guy." Even if he was acting like an asshole. She kept that bit to herself though.

Storm frowned. "Why aren't you questioning her?" he asked. "Why is she still even here?" His eyes were wide.

"My female told me all about her dickhead ex-boyfriend. I know everything, moreover, I know her and I believe her. She was set up. Tammy didn't steal anything. She broke up with the cheating scumbag and he made it look like she broke in, then he destroyed the property and took money out of the safe himself. He ruined Tammy's reputation and needs to pay for his actions."

"I still struggle to trust someone who is not in our fold. She is an outsider."

"All that you need to know is that she is mine," he snarled the word, his arm tightened around her. "I have never claimed a female publicly before." Thunder shook his head. "Do you think I am a fool?"

"No. I think that you might be blinded." Storm didn't look as sure anymore. His shoulders were slumped. "I'm worried about you."

"Don't be," Thunder smiled. "I am a grown male. I'm older than you for fuck's sake. I came to you two days after Lily arrived on our soil. Two days," he held up two fingers. "I told you I was worried about whether or not she was right for our kingdom, for me. I told you that something was off."

Storm nodded.

"I'm not a whelp. You should trust my judgement. Tammy is *my* female. She is mine."

Hearing Thunder talk, Tammy suddenly felt hot in the jeans and sweatshirt she was wearing. The hall suddenly felt a lot smaller. The air felt thinner. This was possessive behavior. It had to be. *Don't panic, Tammy.* It was too soon for that.

"You can go," Thunder said.

"Be careful, brother. One day . . . one day. What does *one day* even mean?" He raised his brows, shaking his head. "You know where I am if you need me." Then he turned his eyes to her. They were the same color and yet, very different from Thunder's. "We are dragons, fema . . . Tamara. It would be best to remember that. I wish you a good day." He picked up the file and left. The door clicked as it shut behind him.

"Sheesh!" Tammy huffed out a breath and fell back into the chair.

Thunder knelt on the floor at her side. "Do not let him

upset you."

"It's fine."

"It's not fine. He had no right."

"Well," she quirked a brow. "As your brother, he kind of does. Like I said, he cares about you. That's where all of this stems from. Why did he feel the need to tell me that you're dragons? I know that."

"Dragons are different from humans."

"No shit!" she smiled.

"No, we know quickly whether someone is compatible as a mate. It can be instant. Certainly soon after sexual compatibility is established."

"Okay." She wasn't sure about this. There was a part of her that didn't want to hear this. It was all too fast for her liking. They had strong feelings for each other. It was all moving in the right direction but it was way too soon to even think about mating one another.

"You look like you're having a quiet, internal meltdown," Thunder smiled. "Look, don't let that get to you. You are not a dragon female and every couple is different. We don't have to rush." He took her hand in his. "We have all the time in the world. I am enjoying dating you. I love having you in my bed."

"Yeah, right," Tammy snorted. "Like Lily." The ugly green monster was back and he was crawling around inside her head, scratching at her skull. She should not have said that. "I'm sorry, that was childish. I guess I'm a bit jealous."

"You have nothing to be jealous about. I meant it

earlier when I said that there is no comparison. I have been with others and yet," he leaned forward, "no one else compares. I have no memory of any of them . . . there is only you." Her heart was beating so hard she was sure her chest might explode. "I want to be a better male because of you. I will prove myself worthy."

"What are you talking about? You are good, you're kind and sweet." She leaned down and kissed him.

"Not that nice," his eyes narrowed. "I would've beaten the shit out of Storm if you hadn't been here."

She gasped. "You wouldn't have."

Thunder stood up and sat back down next to her. "My brothers and I have been in many fights over the years. I would've cleaned this floor with Storm's face," Thunder growled. "He should never have spoken to you that way. I might still go and kick his ass." His lats and traps were roped. His biceps bulged. In short, he looked really tense.

"He cares about you." She got up and walked behind him, Tammy began massaging his shoulders. "Wow! Your muscles are so tight."

Thunder groaned. "That feels so good."

She continued to work his back, finding more than one knot and kneading them out. He groaned and grunted and groaned some more. "You are working magic," Thunder said. "I have never felt more relaxed."

She giggled. "You have."

"No way," he moaned.

"If we weren't in a public place, I would . . ." she felt her cheeks heat and she lowered her voice. "Give you a blow job. I guarantee relaxation like never before, but . . ."

"We're not in a public place," his voice was deep.

She frowned. "I thought we were in the town hall or something."

Thunder smiled. "This is my office."

"What? It's huge."

"This is my conference table," he pointed to the table they were sitting at. "Over there is my desk," he pointed to an area on the other side and sure enough, there was a desk and chair. There were papers and a couple of files on the desk, as well as a closed laptop. "On that side is a lounge area. Through that door is . . ." She kneeled in front of him, putting her hands on his thighs and rubbing. " . . . a small kitchen and through that door are the restrooms." His voice was deep and his words were a bit rushed. Okay, they were a lot rushed. There was a clear bulge in his pants. He swallowed thickly, his Adam's apple bobbed as he did.

"What about your PA?" She let her hand rub higher, just catching his balls with the tips of her fingers.

"I have a VA." His eyes were wide and his breathing had picked up.

"What the heck is a VA?"

"A virtual assistant. We recently got onto the grid. We've had internet for the last six months. We're using satellites to route . . . fuck . . ." he growled as she rubbed over his now very hard member.

She licked her lips. "Maybe I can rub you through your pants. I can't take my sweater off though."

He groaned as she gripped him through the thin cotton.

"I'm sure I could get you off with my hand," she licked her lips again, looking at him from under her lashes. His eyes glowed. The muscles on either side of his neck stood out. She wanted to play with him a little. He liked to talk dirty, she wondered if he liked a little dirty talk right back. She was willing to bet he did.

If she didn't put her mouth on him soon, he was going to have a heart attack. No dragon shifter had ever died in that way before, he would be the first.

Her hand was amazing. She tugged again on his dick and he clenched his butt and fisted his hands at his sides to keep from yanking her head into his crotch.

"I would love to suck on that big cock," she licked her lips.

Fucking hell! Fuck! She'd never spoken like this before. He liked it. He liked the shit out of it. "Tammy," he warned. Then he groaned as she fisted him, giving him another tug from base to tip.

"It would be terrible if someone came in, so . . ." She pouted, he'd never seen her pout before. It made her lips look even more fuckable. Wait a minute. *What had she just said?* He tried to recall but his brain was so lust-soaked. "What?" he croaked.

"I said, someone might come in, so I can't . . ."

"No one will come in," he blurted, stumbling over the words.

She cocked her head to the side and licked her lips, leaving them shiny and plump. "You never know, they . . ."

"I will kill anyone who comes through that door. I am the fucking king. This is my fucking office. They. Will. Not. Dare."

"You're so tense." She pulled her sweater over her head. It was too big for her.

"Fuck!" he growled as he caught sight of her breasts, they were encased in one of her coverings. Thin white cotton. He could make out her nipples. They were hard.

Tammy winked at him. She reached behind her back and unhooked the bra. Her fabulous mammary glands spilled out. She worried that he wouldn't like them, that they weren't firm enough. She was wrong. He loved the hell out of them.

Thunder gripped his lower lip between his teeth and tried not to lunge for her. Everything in him told him to claim her.

Mine.

Mine.

Take.

Fuck.

Claim.

Now.

She gripped her beasts in both hands and squeezed them together. Then she let them go and they bounced. "Don't tease me, Tammy." His loose pants were tented so badly that they were pulling on his ass. His balls throbbed.

She grabbed her flesh, pushing them together. "Do you want to fuck them?" She bobbed her eyebrows.

"Yeah, I do. I want to come all over your chest. Cover

you with my seed." *Must claim. Must mark.* Her eyes twinkled with desire. "But not today."

She frowned.

"I have to have your mouth on me. Please," he added the last.

Then she smiled and gripped his pants. Thunder lifted up so that she could pull them down, all the way down. His dick slapped against his belly and he opened his thighs.

She closed her hand around his cock and gripped his sacs with the other. Thunder tried not to move. He grunted as she squeezed his balls softly. Then she lowered and lowered, it was like she was moving in slow motion. He watched with fascination as she closed her mouth on his tip.

Thunder had to shut his eyes as her wet heat surrounded him. She massaged his balls, tugged on his dick and sucked him into that sweet, gorgeous mouth of hers. Her lips were plump and red. She made greedy little noises as she deep-throated him.

Thunder sat very still. He held onto the backrest of his chair, trying hard not to thrust into her mouth. Trying even harder not to have a heart attack.

"Fucking hell!" he grunted. "Christ! Fuck!" His balls were pulling up. He was trying really hard not to come. It was too soon.

There was a knock on the door.

Tammy stopped moving and he had to stop himself from roaring in anger. "Go away!" he shouted, sounding fairly composed.

His female sucked on him, his tip felt like it knocked the back of her throat. Her hands worked him. Up and down. Fisting the hell out of his shaft. There was no way he was lasting.

There was another knock and she pulled off him completely with a soft pop.

"Fuck off!" he shouted, no longer composed. He could hear the sound of someone leaving. "They're gone," he looked back down at his female.

She smiled. "That wasn't very nice." Then she closed her mouth around him again.

"I don't care, they . . . thank fuck!" he groaned, thrusting into her mouth. *No moving!*

Tammy rocked backwards and forwards. Her hands . . . *Oh fuck those hands.* Her breasts jerked up and down as her head bobbed. The sucking noises made by her mouth on his dick inflamed him.

"I'm going to come," he growled.

Tammy didn't seem to hear.

"I'm coming . . . Christ . . ." he tried to hold off but couldn't. It was impossible. Not with this female. He gripped the chair tighter, crunching forward over his middle as he began to come. Thunder grit his teeth and groaned. His hips jerked forward just a little. It couldn't be helped. "Christ . . . Tammy . . ." There was a cracking noise. She kept going, swallowing everything he had to give. Then she slowed until she finally moved away.

His female licked her lips. She was smiling.

"You're right, I'm so damned relaxed . . ." His tongue

felt thick. His mind fuzzy. Thunder sucked in a deep breath and leaned back. There was a piece of the chair in his hand. "I guess I got a bit carried away." He held up the wood.

Tammy laughed. The sound was music to his ears. "Your turn," his voice was deep and guttural. Thunder lifted his female, placing her on the edge of the table. His scales rubbed beneath his skin. He would force himself to wait, to stay calm. His dragon wanted him to mate Tammy. It wasn't very patient.

He undid the top button on her jeans when another knock sounded. "It's me," Storm said, his voice muffled by the door.

"Don't you dare come in," Thunder shouted, positioning himself in front of his female, just in case his brother was hard of hearing.

"What is it?" Tammy whispered. Her eyes were wide. She had her hands over her breasts.

Storm muttered a curse. "I have an important message for you. It can't wait."

"Give me a minute," Thunder growled. He turned to his female and helped her off of the table. "It's my brother and it can't wait. I'm so sorry, we'll have to finish this later."

She shook her head. "It's okay." Tammy grabbed her clothes. "I'll be in the restroom freshening up."

Thunder clasped her jaw and kissed her. He could taste himself on her lips and tongue. He groaned. Another knock sounded. *Damned Storm.* The male needed a serious lesson in manners. Thunder groaned, the sound laced with frustration.

"Go do your thing," she said as he released her. "Don't hurt him."

Thunder shook his head. She was a mind reader. "I'll try not to."

"You're relaxed," she bobbed her eyebrows. "Remember?"

He gave a nod and grinned at her. "Very relaxed. I . . ." By Claw, he'd nearly told her that he loved her. Only just stopped himself in the nick of time. "Thank you."

"Anytime." She clutched her clothing to her chest and headed for the restroom.

Thunder waited for the door to close behind her. He checked that his pants were on properly. Put the piece of wood on the table and turned to face his brother. "Come in."

Storm walked in immediately. He was frowning deeply. "What is it? What couldn't wait?"

Two males filed in behind Storm. They were fire dragons. Fucking brilliant. This was worse than he had thought.

His brother's nostrils flared for a second. Thunder knew that the male would scent what had just gone down. They all would. Too bad he didn't give a fuck.

"Go ahead," Storm gestured to the closest fire dragon.

The male nodded. "I am Heat, a Pinnacle dragon and high ranking warrior. This is one of my team members, Flame."

The second male nodded. "Blaze sent us to convey a message. You are to return with us to the Fire Castle. The human is to accompany us as well. Blaze wishes to meet with you both."

"I have only just returned to my lair. I request a few days to acclimatize and to rest before having to make this journey." Thunder wanted to buy them some time. It was stupid since the meeting was going to happen whether he liked it or not. He couldn't help but feel it would be beneficial. He wanted to show Tammy around, to allow her to get a feel for what it would be like to live with him here. To become a part of this community. He needed more time with her, period. It looked like that time was up.

"Blaze received your message. It was very detailed. He thanks you for taking the time to write it out."

He hadn't written anything, he'd dictated the report, but Blaze didn't need to know that. Thunder could sense a 'but' coming.

"As much as he would like to grant you time, it is not possible. Are you both in good health?"

For a moment, Thunder was tempted to lie and to say that they weren't but he couldn't do it. "We are fine. My human is tired," he tried not to sound irritated. It wasn't Heat and Flames' fault.

"That is good news," the male smiled. "If that is the case, then you are to accompany us immediately. We are already late but I'm sure the king will understand the reason," he grinned. "I hope to win my own female one of these days."

The male's admission helped calm Thunder down. He was doing his job and following orders. The young buck had no idea what was going on. That much was clear. Thunder nodded. "Okay, fine," he sighed. "Give me a few hours to assemble a team."

Heat shook his head. "Apologies for the confusion, but you are to come immediately. We leave right now."

This was worse than he had originally thought. Way fucking worse. Thunder shook his head. "Cloud is still at large. He is a danger to my female," he worked to keep the menace from his voice and to keep from showing any outward signs of aggression towards these males. It was not their fault. They were clueless. "I would prefer to have a team accompany us in order to protect Tammy."

Flame cracked a grin. It irritated the fuck out of Thunder and he clenched his jaw. "Do not worry, my lord," the male said. "There are two more Fire warriors waiting in the great hall. The five of us will accompany the human."

"My female," Thunder snarled. He cleared his throat. "She is my female; her name is Tammy."

"Apologies, my lord. We will defend and protect your female, your Tammy . . . with our lives. I give you my word." Flame lowered his gaze as a sign of submission. Heat did the same.

His hands were tied.

"I will handle all matters in your absence," Storm said. Thunder expected the male to be happy, but his brother was frowning and looked concerned. "I will be here when you return." He touched Thunder on his arm, already consoling him. *Fuck that!*

"Good, I'm glad to hear it," Thunder said. "I will need a day or two to help my female settle in when we return. I want to show her around the lair, around the whole of our kingdom."

Storm pursed his lips together. It looked like he was trying to hold back a comment. "Whatever you need from me, my lord," he finally said.

"You can begin by organizing a family gathering. Our sisters will want to meet Tammy."

"Are you sure you—"

"Do it!" he shouted. "We will be back before nightfall. Have someone clean my chamber and prepare a meal. Something intimate and romantic." He couldn't quite catch his breath.

"Brother," Strom touched the side of his arm. He looked sad. Thunder gave a small shake of the head. He couldn't handle negativity. Not right now. Not when his own mind was running at a mile a minute, screaming things he didn't want to hear. "I will arrange everything. I look forward to your return. The both of you," he quickly added. "Have a safe journey.

"We will, thank you." Thunder turned back to the males. "Give me fifteen minutes. I need to inform my female and fetch warm clothing for the journey. As you know, humans are soft and weak."

Heat smiled. "Yes, they certainly are. Soft is a good

thing though," the male grinned. He turned serious. "I can only give you five minutes. We have delayed too long already. I must warn you, Blaze is in a bad mood. He was very clear about this meeting and stressed the urgency around seeing you both."

Fuck! A knot formed in his belly. Thunder was not looking forward to seeing Blaze. Although things were much more cordial between them, there was still a lot of water under the bridge. He was sure that he hadn't simply forgotten how Thunder had crossed him. At least, that's how the male would see it. Although things had worked out better for Blaze in the end, so maybe it would all be okay. The male might not have mated one of his sisters but he had ended up with Roxy. Blaze should thank him. *Yeah right, and Father Christmas was a dragon shifter.*

"I will meet you in the great hall in a few minutes," Thunder looked at Heat as he spoke. The male nodded. Thunder turned and headed for the restroom. He knocked. Tammy opened within seconds. "I'm sorry, I was hiding out. I heard all that. We should be worried, shouldn't we?" Her eyes were wide.

Thunder shook his head. "I won't let him take you. I told you that and I mean it."

She pulled in a deep breath. "I'm worried. I can't believe he would enforce a silly rule."

"We'll get through this," he injected confidence into his words. There wasn't much he could do. If Blaze was setting this whole thing up so that Tammy could be removed from the four kingdoms, physically if need be, then there wasn't a damn thing he would be able to do about it. His hands would be tied. He'd have none of his males at his side. He was hobbled. "If you are forced back, know that I will come for you," his voice hitched.

Tammy nodded, her eyes brimmed with unshed tears. She gave him a sad smile and gripped his hand. "You need to know that I don't want to go."

"I know."

"We'd better get going. I've got less than three minutes to grab my coat and brush my teeth."

Thunder kissed her nose. "I . . ." *love you,* "agree, let's move."

CHAPTER 20

Tammy hung between Thunder's claws. This mode of transport was becoming situation normal for her. She'd put on a woolen beanie and gloves, as well as a fur-lined winter jacket, not to mention the rest. Thunder had grunted some commands to one of his men and the stuff was delivered half a minute later. She was lost in the oversized jacket but she was very warm. *Toasty.*

There were two Fire warriors up ahead and two to their rear. She could hear their wings flap almost in unison. If it weren't for the sick feeling in her stomach, she would sit back and enjoy the beautiful scenery. They were headed straight for the biggest mountain range, slowly gaining altitude. There was a narrow pass between two of the smaller peaks. She'd get to see all that ice and snow up close. Her heart beat way too fast but only because she was afraid of losing Thunder. She'd meant to ask him what he was to her. They were dating . . . so was 'boyfriend' appropriate? It didn't seem enough, yet how could he be anything more after only knowing him for a week and a half?

She should also have been excited at the prospect of seeing the Fire Castle again. Of seeing Roxy and maybe one or two of the other women who had left with her on the hunt.

This didn't bode well for them though. She could see it in Thunder's eyes. He was really nervous. It was the first time she'd seen him like this.

Tammy wasn't ready to go home yet. Their relationship was still so new. In its infancy, but the more she got to know him the more she wanted to know. The more time she spent with him the more she wanted to spend with him. She needed to trust that he would sort this out. He had to.

They neared the pass, which looked thick with snow. It was untouched. Pristine. She could almost see the individual ice crystals twinkling and blinking. They were flying pretty low. Low to the ground, but many miles above sea-level. The air felt thinner. She was breathing heavily, even though she wasn't exerting herself. The dragons in front of them released great plumes of white with every breath.

She looked back down and to the right. What was that? It looked like a single foot print in the snow. It couldn't be though. Not all the way up here. She squinted her eyes up, trying hard to see.

Suddenly one of the dragons ahead of her fell. He landed heavily in a flurry of limbs and wings. She screamed as the dragon next to him dropped as well, falling just as hard and just as fast. Thunder veered sharply to the left but not before she saw them. Crimson drops in the snow directly below. Tammy couldn't breathe. Her stomach felt like it was left behind as they did another sharp dive. None of that mattered. Thunder had been hurt.

There was an almighty crash behind them together with the heavy crunching sound of snow. In front of them, the cliff wall grew closer and closer, Thunder set her down carefully, considering the circumstances they found themselves in. The snow was thick, quickly swallowing her feet and calves. Thunder changed back into his human form. Blood gushed from a hole in his arm.

"You're hurt."

"I'm okay." He ushered her towards an outcrop of rocks at the cliff wall. Her teeth chattered, she had to lift her legs high because of the snow, so the going was slow. Her ski pants were wet. Again, none of that mattered.

The fourth Fire dragon, the only dragon still standing, came to a halt behind Thunder, its great back to them, its huge tail swishing from side to side, reminding her of an angry cat. It was on the lookout. Not that the beast stood much chance.

"Is it silver?" She pointed to his arm.

Thunder didn't answer her, he didn't have to. "We need to get you safe."

"I don't see an exit wound. We need to get it out of your arm," she said, as he shoved her behind the rocks. She glanced around them. There was a fissure in the rock. Thunder gripped her by the arm and pushed her into the narrow space. She pulled up her jacket and using her mouth, pulled off the glove on her right hand.

"You'll freeze," Thunder frowned, looking at her hand.

Tammy unsheathed her knife. Taking it with her had been purely out of habit. She'd grown so used to pushing the sheathed blade into the front of her jeans, it was second nature. "You'll die if I don't sort this out."

The dragon roared loudly. It was a deafening sound.

"We're out of time," Thunder pulled back but Tammy gripped him by the arm and he held still. She sliced across the wound, which was at the top of his bicep. There was no time for being careful. The longer the silver was inside him, the more of its poison would enter his bloodstream and the weaker he would become.

The dragon screeched as she dug the knife in the hole. It was right there, just below the surface. She gripped the edge and pulled out an oval shaped piece of silver. It was sharp on one side

"It's a bolt," Thunder growled. "He has a crossbow."

"I'm sure he has more than just a crossbow."

Thunder's eyes were dark. His muscles bunched. "He had better have more. A whole lot more." He gripped her arms and kissed her. It lasted all of a second but still left her a little breathless and a whole lot worried. "Stay here," he pushed her further into the narrow space. "Do not move unless I come for you."

"Be careful," she called after him.

There was a crunching noise and a wail that was more animal than human. It was the last dragon. The last barrier between Cloud and Thunder had fallen.

"It's over!" Thunder yelled. "Surrender or die!"

Tammy heard the sound of laughing. A sound so eerie it chilled her blood. "I should say the same," Cloud said. She had known it was him but hearing him still had her heart racing. She was tempted to run out there and to let him have a piece of her mind but doing so would put Thunder even more on the back foot, so she stayed put. Besides, it wasn't as if a crazy-ass person like Cloud would be able to rationally comprehend what she had to say. The guy was too far gone.

"Last chance, Cloud. I don't want to kill you." She could hear the anguish in Thunder's voice.

"I have a bolt aimed at your chest. At your heart to be more precise."

Tammy squeezed her eyes shut. *Oh god!* She could only hope that Thunder knew what he was doing. He hadn't looked in the least bit afraid. Not even a tiny bit nervous. Maybe he had a plan.

It was Thunder's turn to laugh. The sound was deep and filled with confidence. "That would be a first. You're someone who prefers a male's back to facing him head-on. You play dirty. You break rules to get ahead. You'd step on your own mother to get ahead if she was still alive. Face me like a male."

"We both know that I would lose, so what would be the point?" Cloud's voice was clipped. "I need you dead. I promise to take good care of your female."

Thunder roared. For a moment she was sure that Cloud had attacked, but then he spoke. "You are a coward.

Hiding in the shadows. You are not the male I thought you were. You talked your mate into taking a drug that had a fifty percent chance of killing her. It is your own—"

Cloud screamed. He sounded like a man possessed. Thunder roared again. There was the sound of running. She heard two dull thuds over the crunch of the snow. *What was that? What had happened?* The dull thuds were followed by a loud thud and a crunch.

Then silence.

Her chest heaved. It was the only sound that reverberated around the small space. She wanted to call Thunder's name. She wanted to move. Thunder had told her to sit tight though. He'd been very clear about it. Another minute ticked by agonizingly slowly.

Screw it.

They were no longer fighting, which told her that one or both was too injured to keep on going. If Cloud was still fine, it was only a matter of time before he came for her. Maybe Thunder needed her. She rushed from the opening. Maybe Cloud was still alive but vulnerable. She could help. The snow crunched beneath her fur-lined boots. Thank god Thunder had insisted she wear them. She rushed – although rushed wasn't the right word since the snow was so thick – she maneuvered around the rocky outcrop, going as fast as the terrain would allow.

When she saw the scene that unfolded before her, she stopped. Thunder was crouched over Cloud. His shoulders were hunched and his face bowed. Cloud's eyes were open, unseeing. The crossbow lay a short distance away from him. His neck was at a strange angle.

Thunder's chest and arms were covered in blood. He turned to her as she slowly closed the distance between them. "I told you to sit tight," his eyes glistened and his voice was thick.

"It wasn't your fault." She knelt beside him. "You had to do it."

"I know but . . ." he shook his head. "It has been many years since a dragon was put to death by its own. I had hoped never to have to . . ." he sucked in a deep breath. "It was not to be avoided."

"The guy may have been really great once upon a time, but he changed. He lost his mind when his wife and unborn child passed."

"Or maybe he was a great actor."

She frowned.

"I checked in with the healers soon after I arrived at the lair." He rubbed his eyes. "I don't know that Cloud was the good male I thought he was, or maybe the madness started before he lost his female."

"Is that where you disappeared to, the healers?" He'd left ten warriors to guard her. Ten. Five on the balcony and another five outside his door. He'd been gone a total of fifteen minutes. She'd found it a little extreme at the time. Now, not so much. "What did they tell you?"

"I don't even know why I went. I guess I needed more clarity. I asked a few questions about Cloud and his female. I didn't really know what I was looking for at the time. One of the healers remembered them coming in for the drug. His mate was crying heavily. The healer checked several times before administering the herb. It was at the insistence of Cloud. I don't think his female was comfortable taking the drug, I don't think she wanted to."

"You mean he forced her?" That poor woman. Tammy couldn't imagine.

"Yeah, that's exactly what I'm saying. I think he forced her and then his sick mind twisted everything to blame me."

"But you still feel bad about killing him."

Thunder nodded. "I would do it again in a heartbeat. I'm glad you are safe." He gave a tired smile and her chest did a funny tightening thing. Then he held up his hands. There was a bolt through one of his palms and another through his forearm.

She pulled off her glove and unsheathed her knife. "I should start charging for this. I'd make a fortune."

Thunder laughed. "Don't let Storm hear you say that. He'll think you're serious."

"You stopped the bolts with your arms."

He nodded. "Better than stopping them with my chest. I got him talking so that I could pinpoint his location and then I got him mad. An angry male doesn't think clearly. Once he loosed—" he winced as she pulled out the first bolt. Thankfully the ends weren't barbed. "the first bolt, I was already halfway to him. He didn't have much time to reload. I stopped the second bolt with my arm. There was no time to change weapons or reload after that, I had him."

Tammy pulled out the second bolt. The wound gushed blood, which was probably a good thing. Hopefully some of the poison would bleed out.

There was a scraping noise. It was one of the fire dragons, it was trying to stand.

"We need to help them as well," Tammy said.

Thunder nodded. "Let's get the bolts out and then we're going to fetch help. It's only about a half hour from here to the Fire Castle."

Tammy sheathed the blade and started walking towards the conscious beast. She was startled to see that the dragon that had fallen close to this one was back in his human form. There was a bleeding wound in the middle of his chest and another in his thigh. He looked like he was still breathing but she didn't need a medical degree to see that he was in a bad way.

"We need to hurry." Thunder came up behind her.

"Are they dying?"

Thunder's only response was a deep frown.

She'd done this a few times, she fell on her knees beside the bleeding shifter. Tammy's hand shook as she unsheathed the blade once again. She sucked in a deep breath and got to work.

CHAPTER 21

A few hours later...

They'd barely had a chance to wash up and eat when Blaze summoned them. The male sat at the head of a long table; he watched as they entered, his expression unreadable. Coal was in attendance. At least the younger male gave a nod of the head as greeting.

Both males rose to their feet as they entered. Thunder had to force himself to breathe slower, to unclench his fists.

"My healers advised me that you are doing well, that the wounds were superficial," Blaze said. He turned to Tammy before Thunder could reply. It was the male's way of establishing immediate hierarchy. It pissed him the hell off.

Tammy clasped his hand tighter, as Blaze locked eyes with her. "I am Blaze, King of Fire and ruler of the four kingdoms. This is my brother, Coal, my second in command. We are royal." He touched his marking as was customary.

"I'm Tammy," her voice shook ever so slightly and Thunder had to stop himself from putting an arm around her. This was a formal meeting, such a gesture would be frowned upon.

Blaze finally looked him squarely in the eye and Thunder was taken aback by what he saw written in the male's eyes. He looked sad. His face had a pinched look, even his shoulders were slightly hunched.

Thunder stepped forward. "Are your warriors okay? It was my understanding that all of them would pull through. Is that not the case?"

Blaze put up a hand. "Thanks to your quick thinking, and to the human's," he motioned to where Tammy was standing, "skill at removing the bolts, the males will be fine."

"Thank fuck," Thunder blurted, he had thought the worst. He gave a sigh. "I am sorry it happened. I wish I had known, wish I could have—"

"There was nothing you could have done," Blaze interrupted him. "You saved my males. You saved the human from certain death. You righted wrongs in accordance with the lores." In other words, he'd killed Cloud.

Thunder gave a nod. He wanted Blaze to get on with it. To tell him the reason he had been summoned. Like he didn't already know.

Blaze gestured to the table. "Let's take a seat."

They all sat down, everyone but Coal. "Something to drink?" The male held up a jug of water.

"No," Thunder practically snarled. "Thank you," he quickly added. He was not beyond licking ass. Doing anything it took.

"I read your report, but after today's events, I can better understand what you were up against." He looked solemn. "I poured over the rule books but the lores are clear. I could find no loopholes. You shifted during a hunt, before making it back to the castle. According to the lores, your indiscretion calls for an instant disqualification."

Thunder held his breath. He willed his heart to slow. Adrenaline coursed through his veins. He wanted to put Tammy over his shoulder and run. Despite the situation, his dick hardened up. Not all the way there but enough that he could feel a tightening in his pants. The need to claim rode him hard. He sucked in another lungful of air and forced himself to listen to what Blaze was saying. "You are also banned from competing in the next hunt."

Not that he gave a fuck about the next hunt.

"I had my brother take a look, just in case I was missing something."

Coal clenched his jaw and looked away.

"Hell, I had my mate look through several lores that I hoped I had wrongly interpreted. The three of us spoke about it at length."

The male was dancing in circles. He was dressed for battle, he had his sword but instead of coming in for the kill, he was dancing. It wasn't like Blaze. Thunder was out of patience. "Your point, my lord? Not that I have to ask." It was insolent of him but he didn't give a fuck.

Blaze frowned. "I'm sorry, there is nothing I can do."

"Bullshit!" Thunder rose to his feet. The chair scraped loudly against the floor. "You are the king of the four kingdoms."

"Sit down," Blaze said, his voice even.

Thunder kept his eyes steady on the other male. His jaw was locked and his muscles bunched, he was ready for battle.

"Sit!" Blaze said again, this time using a commanding tone.

For a second he almost obeyed, every part of him wanted to do as the ruling king commanded but he forced himself to stay where he was.

"Do as he says," Tammy touched him on the side of the leg. "Please."

There was nothing he wouldn't give this female. Not a damn thing. He looked at her, at her dark eyes, silently pleading, her skin looked pale. He felt himself calm and did as she said.

Once he was sitting, Blaze continued. "I wish it could be different. I feel for you . . ." He looked at Tammy. "For both of you, but I don't make the rules, I enforce them. The lores are clear."

"It's not fair," Tammy said.

"What happened with Cloud was an anomaly. He made a mockery of the lores. I did what I had to do under the circumstances. I would never have shifted unless there was no other choice," he was breathing heavily, still trying hard to keep himself under control. His scales rubbed, he could feel his power simmering below the surface. "Given what I know now, I would do it again because we wouldn't be having this conversation if I hadn't acted. My Tammy would be gone."

"I take it you want to be together?" Blaze asked.

The question was completely unexpected. Thunder felt something lift. "Yes, of course." He was too afraid to breathe, too afraid to hope.

Blaze folded his arms and leaned back in his chair. He scrutinized them. His nostrils flared. "You are actively rutting."

Tammy gave a gasp and shifted in her seat.

Blaze ignored her discomfort. "You recently," his nostrils flared again, "marked this female and yet you haven't mated." He frowned. "Why?"

Thunder swallowed hard. "My female . . . Tammy isn't ready. She was jilted by her previous . . . by a dickhead and is worried about rushing into another relationship. We are headed in the right direction, but we need time," he cleared his throat. "She needs time and I want to give it to her."

"I understand . . . trust me . . ." he widened his eyes. "Out of everyone in the whole damned lair, I understand better than most. If you had arrived here already mated, there was nothing I could have done. You would've received twenty lashes for breaking a lore but the female could have stayed," Blaze looked at Tammy. "You could have stayed."

His female lowered her gaze to the ground. A strained

breath left her lips. "I don't understand your lores. I've only known Thunder for just over a week, it's too soon to take such a big step. I love being with him and we've been through so much together. I feel like I've known him for way longer but in reality, it hasn't been long at all," Tammy spoke quickly, giving away how nervous she was. "It would be nuts to marry, mate one another after such a short time. What if one of us is wrong about the other or our feelings?"

It hurt to hear her say it, and yet he understood where she was coming from. She'd been badly hurt. Betrayed by someone she loved.

"Why can't we date?" Tammy shrugged. "Spend time together? It's far more normal to do things that way. Maybe in a few months, a year . . ." Tammy went on and Thunder felt himself cringe with each admission. He didn't mind, he'd do anything for Tammy but he worried about how Blaze would see things.

Blaze all out frowned. "Date? Normal?" He huffed out a breath. "Dragons don't date."

"Why not?"

"We just don't. We mate or we move on. Either you love this male and want to be with him or you don't, it's that simple."

"It's not that simple," she looked mortified.

"It is if you're a dragon," Blaze frowned.

"I'm not a dragon. I keep having to defend that important fact."

"No, but Thunder is and you are on our turf. Again,

either you're down with that or you need to go home." Again, Thunder cringed at each statement. He worried how Tammy would take the statements this time.

"Now, I'm going to give you this one chance and one chance only," Blaze narrowed his eyes. "I shouldn't but I will. I can see that the two of you are crazy about each other and I don't like the idea of tearing you apart." He locked eyes with Thunder, whose heart was beating wildly. "Are you willing to take twenty lashes with a silver-tipped whip?"

"Yes," he growled. "I'd take a whole lot more than that, although I didn't think we possessed such a weapon."

Blaze smiled. "The vampires have plenty. Their kind are far more prone to breaking the lores, or so it would seem. Alternately, you could spend a week in the cage. It's your choice."

"What is he talking about?"

Thunder squeezed Tammy's hand, excitement coursed through him and a silly smile had taken up residence on his face. He could feel it. "I'll take the lashes, I don't want to be separated from my female for so much as a day. A week would feel like a lifetime."

Blaze nodded, looking like someone had pissed on his parade. Thunder felt his smile wane. The male looked at Tammy. "If you agree to mating tonight, I will overlook this meeting ever took place."

"Oh my . . ." Tammy gasped. She was frowning and shaking her head like she couldn't believe what she was hearing.

Thunder's hope plummeted, for whatever reason he had expected Blaze to say that they could date. That they could have as much time as they needed, but he was an idiot for believing it. "It's fine," he turned to face Tammy. "I know that you cannot agree to such a thing." He swallowed hard.

Her eyes welled with tears. "I don't want to leave you. It's too soon though. I can't leave you . . . I don't want to."

"And I don't want you to go, but unless we mate tonight . . ."

She shook her head, a tear fell. "You're nothing like him and this last week has been the best of my life," her voice caught. "I'm one hundred percent behind being with you for the foreseeable future. I never thought I would want to live with someone so quickly again but I'm fully behind doing that too." She sniffed and another tear fell. "I don't want your family jewels . . . okay, not the diamond and gold ones," she gave a nervous laugh. It held zero humor.

Thunder felt his throat close and his eyes sting.

"This thing between us is already moving so quickly . . . too quickly. I can't mate you so soon, it wouldn't be right because I'd be doing it for the wrong reasons. I'd be doing it to stay and not because . . ." she shook her head. "I have strong feelings for you, but I can't be in love with you already. It's not possible. Not after such a short time. I can't do this . . . I just can't."

Fucking hell! So this is what a broken heart felt like. He completely understood where she was coming from. After everything she had been through, it was a miracle she'd made it this far this quickly. She had strong feelings for him. He knew she did. If she wasn't all the way there already, she would be soon. It was a damn shame. A crying shame.

"Are you sure, female?" Blaze asked. "There is no going back. If you decide to leave, the two of you may never see each other again. The penalty would be your throne," Blaze looked him head-on. "You stay away from this female or you will be banished."

Thunder hadn't been aware that the penalty was so harsh. It felt like he was drowning without a drop of water in sight. Like his world was collapsing.

"I thought you said you would come for me," Tammy's eyes were wide and tear-soaked. Her lip quivered.

"I will," he choked out.

"You will not!" Blaze smashed the table with his fist. "You would give up everything for a female who won't take a chance on you? She doesn't love you, she said it herself." It hurt to hear the male say it. "You would be fucking crazy. This is how it's going to be, the human will stay the night, at first light . . ." Blaze locked eyes with Tammy. Her chest rose and fell in quick succession. "You will be taken back to your human settlement. Do not try and contact Thunder. If you have any feelings for the male, you will turn him away if he ever goes to you. He is needed here, he has a kingdom to run, heirs to produce. He has family and friends here who do love him. There will be someone in his future who will deserve him and cherish him . . . ask me, I know." Blaze clasped a hand over Thunder's wrist. Thunder's first instinct was to pull away. To punch the male, but he couldn't do it on both counts. Blaze had tried. The male had been willing to bend the rules. To bend them so hard that they might even be considered broken afterwards. He was trying to show Thunder that he cared even if his methods sucked.

"Don't let him do this," Tammy was crying openly. Her shoulders shook. "Please, don't. I'm not ready for marriage but it doesn't mean I don't want to be with you, because I do. You do understand that, don't you? Please understand." She sounded desperate.

Thunder nodded, his eyes were hurting so damned badly. "I understand," his voice sounded funny as well. "I do."

"Thunder," Blaze drew his attention back to him. "You will also stay in my lair tonight. You are in no state to return to your kingdom and when you do," he paused, "you will be watched day and night. Storm can take over your duties for a while. I won't let you fuck your life up, do you hear me?"

Thunder nodded, he was feeling numb. This wasn't happening.

"You *will* take place in the next eligible hunt and you *will* win a female."

"No!" Tammy gripped his arm, using both of her hands. "This is crazy! I can't believe this is happening." She mirrored his feelings in that regard.

"He doesn't have a choice. You made your decision and now you must accept it."

"I won't!" Tammy shoved her chair back. Within seconds four Fire warriors surrounded them.

"Don't fucking touch her!" Thunder shot to his feet as well. Two of the males grabbed each of his arms, another wrapped his arms around his chest. "Blaze!" he yelled. "Don't let them touch her."

"I'm sorry," Blaze paused for a moment, "it's going to be a long night." The Fire king shook his head. "Take him to his chamber," Blaze commanded the warriors. "Make sure he stays put."

Tammy was trying to pull free from the fourth warrior. "Take her to her chamber," Blaze addressed the warrior.

"Get your fucking hands off of her!" Thunder roared.

His female screamed his name, the sound was filled with anguish.

Adrenaline pumped through him and he fought against the three males but together they were too strong for him. They dragged him from the chamber. His female kept screaming for him all the while. The male who was holding her grunted. "Stop kicking," he ordered.

"Fuck you!" she screamed, before shouting Thunder's name. Each time she said it, it was like a silver-tipped spear to the heart.

CHAPTER 22

There was a knock at the door. Tammy pulled the pillow over her head. It wasn't Thunder and she didn't care about anyone else. She didn't want to see anyone else, so she buried her head even deeper. She went from feeling like an idiot for letting Thunder go, to feeling angry they had been torn apart because of some ancient rule.

The pillow was tugged off of her head and a sympathetic stare greeted her. "I'm so sorry this happened."

"I don't really want to talk about it," her voice broke and fresh tears rolled down her cheeks. She didn't think it would be possible for a person to cry this much. Tammy rolled onto her side and away from the other woman.

"That's too bad because we are going to talk about it." Roxy's voice was stern.

Tammy turned back. "Thank you for your concern, but..."

Roxy narrowed her eyes. "I am not here to show my concern or to rub your back and dry your tears."

Tammy could feel she was frowning. She used the back of her hand to wipe her nose.

"I'm here to kick your ass." Roxy lifted a hand. "Not literally." She looked down at her belly, which was rather large. "Obviously. I am due pretty much any minute, so I would appreciate it if we kept my stress levels down."

"Go right ahead," Tammy snapped. "Do your worst. There is nothing you could say to make me feel any more shit than I do."

"You love him. Why couldn't you just admit it?" She took a seat on the edge of the bed.

"It's too soon for that." *Why did these people keep making her repeat it?* It was getting annoying.

"You wouldn't be reacting like this," Roxy made a flourish with her hand, "completely devastated if you didn't have strong feelings for him."

"I do have strong feelings for him, but marriage . . ." she pushed out a breath. "We're not ready to take that step."

"We?" Roxy raised her brows and cocked her head. "Really, Tamara? Are you sure you can speak for him when you say that? Have you even asked him how he feels? Asked him his opinion on all of this."

"Yes, we agreed on this. We agreed we would take it slow. Thunder has told me more than once that there's no rush."

"Did he tell you that because it's what he wants or did he say it for your benefit?"

Tammy lifted her eyes in thought. She went over their

conversations. "It may have been more for me, but he was fine with it . . . more than fine. What are you trying to get at?" She sat up.

"I can safely say that Thunder is more than ready to mate you." Roxy rubbed her belly. Her back was straight.

"I know that he would mate me in a heartbeat if it meant keeping me here, but he might regret it." Her lip quivered so she bit down on it. "We both might end up regretting it. I don't know him that well yet. He hardly knows me. I would hate it if he regretted the decision. Either one of us for that matter."

"Would you ever blatantly hurt the guy or cheat on him or . . . ?"

"No!" Tammy yelled. "Of course not." Softer this time. "What are you trying to get at?"

"You say that he hardly knows you, but I can guarantee that he knows enough. He's a dragon shifter. They know pretty quickly when someone is for them."

She shook her head. "He just thinks he knows, but—"

"No!" It was Roxy's turn to yell. "He's a shifter. When I tell you he knows, he knows. He is calling you his female. He's biting your neck, fighting for you, he's willing to throw everything away for you and probably will because he already sees you as his mate. It's not my place to tell you all this but someone has to before it's too late. Thunder loves you, you idiot!" She sucked in a breath through her nose and grimaced. Then she rubbed her belly. "It's a Braxton hicks . . . it's a fake contraction." She took a couple more deep breaths before continuing. "If the two of you mate, he will never stop loving you. He will never cheat on you."

"You can't know that for sure."

"I can and do." She grimaced again. "I swear, if you make me go into labor . . . ! It's shifter DNA. It's how they are wired. You can stop speaking for Thunder because you don't know what you're talking about."

"Why didn't he tell me all this?"

Roxy rolled her eyes. "Because he loves you. He doesn't want to scare you off. Blaze mentioned that you were with some dickhead who broke your heart and that it's part of the reason you are running scared. I get it. But Thunder loves you," for the first time her voice softened, it sounded coaxing. "He's completely smitten. He'd do just about anything for you, including going against his own instincts. In other words, he would've given you as much time and space as you needed even if it killed him. He would've given you space to figure things out."

"Yes, space," Tammy said, another tear rolled down her cheek. "That's exactly what we need."

"No," Roxy shook her head. "It's what *you* need. Thunder would've taken some serious strain. It might've killed him—not literally," she rolled her eyes again. "But close enough. You have no idea what agony it is for a shifter to go against his instincts."

"Physical pain?" Thunder would've suffered, for her. He wouldn't have told her either. He would've waited because he was sweet like that.

Roxy nodded. "Physical. Mental. All of it. In some

ways, this whole thing has been a blessing in disguise."

Right. Tammy didn't say it. She didn't feel it either . . . not really. It killed her to think of Thunder suffering though. Especially if his suffering was because of her.

"So, this has nothing to do with Thunder. He loves you and he wants to mate with you yesterday. You need to decide what you want. What are your feelings for him? You need to set your fears aside, don't let bullshit clutter your thinking. Listen to your heart."

"It's too late," she whispered. "I'm leaving in the morning. Thunder will come for me . . . he has to."

Roxy made a sound of disgust. "You would let him destroy his life? He'll be banished. A dragon shifter cannot be complete without his tribe. He will suffer. You would allow for that to happen?"

It was so selfish, she felt guilty for saying it. "I can't live without him."

Roxy smiled, she put a hand on Tammy's arm. "You have your answer then. You can't live without him. Thunder can't live without you. Surely you have your answer. Don't make me call you an idiot again."

Tammy felt like she couldn't catch her breath. "It's too late though. I do want Thunder. I can't live without him." She rubbed her temples. It felt like the start of a serious headache. Then she rubbed her sternum and anticipated some serious heartache too. "It's too late to do anything about it."

Roxy put a hand to her back and another anchored behind her, then she stood up slowly. "My back is killing me." Once she was fully upright, she gave another tired smile. "Thunder is in the chamber next to you," she pointed to the wall on the left.

Tammy gasped, clasping her hand to her mouth for a moment. "So that's why I keep hearing banging?"

Roxy nodded. "He's tried to escape a couple of times."

Thunder was right next door but that didn't mean anything. "But there are guards outside. They'd never let me . . ."

"The guards have been instructed not to let Thunder leave. They have no orders to prevent someone from visiting him." She feigned shock. "I guess my darling husband forgot to tell them that part."

Tammy jumped up and hugged Roxy. "Thank you! Please thank Blaze for me."

"You can invite me to the official mating ceremony when you take the plunge," she grinned.

"Thunder has to forgive me first. I pretty much told him I didn't want him."

Roxy's smile didn't waver. "There's nothing to forgive. Love and forgiveness go hand-in-hand. Let me tell you a few more things about dragon shifters, they . . ." Roxy sat back down on the bed.

Thunder's muscles bunched as he gazed out over the terrace. Three shifters paced out there, blocking his exit. Three more were outside the door. There was fuck all he could do about it. He wasn't sure what he would do if he managed to escape anyway.

Tammy wasn't ready to commit to him. He would be wasting his time but he had to try to talk to her. Maybe he could convince her. He strode towards the door, ready to tear it from its hinges – yet again – when it opened. Thunder stopped in his tracks. His mouth fell open.

One of the Fire dragons held the door so that Tammy could enter his room. He was tempted to rub his eyes. Had he hit his head? Maybe he had fallen asleep and he was dreaming. "Tammy," he whispered her name.

She thanked the Fire dragon and he growled. It couldn't be helped.

The Fire dragon smiled. *Fucker!* "It is my pleasure, female. If there is anything that . . ."

Thunder took a step towards the male, he rumbled low and extra deep. The lesser male's eyes bugged out of his skull and he lowered his gaze, backpedaling as quickly as his legs would take him. *That's more like it!*

Air filled his lungs again as soon as the door closed.

Thunder picked Tammy up and pulled her against him. "I don't know how you managed to escape, but I'm so fucking glad you did. Although I'm not sure why that male let you in."

"Me too." She put her arms around his neck. "I can't believe you even want to see me . . . then again, I can believe it."

"Of course I want to see you!" He lifted her so that they were eye to eye, only about an inch apart. "When I said that I would never get enough, I meant it. I understand why you couldn't commit right now." He clenched his jaw. It hurt but he understood. "You aren't ready. I'm not angry. It's not either of our faults there are stupid lores. I guess no one could predict something like this happening. You need to know, I meant it when I said I was coming for you. They can't stop me. Can't watch me twenty-four seven indefinitely." Tammy was his female. The last thing he wanted was to be banished, but what choice did he have?

"You really would give everything up for me?" Her voice was soft and timid, her eyes filled with tears. Her eyes were puffy and red-rimmed. He could see that she had been crying. It got his back up.

Thunder nodded. "Most definitely." He hugged her close for a moment. "Please don't cry, I can't take it."

She sniffed. He felt her head nod so he drew back, needing to look into her eyes. "Do you remember when you said that that my asshole ex didn't deserve me?"

His eyes darkened up. "Yes, I do. You were far too good for him."

Tammy cupped his cheeks, his stubble caught against her fingers. "Well I don't deserve you. I'm the asshole in this relationship."

What? She had this all wrong. Just like when she thought she was a gold-digger. "That's not true."

"You are far too good for me, although . . ." she narrowed her eyes on his. "I do need to give you a piece of my mind for not telling me a few things."

"Like what?" he blurted, frowning. "And for the record you do deserve me, you're fucking perfect for me."

Her stern look softened up a whole lot. "Why didn't you tell me that shifters have this mating urge? Roxy spoke about it in our crash course training but I had no idea how bad it could get for you."

"You weren't ready. I can wait. I'm a grown male."

She ran a hand through his hair. "It would've hurt you. Physically hurt you. Mentally hurt you. Pure torture."

He nodded. "It isn't easy to dismiss your instincts, but I would've been fine," he tried to sound nonchalant.

"You should've told me. You also should've mentioned that shifters become really attached. That you can't end up cheating."

He put her down, breaking the contact. "If I had told you, it would've been hot air. You needed to figure that out for yourself. You would've figured it out . . . you will. I meant it when I said I was coming for you. There will still be time for that to happen."

She shook her head. "You're not giving up your life for a woman who's not willing to take a risk on you. Blaze was right."

Thunder's jaw ticked. "Blaze doesn't know what the fuck he's talking about." This was her attempt at a 'Dear John.' Tammy was going to try and talk him out of giving up on his people for her. It wasn't what he wanted but he couldn't help what he needed. Tammy had become a part of him.

"Blaze is right. I'm the one who was wrong." She grabbed both his hands. "I love you too. Very much." She pinched her lips and seemed to hold her breath.

Thunder frowned. What was Tammy trying to say? Then he smiled and squeezed her hands as hope unfurled. Then he frowned some more. Did she mean it? Was this a trick, a test? *What the hell was this?* "What do you mean *too?* I never got a chance to tell you."

"Yeah, you did. You've shown me what I mean to you. Through your actions, those little gestures. They mean so much to me. You mean so much to me. Thank you for showing me your love. I'm here to tell you that I love you too and I plan on showing you right back . . . every day if you'll let me. I plan on doing a much better job of it."

Thunder grinned. "You love me*?*" *She loved him. His female really and truly loved him!*

"Yes, I do. I'm sorry it took me so long to figure it out."

He picked her up and swung her around. "I'm so happy. So unbelievably . . . Wait a minute. You leave in the morning. This doesn't change anything." *Fuck!*

"Yes it does. Blaze is a sneaky sneak."

"A what?" he growled.

"He's a sneaky shit," she grinned. He didn't catch her point but Blaze *was* a sneaky motherfucker.

He had to cringe though. "Don't let him hear you say that."

"I happen to really like the guy."

"You do?" It came out sounding like a grumble. His female liked the fucker. Thankfully Blaze was mated or Thunder might get jealous. Who was he kidding, he was seriously jealous.

"Not in that way . . . sheesh! This whole mating instinct

thing is affecting you badly."

"Yeah, it is," he gave a half smile and he could see that she forgave him in an instant.

"Blaze put us in rooms right next to each other. He sent Roxy to set things straight with me. I needed to know a few things."

"Like what?" He didn't look too sure.

"Like what an ass I am. Like how sweet you are."

"You're not an ass," his eyes glazed over a little. "You have a stunning ass though."

"Let's not talk about my ass just yet. He did all of this in the hope that I would come to my senses, and I have. We have until first light to make this official." She chewed on her lip. "If you'll still have me, you can mate me now."

"As in, right now?"

"Yes." She was suddenly nervous that he would turn her down. "It's now or never because I won't let you give up your throne. I can't let that happen."

CHAPTER 23

Thunder looked thoughtful for a moment. Three steps later and he was tossing her on the bed. The need to claim her was overtaking everything. His scales rubbed like mad. He ripped his pants off. Couldn't get them off fast enough. Tammy's eyes widened. There was excitement in their depths. Then he got onto the bed, unable to take his eyes off of her. Thunder straddled her. *Claim. Now.* He ripped her clothes off as well. Buttons went flying and fabric tore between his fingers like paper.

"I can't promise to be gentle," he growled.

"Please don't be." She gripped his shoulders.

"I love you, Tammy."

"I know." She reached up and kissed him. "I love you too."

Claim.

Now.

"I'll try not to hurt you." His hands shook.

She squirmed, her eyes glinted. "You won't."

"I might." He was worried. "Turn over," his voice was guttural, his beast taking over. It wanted her on all fours.

Tammy rolled over, his female put that lush ass of hers in the air. Her pussy glistened. "I'm going to mate you now and you need to know upfront that I will bite you. I will hold you down but I swear I'm going to make you feel good." His mouth watered, his teeth felt sharp against his tongue.

"Sounds good," she was out of breath even though they hadn't done a damn thing yet. She pushed her lush ass towards him.

"You are perfect for me." He gripped her hips.

"We're perfect for each other." She cried out as his thumb skimmed over that tiny little bud of nerves. All he wanted was to take her. His dragon was still insisting he do it now but he needed to prepare her.

He dipped the tip of his finger into her snug pussy. "So fucking wet." His scales rubbed a whole lot more. His teeth felt sharp against his tongue. He strummed her clit and she mewled. Arching her back.

"I'm going to mate you now, Tammy."

"Please. I need you," she sounded breathless and needy. Her legs were splayed wide but he pulled them wider still. He needed her open and submissive. He needed her, period.

"Don't fight me," he growled as he positioned his dick against her slick channel. "I'll try and go easy."

"Need you. Please." His tiny human knew how to beg. "Oh God!" she shrieked as he sheathed himself inside her in one hard thrust. His hips hit her ass. Her lush ass.

"Say my name," he growled.

"Thunder," her voice quivered.

"Do you want this?"

"Yes." A whimper.

"You are mine, Tammy and I'm yours." He struggled to stay still. His whole body vibrated with need.

"Yes." A breathy whisper. "I love you, Thunder."

"I'm very far fucking gone. I need to claim you but I'm scared of hurting you."

"I won't break," she moaned loudly and he realized that his thumb was turning lazy circles on her clit. His other hand held on tightly to her hip, his fingers making indents on her flesh. "Please, Thunder. I want you. I need you. I won't fight you. I know this whole mating instinct thing is driving you nuts. Believe it or not, I feel it too. You can fuck me hard and hold me down and do any of the other things you want to do. I'm yours, let's make it official."

He pulled out on a low growl and plunged back in. Thunder pushed her down on the bed, he continued to thrust into her welcoming flesh. He could feel the sweat bead on his brow. "Feels so good," his voice was gruff. Her ass bounced each time his hips collided with the lush mounds.

She arched her back. His dragon didn't like it. In the beast's mind she was trying to get away. He gripped her shoulder, holding her down, using his other hand to push her flush onto the bed. *Take it easy!* He loosened his grip. His female moaned. Thunder crouched over her, caging her in with his body. His female mewled and her pussy fluttered. It felt like she was about to come. He couldn't be sure though and it worried him. Tammy was breathing heavily, her eyes were wide, her mouth was open. She might also be panicking. He tried to ease off but couldn't do it. If anything, the need to fuck her harder coursed through him, took ahold of him.

"Yes!" she screamed. "Please."

Her sex tightened around him and she made a strange, high-pitched keening noise that told him she was diving over the edge. *Thank fuck!* At last, a feeling of calm descended. At the same time, his blood rushed and his balls pulled tighter than ever before.

"Mine!" he snarled as he sank his teeth into her neck.

Mark.

Claim.

Take.

His own pleasure rushed through him in that instant. He released her neck as power surged through him and into her. Tammy went ridged for a split second, her sheath so tight he physically hurt. Then she screamed. Thunder kept moving, or at least tried to, his whole body felt like it was spasming around her, in her.

At long last, he was able to slow, he moved in slow easy, circular thrusts wringing out the last drops of pleasure for his female. He was dripping with sweat. They both were. He was sure to keep his weight off of her. Thunder was loath to pull out. He wanted to stay joined with her but he needed to make sure she was fine.

Her eyes were closed, her breathing had evened out. Her mouth still hung open. The bite wound was raw. It was more severe than he had planned. It would leave a scar, which was customary for a dragon female. Tammy was a human. She was fragile and weak. Something lodged in his throat and his chest hurt.

Thunder laved at the wound. It would seal quickly. Now that they were mated, her senses would improve, her healing capabilities would improve as well. It didn't make him feel any better. Tammy didn't react, she looked unconscious. He felt his brow knit as worry tightened his chest.

"Tammy?" With a grunt, Thunder withdrew from her heat. He moved in next to her and cradled her in his arms. "Sweetheart," he tried again.

She moaned and her eyelashes fluttered.

"Tammy!" his voice held a more frantic edge, he lifted her into a sitting position, still cradling her in his arms. Her head lolled for a moment before she rested her cheek against his chest.

"That was . . ." her voice croaked, her eyes were still closed. She swallowed thickly.

"Too much. I hurt you." He wiped the hair from her brow. Her face was flushed. "I'm so sorry. My dragon . . . I just . . ."

"No," her voice was thick, she sounded half asleep.

"Yes." He cradled her closer.

She gave a drunk looking smile and cracked her eyes open for a second. "That was amazing," she whispered, closing her eyes again.

"I didn't mean to hurt you. I was too rough and I . . ."

"You were very naughty." She nipped at his pec and he grunted as her teeth sank into his flesh. His dick took note.

Not now! Down, boy! She was obviously delirious. "Should I get a healer?" His heart beat wildly.

Tammy giggled, she wrapped her arms around his neck and she finally opened her eyes. "You've been holding out on me."

Thunder cupped her cheek, he looked deep into her eyes which were glassy. "I think you might be running a fever. I must have hurt you. You . . ."

She gripped his hand and kissed the palm. "I'm perfectly fine. Please can you explain what just happened and why you lied to me." She had a goofy smile on her face and had a slow blink going on. In short, she looked tipsy. He'd seen females after they'd had too much to drink.

"I never lied. Tammy," he could hear the frustration in his voice. "What's wrong with you?"

"I'm fine . . . it's the sex . . . oh my God!" she smiled, looking more like herself. "You lied when you said I only have two G-spots. That felt like I have a whole lot more, like all over my body. What was that?" she spoke quickly, her eyes wide. "Holy shit! I think I was unconscious for a minute there."

"Yeah," he touched her brow. "That isn't happening again."

Tammy slapped his hand away. "Oh yes it is. I loved it." She straddled him, her nipples abrading his chest. "Remember that vacation you told your brother we were taking? Well, it's happening and we're doing that . . . lots and lots of times."

Something eased in him. "I wasn't too rough then?"

She shook her head, threading her fingers around his neck. "No way."

The wound on her neck was already healing. It didn't look as bad. Then again, maybe he had been so worried earlier that it seemed worse than it really was. "I won't bite you quite as hard." He touched the bite mark.

"I like the whole biting thing." She bobbed her eyebrows and bit his neck. Thunder growled as her teeth sunk into him. "Do you like that?" Her voice held a timid edge.

"Very much," the words left him in a deep rumble and his dick gave a twitch between their bodies.

She pulled her lips into her mouth for a moment. He could see that she was thinking about something. "You need to tell me what you like. What makes you happy. I want to make you happy, Thunder."

"You do," he answered without hesitation. He turned her so that he was between her legs with Tammy flat on her back. She gave a squeal.

"I fucking love anything to do with you," his voice was deep, his chest vibrated against her soft breasts. Her nipples hardened. "I love being inside you, your mouth on me, your teeth on me . . . all of it and everything."

"Oh . . . good." A breathy sigh. "I feel the same," she smiled shyly.

"For the record . . ."

"Yeah?" She pulled her lower lip between her teeth.

"I never lied, you only have two G-spots . . . but you also have five hundred and twenty-three erogenous zones."

She sucked in a breath. "Show off! I can't believe you know the exact number," she shook her head.

Thunder chuckled. "I'm only joking! I don't know the exact number but there are a lot. All I know is that when I activate my power," he kissed her neck, "a minute electrical surge goes through your body and stimulates them all."

Tammy groaned. "It sure does. It was so good." She reached up and brushed a kiss on his mouth.

"I'm glad you can handle it." Thunder was sure that his female was sore after such rough lovemaking. He tried to ease off of her.

Tammy had other ideas. "Where do you think you're going?" Her hand slipped between them and wrapped around his cock. Tammy gave his length a light tug.

Thunder's eyes closed for a moment and he groaned, pumping into her tight fist.

"I'm ready for more," a breathy whisper, so full of promise he couldn't help but pumping into her fist, making a grunting noise this time.

"I'm glad, because there is a lot more where that came from," Thunder kissed his female. His heart felt huge inside his chest. It beat for her. For his Tammy.

The next morning . . .

The door creaked open. It crashed as the broken hinge gave. Thunder sat up, ready to spring into action. To defend his female.

It was Blaze. The male smiled broadly. "I'm glad to see that the two of you came to your senses." The male kept his gaze on Thunder, who glanced down at his female. She was sleeping soundly. Thunder made sure that the blankets were tucked firmly around her.

"Congratulations!" Blaze was grinning from ear to ear.

"Yeah, thanks," Thunder couldn't help but smile back.

Tammy buried herself deeper into the blankets and gave a soft sigh. They had made love all night. The sky had been streaked with oranges, blues and purples when they'd finally fallen asleep.

Judging from the height of the sun, it had to be mid-morning already. Thunder bit back a yawn and rubbed his eyes with the heel of his hand.

"Roxy gave birth to a beautiful, healthy egg." Blaze's grin widened.

"Oh wow!" Thunder grinned right back. "That's great! You guys must be thrilled."

"It's hard to believe that we're going to be parents soon." He clenched his jaw, looking emotional for a second or two. He'd never seen the male like this but Thunder couldn't blame him. Not even a little bit. He would love to be in the other male's shoes.

"Congrats! Please congratulate your mate as well for

me."

Blaze nodded once, his expression turned more serious. His body tensed. "About those lashes . . . when would be a good time for you?"

"I'd say right now but we don't have a whip."

Blaze smiled. "We do. I sent for one."

Thunder raised his brows. "When?" he frowned.

"Yesterday, after our meeting."

"But that would mean . . ." Thunder shook his head. "Tammy was right, you're a sneaky sneak."

"A what?"

Oh fuck! What the hell was he saying? "Um . . . what I meant was . . ."

Blaze choked out a laugh. Thunder laughed along with him. His female didn't so much as blink through the commotion. He really had worn her out.

It was Thunder who pulled himself together first. "If you don't mind us staying on for a couple of days, I'll get my punishment over with now."

"You sure?" Blaze smirked. "You are newly mated. Your female might not be happy if you're out of action for a day or two."

Tammy needed the recovery time. His female had been insatiable. She had matching bite marks on her breast and one on inner thigh. Not as deep as the first, but still. "This morning would be good." He also didn't want her to worry. This way it would be over with before she even knew what was happening.

"Okay. I'll have one of my warriors fetch you in an

hour."

Thunder pulled a face. "Can we make it a half hour?"

Blaze looked at him pointedly. "She's going to be pissed," he gave a nod towards the sleeping female. "But I do understand why you're moving so quickly. Humans are squeamish about this sort of thing." He sighed. "I'm sorry there's no way around this. It's . . ."

"You do not need to apologize, my lord. It is I who should be thanking you. I'm deeply grateful for all you have done for us. My female is worth it."

"I would do the same for Roxy," Blaze looked thoughtful for a moment. "I will send my best healer since my four warriors are doing so much better."

"I'm glad to hear it."

"I'll leave you to prepare." The male's nostrils flared. He sucked in a breath like he wanted to say something. Instead, he gave a small shake of the head and left.

Thunder knew what the male could scent. His female was at the start of her heat.

CHAPTER 24

Three months later . . .

Tammy straightened the cutlery on the table. She poured the wine, putting the bottle on the table. It was a rich burgundy that, according to the bottle, was robust and opulent. The table looked perfect.

The roast was resting. Everything else was ready and waiting. She'd prepared the meal herself and it smelled delicious. They were having chocolate fondant for dessert. It was Thunder's favorite. A flutter of nerves hit, her stomach gave a little clench. She wanted this to be perfect.

Tammy smoothed her dress, she walked to the full-length mirror just to be sure. The dress was blue silk, it clung to her every curve like a second skin. She'd put on some weight since coming to live in her new home. Her boobs were more out there and her hips more flared. Thunder loved it. He couldn't stop touching her and kissing her. He loved how everything bounced when they made love. Loved that there was more to hold onto. He just loved her full stop. The butterflies in her stomach slowed their roll.

She'd never been happier. She touched one of the diamond and ruby earring. It sparkled in the dim light. They were those elaborate chandelier type earrings. For a second she was tempted to take them out. They were too much.

There was a knock at the door. She frowned. Who could that be?

Storm leaned up against the doorframe. His whole face lit up when he saw her. "It's my favorite sister-in-law," he grabbed her in a bear hug. "Happy three-month anniversary."

"I'm your only sister-in-law, but thanks," she hugged him back. "You're about to ruin my surprise." She looked up and down the outside hallway.

Storm chuckled. "Surprise?" He shook his head. "Hardly."

Tammy grabbed his wrist and pulled him inside. "What's so funny?"

"You celebrated your one-week anniversary. Same with your one-month anniversary. Then," he lifted his eyes in thought, "there was your two-month anniversary, so it stands to reason that you would celebrate this one as well."

She folded her arms. "Are you done mocking me?"

He smiled. "I'm not mocking you. I think it's really sweet. I only hope my female is as lovely and half as caring."

She gave him a light touch on the arm. "I'm sure she will be. Is there something I can help you with?" She tried not to sound impatient. The last thing she wanted was to kick him out but Thunder would be arriving at any second.

Storm tapped her on the side of her arm with the rolled up newspaper in his hand. "You can relax. He's finishing up. Thunder will be at least another ten or so minutes. They're working on the new project. All the kings were on a conference call."

"The new project, as in the whole silver thing?"

Storm nodded. "You are a genius as well as being the nicest female I know. They're moving forward with the project and it's all your doing."

She made a noise of embarrassment and waved her hand. "Hardly."

Then Storm frowned, looking worried. "The next step is deciding who gets to play guinea pig. Granite has put the Earth dragons forward."

"Someone's got to do it. What's the big deal?"

He exhaled. "What if it works?"

"That would be wonderful," her voice was filled with excitement.

"The four kingdoms are united but it wasn't that long ago that we were at each other's throats. The kingdoms have little trust for one another. If the Earth dragons find a cure for our silver affliction, it puts the rest of us on the back foot. It puts Blaze one rung lower than them and the male will never stand for that. I foresee bloodshed before a decision is made. We all want to take on this project and yet to bring a team of human doctors into our lair would mean more risk. It is a tough one."

"I hear you," her voice was soft and filled concern. Mirroring the worry she felt inside. Storm was right, the dragons might be barbaric sometimes in the way they did things but they were a fair species, a just species. Humans could be cruel. No wonder Storm had been so cagey during that first meeting. If the humans ever found out about the dragons, about where they obtained their wealth, it would be over. They would be wiped out. She shivered. "We need to find a cure. You need to work together. Stick together."

"I know," he gave a shake of the head. "I am with you on that one. Enough doom and gloom. It's a celebration. Thunder will be here soon. There is something I wanted to show you." He unrolled the paper. "I know my brother won't want you to know about it but I think that you should."

"Know about what?"

The paper crinkled in his hand drawing her attention.

"This," he gave the front page of the *Walton Springs Press* a slap with the back of his hand.

There was a picture of her ex-boyfriend on the front cover. One of his eyes was swollen shut, his lower lip was cut and his arm was in a sling. He was barely recognizable but it was definitely him. "What the hell?" she muttered, taking the paper from Storm. "Local business man, Christopher Collins, made a startling confession earlier today," she read aloud, not quite believing what she was reading. "In 2014, he accused one of his employees of breaking into his place of business, destroying his property and making off with an undisclosed amount of cash. Tamara Schiffer was arrested for the crime. Collins later dropped the charges under suspicious circumstances. Oh my God!" She clasped a hand over her mouth, skimming the rest of the article. There was a quote from her arresting officer saying that he never believed Tammy was guilty.

Her eyes felt wide in her head and she felt them stinging. "Collins confessed to everything. He handed himself in to local police begging to be arrested for his crimes." Her eyes ran over the rest of the page. A tiny article in the bottom corner caught her attention.

"Man sees dragons," read the headline.

PETER THOMPSON was walking his dogs when two large dragons took flight from a nearby garden.

"They scared my little Harry half to death," said Thomson, who described the mythical creatures as being at least as big as a delivery van, with scales, wings and gleaming golden chests.

"It was the two of you," she looked up at Storm who cocked his head.

"I thought you should know. It was Thunder's show. I went along for the ride."

"Wow!" She gave a quick laugh and held the paper to her chest. "I can't believe it. Thank you."

Storm gave a shrug, as if it was nothing. "I love it when they piss themselves. Bullies always cry the loudest."

"Chris peed himself?" Tammy knew it was wrong of her to take glee in another person's suffering but in this case she couldn't help it. Christopher deserved everything he got.

Storm nodded. "He refused to listen to Thunder. Idiot had a lot to say, should've kept his smart mouth closed," he clenched his jaw for a second. "Fucker crapped himself in the end."

"He crapped himself, as in . . . ?" She tried not to smile. It wasn't right. "Surely not."

Storm had no such qualms. He grinned and gave a slow nod. "Yup. He deserved everything he got . . . you can trust me on that one. The male is bad news."

"Yeah, he is." She didn't know what she'd seen in him.

"He also made a sizeable donation to the local orphanage to make up for what he stole from you."

"Thank you." She gave him another tight hug. "You really are the best brother-in-law."

Storm put a hand to her back but otherwise didn't reciprocate. "You can thank Thunder. Like I said, it was his show."

"By the way," he took a step away from her, towards the door, "you look really amazing. My brother is one lucky SOB. You also smell really . . ." then he made a groaning noise. "Your surprise," he lifted his brows.

She nodded.

He held up both his hands. "I'm out of here."

She giggled and folded her hands over her chest. "Thanks again."

Storm was already on his way to the door. He glanced back at the last minute. "Those earrings look really good on you."

"Thanks." She fingered one of the pieces.

"You should wear more of our family heirlooms. My mother would have really liked you." Then he winked at her, reminding her of Thunder. "Enjoy your anniversary." She thought she heard him say 'My brother is one lucky fuck' but she couldn't be sure.

Within three minutes Thunder walked in. Tammy launched herself into his arms and wrapped her thighs around him.

"Now that's a welcome home." He planted a kiss on her lips.

"You're the best and I love you."

"I love you too," his voice was a deep, rich baritone. He clutched her ass and buried his face in her neck. She heard him inhale deeply a couple of times. Thunder lifted his head, his brows were raised but there were also two deep grooves on his forehead. "I thought you were taking the Pill?" He didn't wait for her to reply. "Your last heat nearly killed me."

It was all true. They'd ridden it out together. The first day had been pure torture for both of them since Thunder's back was still healing and well, she was a little tender. After that, it had been one sweaty bout of sex after another. Thankfully it was over in three days. They'd gone through a ton of condoms. She smiled just thinking about it.

He shifted her in his arms and for a second she thought he might put her down but he didn't. His frown deepened. "You said you would only stop taking those things when you were ready to become pregnant."

She sucked in a deep breath. "I know."

His mouth fell open. "Does that mean . . . ?" His eyes lit up.

She nodded.

Thunder smiled, his whole face lit up. "You want to get pregnant?"

"I do if you do?" She raised her brows.

Thunder smiled. He swallowed hard. "Are you sure?"

"I'm very sure." She brushed her lips against his. "I've never been more sure of anything."

Thunder's chest expanded as he pulled in a hard breath. "I don't think I've ever been happier." Then he squeezed her ass. "Let's get started right now."

"After dinner."

"You might just kill me." Thunder put her down, groaning when he noticed her footwear. "I want those heels to stay on, you can wrap them around the back of my neck while I fuck you."

Tammy felt that familiar heaviness in the pit of her belly and between her thighs. "I'm not wearing any panties," she whispered.

Thunder groaned again. "You are evil." She noticed how he clasped his hands together and rocked from one foot to the other, like he was trying to stop himself from touching her. She loved how much he desired her. His gaze softened. "You're going to make such an amazing mom."

She swallowed thickly and opened her arms. "Maybe one quickie before dinner."

"Thank fuck!" he lunged for her, picking her up off of her feet and holding her close. Instead of ravaging her like she expected, he kissed the tip of her nose. "I can't be gentle," he declared.

Tammy had to giggle. "Good. I want it all." She wrapped her legs around his waist.

He walked to their bed. "Good, because you have it all."

AUTHOR'S NOTE

Thank-you for reading the fourth book in this series. It is a spin off from my bestselling series The Chosen and The Program.

This book would not have been possible without the assistance of my editors and beta readers. Thank you KR, Bridgette Aisha and Enid.

Also, a big thank you to my ARC readers for your invaluable input and support. Especially those of you that review my books every time without fail. I'm talking about you Judy, Bridgette, Gretchen, AJ, Brenda, Stephanee, Mrs Duff and Ana . . . there are more of you. Thank you all!!

A big and heartfelt thank you to you . . . my readers. For reading my work and for all your messages and emails. Also, to those of you that take the time to review my books. It means the world to me. You are what keeps me writing on days that I might not feel like it so much.

If you want to be kept updated on new releases please sign up to my Latest Release Newsletter to ensure that you don't miss out http://mad.ly/signups/96708/join. I promise not to spam you or divulge your email address to a third party. I send my mailing list an exclusive sneak peek prior to release. I would love to hear from you so please feel free to drop me a line charlene.hartnady@gmail.com.

Find me on Facebook—www.facebook.com/authorhartnady

I live on an acre in the country with my gorgeous husband, our three sons and an array of pets.

You can usually find me on the computer completely lost in worlds of my making. I believe that it is the small things that truly matter, like that feeling you get when you start a new book or a particularly beautiful sunset.

BOOKS BY THIS AUTHOR

The Chosen Series:
Book 1 ~ Chosen by the Vampire Kings
Book 2 ~ Stolen by the Alpha Wolf
Book 3 ~ Unlikely Mates
Book 4 ~ Awakened by the Vampire Prince
Book 5 ~ Mated to the Vampire Kings (Short Novel)
Book 6 ~ Wolf Whisperer (Novella)

The Program Series (Vampire Novels):
Book 1 ~ A Mate for York
Book 2 ~ A Mate for Gideon
Book 3 ~ A Mate for Lazarus
Book 4 ~ A Mate for Griffin
Book 5 ~ A Mate for Lance
Book 6 ~ A Mate for Kai

Demon Chaser Series (No cliffhangers):
Book 1 ~ Omega
Book 2 ~ Alpha
Book 3 ~ Hybrid
Book 4 ~ Skin
Demon Chaser Boxed Set Book 1–3

Excerpt

A MATE FOR YORK
The Program Book 1

Chapter 1

Cassidy's hands were clammy and shaking. She had just retyped the same thing three times. At this rate, she would have to work even later than normal to get her work done. She sighed heavily.

Pull yourself together.

With shaking hands, she grabbed her purse from the floor next to her, she reached inside and pulled out the folded up newspaper article.

Have you ever wanted to date a vampire?

Human women required. Must be enthusiastic about interactions with vampires. Must be willing to undergo a stringent medical exam. Must be prepared to sign a contractual agreement which would include a non-disclosure clause. This will be a temporary position. Limited spaces available within the program. Successful candidates can earn up to $45,000 per day, over a three day period.

All she needed was three days leave.

Cassidy wasn't sure whether her hands were shaking

because she had to ask for the leave and her boss was a total douche bag or because the thought of vampires drinking her blood wasn't exactly a welcome one.

More than likely a combination of both.

This was a major opportunity for her though. She had already been accepted into the trial phase of the program that the vampires were running. What was three days in her life? So there was a little risk involved. Okay, a lot of risk, but it would all be worth it in the end. She was drowning in debt. Stuck in a dead-end job. Stuck in this godforsaken town. This was her chance, her golden opportunity, and she planned on seizing it with both hands.

To remind herself what she was working towards, or at least running away from, she let her eyes roam around her cluttered desk. There were several piles of documents needing to be filed. A stack of orders lay next to her cranky old laptop. Hopefully it wouldn't freeze on her this time while she was uploading them into the system. It had been months since Sarah had left. There used to be two of them performing her job, and since her colleague was never replaced it was just her. She found more and more that she had to get to work way earlier and stay later and later just to get the job done.

To add insult to injury, there were many days that her a-hole boss still had the audacity to come down on her for not meeting a deadline. He refused to listen to reason and would not accept being understaffed as an excuse. She'd never been one to shy away from hard work but the expectations were ridiculous. Her only saving grace was that she didn't have much of a life.

There had to be something more out there for her and a hundred and thirty five thousand big ones would not only pay off her debts but would also give her enough cash to go out and find one. A life that is and a damned good life it would be.

Cassidy took a deep breath and squared her shoulders. If she asked really nicely, hopefully Mark would give her a couple of days off. She couldn't remember the last time she had taken leave. Then it dawned on her, she'd taken three days after Sean had died a year ago. Her boss couldn't say no though. If he did, she wasn't beyond begging.

Rising to her feet, she made for the closed door at the other end of her office. After knocking twice, she entered.

The lazy ass was spread out on the corner sofa with his hands crossed behind his head. He didn't look in the least bit embarrassed about her finding him like that either.

"Cassidy." He put on a big cheesy smile as he rose to a sitting position. The button on his jacket pulled tight around his midsection which was paunchy. He didn't move much and ate big greasy lunches so it wasn't surprising. "Come on in. Take a seat," he gestured to a spot next to him on the sofa.

That would be the day. Her boss could get a bit touchy feely. Thankfully it had never gone beyond a pat on the butt, a hand on her shoulder or just a general invasion of her personal space. It put her on edge though because it was becoming worse and worse as of late. The sexual innuendos were also becoming highly irritating. She pretended that they went over her head, but he was becoming more and more forward as time went by.

By the way his eyes moved down her body, she could tell that he was most definitely mentally undressing her. *Oh god.* That meant that he was in one of his grabby moods. *Damn.* She preferred it when he was acting like a total jerk. Easier to deal with.

"No, that's fine. Thank you." She worked hard to plaster a smile on her face. "I don't want to take up much of your time and I have to get back to work myself."

His eyes narrowed for a second before dropping to her breasts. "You could do with a little break every now and then . . . so could I for that matter." Even though she knew he couldn't see anything because of her baggy jacket, his eyes stayed glued to her boobs anyway. Why did she get the distinct impression that he was no longer talking about work? *Argh!*

"How long has your husband been gone now?" he asked, his gaze still locked on her chest. It made her want to fold her arms but she resisted the temptation.

None of your damned business.

"It's been a year now since Sean passed." She tried hard to look sad and in mourning. When the truth was, that if the bastard wasn't already dead she would've killed him herself. Turned out that there were things about Sean that she hadn't known. In fact, it was safe to say that she'd been living with and married to a total stranger. Funny how those things tended to come out when a person died.

Her boss did not need to know this information though. So far, playing the mourning wife was the only thing that kept him from pursuing her further.

"What can I do for you?" His eyes slid down to the juncture at her thighs and again she had to fight the urge to squeeze them tightly together. Even though it was damn near scorching temperatures outside, she still wore stockings, skirt to mid calf, a button-up blouse and a jacket. Nothing was revealing and yet he still looked at her like she was standing there naked. It made her skin crawl. "I would be happy to oblige you. Just say the word, baby."

She hated it when he called her that. He started doing it a couple of weeks ago. Cassidy had asked him on several occasions to stop but she may as well have been speaking to a plank of wood.

She grit her teeth for a second, holding back a retort. "Great. Glad to hear it." Her voice sounded way more confident than what she felt. "I need a couple of days off. It's been a really long time—"

"Forget it," he interrupted while standing up. "I need you . . . here." Another innuendo. Although she waited, he didn't give any further explanations.

"Look, I know there is a lot to do around here especially since Sarah left." His eyes clouded over immediately at the mention of her ex-colleague's name. "I would be happy to put in extra time."

As in, she wouldn't sleep and would have to work weekends to get the job done.

"I'll do whatever it takes. I just really need a couple of days . . . It's important."

His eyes lit up and she realized what she had just said and how it would've sounded to a complete pig like Mark.

"Anything?" He rolled the word off of his tongue.

"Well . . ." It came out sounding breathless but only because she was nervous. "Not anything. What I meant to say was—"

"No, no. I like that you would do anything, in fact, there is something I've been meaning to discuss with you." His gaze dropped to her breasts again.

Please no. Anything but that.

Cassidy swallowed hard, actually feeling sick to her stomach. She shook her head.

"You can have a few days, baby. In fact, I'll hire you an assistant." Ironically he played with the wedding band on his ring finger. His voice had turned sickly sweet. "I'd be willing to go a long way for you if you only met me halfway. It's time you got over the loss of your husband and I plan on helping you to do that."

"Um . . . I don't think . . ." Her voice was soft and shaky. Her hands shook, so she folded her arms.

This was not happening.

"Look, Cass . . . baby, you're an okay looking woman. Not normally the type I'd go for. I prefer them a bit younger, bigger tits, tighter ass . . ." He looked her up and down as if he were sizing her up and finding her lacking. "I'd be willing to give you a go . . . help you out. Now . . . baby . . ." He paused.

Cassidy felt like the air had seized in her lungs, like her heart had stopped beating for that matter. Her mouth gaped open but she couldn't close it. She made a croaking noise but couldn't seem to actually talk.

She watched in horror as her boss pulled down his zipper and pulled out a wrinkled, flaccid cock. "Suck on this, or you could bend over and I'll fuck you . . . the choice is yours. I would recommend the fuck because quite frankly I think you could use it." He was deadly serious. Even gave a small nod like he was doing her a favor or something.

To the delight of her oxygen starved lungs, she managed to suck in a deep breath but still couldn't get any words out. Not a single, solitary syllable.

"I know you've had to play the part of the devastated wife and all that but I know you really want a bit of this." He waved his cock at her, although wave was not the right description. The problem was that a limp dick couldn't really wave. It flopped about pathetically in his hand.

Cassidy looked from his tiny dick up to his ruddy, pasty face and back down again before bursting out laughing. It was the kind of laugh that had her bending at the knees, hunching over. Sucking in another lungful of air, she gave it all she had. Unable to stop even if she wanted to. Until tears rolled down her cheeks. Until she was gasping for breath.

"Hey now . . ." Mark started to look distinctly uncomfortable. "That's not really the sort of response I expected from you." He didn't look so sure anymore, even started to put his dick away before his eyes hardened up.

Cassidy was wiping the tears from her face. She still couldn't believe what the hell she was seeing and even worse, what she was hearing. What a complete asshole.

Her boss took a step towards her. "The time for games is over. Get down on your knees if you want to keep your job. I'm your boss and your behavior is just plain rude."

Any hint of humor evaporated in an instant. "I'll tell you what's rude . . . you taking out your thing is rude. You're right, you're my boss which means what is happening right here"—she gestured between the two of them, looking pointedly at his member—"is called sexual harassment."

He narrowed his eyes at her. "Damn fucking straight, little missy. I want you to sexually harass this right now." He clutched his penis, flopping it around some more.

A Mate for York (The Program Series)—available now

Printed in Poland
by Amazon Fulfillment
Poland Sp. z o.o., Wrocław